M000111026

A Feast of Narrative

VOLUME 2

Copy Editor: Tiziano Thomas Dossena
Cover Design & Layout By: Dominic A. Campanile
On the cover: Girls with goat on the grass,1969; oil painting
by Emilio Giuseppe Dossena (1903-1987)

ISBN: 978-1-948651-17-2
Library of Congress Control Number: 2020945587

Published by: Idea Press (an imprint of Idea Graphics, LLC) — Florida (USA)
www.ideapress-usa.com • email: ideapress33@gmail.com • editoreusa@gmail.com
Printed in the USA - 1st Edition, Autumn 2020

A Feast of Narrative

VOLUME 2

An Anthology of Short Stories by Italian-American Writers
Edited by Tiziano Thomas Dossena

To Robert Viscusi,
an award winning novelist and poet,
but most of all a friend

ACKNOWLEDGEMENTS

I would like to thank my family for understanding that editing an anthology would force me to sit at the computer at the weirdest hours and my friend Leonardo Campanile for agreeing on the necessity of this project.

The Organization of the Sons of Italy, through their National magazine *Italian America*, which cooperated in the advertisement of this project, allowed us to reach a wider audience, and I thank them for it. Most of all, though, I thank all the contributors to this anthology for showing me how creativity can truly express its existence in so many ways.

INTRODUCTION

Tiziano Thomas Dossena
Editor

When I started with the first Italian American Writers anthology, I was delighted to see that most writers realized this was an effort on my part to focus on our own ethnic group's copious literary production, and participated enthusiastically.

Until recently, no spotlight has been put on them as a group specifically and I believed, and still do, that more of these projects should be initiated and supported by the various Italian American associations. It is, after all, a tenet of most of these organizations to assist their own kind in cultural activities. Somehow, though, I don't see it happen that often, and it's disappointing to realize that there is no awareness of this need to promote our writers, artists, dramatists, and composers so that they may leave a mark of their own.

Anthologies are just one of the tools to allow writers to be known, but they are much more, because they allow writers to 'belong' to a group of 'chosen' people like themselves, people who enthusiastically write because they want to and believe their innermost feelings need to be shared, at least on paper. It makes them realize that, regardless of whether their name is famous or not, they were chosen to be part of something that makes them shine just as much as the other contributors.

A copious number of contributors to this Volume Two made it impossible to fit them all in a tome of less than 300 pages, therefore we created a Volume Three, which will be published a very short time after this Volume.

Most of the writers of this anthology have an extended resume and their name may be well known even outside of the Italian American community, while some are at their early stages of writing; all of them wrote marvelous stories.

The additional detail that distinguishes Volume Two and Three from Volume One is that the participants are from all corners of United States, which was the original goal of this project.

We hope that with this anthology we helped, even just a bit, in promoting the writing of Italian Americans to the world.

PREFACE

Tiziano Thomas Dossena
Editor

This anthology contains a very interesting amalgam of different stories and authors. What is common, other than their belonging to the same ethnic group, is the validity of their content and the message they send to the readers. Some stories are funny commentaries on social gatherings of some kind, wakes included, while others address different topics with a more somber tone, such as war events, the constant search for our roots, the changing of neighborhoods, the Covid19 crisis, and so on. Regardless of the topic, these writers prove that passion for writing is another element they have in common with each other. This is their message and it proves that having them together in this anthology is the proper decision.

I am more than happy, therefore, to present you the authors of Volume Two of "A Feast of Narrative."

With true-to-life observations and descriptions of a teenager's interactions with a friend and a prospective date, **Peter Alfieri** gives a masterful example of how life's events can change fast and unpredictably in "Birches." A powerful depiction of teenager's fears and angst.

"Mr. Capri" is the account of an encounter of a young lady with an Italian speaking man who is lost and the help the woman gives him to reach his destination. But what she does may influence her near future, even though only temporarily. **Lucia Antonucci** does a great job at constructing a simple action into an interesting situation.

Marylin Antenucci's "Barely There" is a humorous look at older people's conversations and awkward situations arisen because of their old way of communicating and dealing with each other. You may wonder where in the narration of the protagonist reality ends and fantasy starts. It will certainly make you smile.

The interactions of the surviving family and friends are the focus of **Joseph Cacibauda**'s "The Wake," a marvelous tale narrated with directness and the awareness that life goes on regardless of everything and everyone. The fine sense of comicality that is embedded in the realistic conversations is even more emphasized by the scattered use of Sicilian words. Interesting the reflection on how ethnicity may influence the way the clergy operates and interacts with the parishioners.

Presented almost as a fable or a fairy tale, **Debbie DiGiacobbe**'s "Happily Ever After" is a brief account of the management of a young woman's recycling duties in a condominium trash area and the changes in her life that arose from it. Having a distorted attitude toward society on her part, and feeling that rules are for everyone else, the protagonist lives in a town called Neighborly; a fascinating notion.

Patricia Rispoli Edick introduces us to the unknown in "A Conversation with a Stranger," a story that introduces a stranger with not-so-mysterious goals and unlimited implements for his plans to work. Who he really is may not surprise everyone, but it certainly will confirm that a war of some sort has been going on for a long while. Well developed and structured narration.

The interesting comments and clarifications about serving as altar boys in a catholic church in the 60s make "Alter Boys" a wonderful, well-knit story that will definitely make one smile throughout the reading and openly laugh at certain passages. This witty recitation of these young boys' justifications for their actions makes this story by **Fred Gardaphè** a must to read.

Cecilia M. Gigliotti offers us a concise but poignant story in "Mia Slept Over," which could almost be a poem for its sensitivity and cadenced style.

Joe Giordano's "A Requiem for Guido" is a remembrance of someone who helped the main character in Italy when no one else would. Guido left a mark into his heart that even death cannot erase. Brief and to the point, it will trigger memories to people who travelled abroad to study.

Imagine having been told "that the drug carriers often used oregano to mask the smell of marijuana" and having a package of oregano in your suitcase! Those are the funny premises of "Arrivederci Oregano" by **Mary Lou Amato Johnston**. The developing actions are typical of people who are innocent and are afraid of having inadvertently done something wrong or illegal. A very entertaining story.

"Responses" is a particularly thought-provoking narrative based on an extremely obese man who realizes someone entered his apartment while he is occupied at necessary corporal tasks in his bathroom. **Thomas Locicero**'s story is an amalgam of comedy, social commentary and unexpected turns.

How much can life be altered by an accidental delay and the betrayal of someone close to you? Very much indeed. It can take a completely different turn, and that is what "Diana's Storia Segreta" by **C.J Martello** presents in a quick-paced and mesmerizing style. The story also sheds light on the abominable and unprovoked internments of Italians during WWII.

Edward Albert Maruggi's "Alberto's First Date" explores the tortuosity of the thoughts of a young Italian man's blind date with an American girl. The outcome is far from expected and it's a pleasant surprise both for Alberto and the reader.

"New Corners" by **Maria Massimi** has the protagonist travel in her mind to reconstruct her youth in a city neighborhood, interrupted suddenly by her family's moving to the suburbs. A deep and heartfelt analysis of what friendship and a neighborhood mean to a child, the story will appeal to many readers who have lived a similar transition in their lives. A true New Yorker's tale of social and economic progress.

The dream of America and all the expectations connected to it is the topic of "The Sister Left Behind," an emotional tale by **Suzanna Rosa Molino** with excellent rendition of the dialogues in Italian. The process of passing through the inspectors before departing for the United States is a process that not everyone is aware of. It belongs to an age when Ellis Island was the known filtering agent for immigration. To get there, though, you first had to get on a ship and that's when the first examination occurred. The inspectors, however, took somewhat approximate or arbitrary decisions when encountering candidates who may have seemed sick. This story is an account of one of those would-be immigrants' vicissitudes.

"From Train to Tradition" shows how a small decision taken to save a train fare brought one of the protagonists to be involved in a competition, a participation that became a family tradition. **Sharon Nickosey** tells this story in a lively and enjoyable style.

"White Mountains," by **Marge Pellegrino**, is the description of the first day in a vacation house, or bungalow, somewhere in the White Mountains. It shows how similar most of us are by presenting the main character's thoughts along with his conversation with the wife. Many of us will recognize those very charming and amusing thoughts and interactions.

Annadora Perillo's "La Befana" offers shimmering images of a summer day in Tuscany, with superb poetic descriptions of the environment, and the happy exchanges of a potential young family in a dream by the main protagonist. Awakened, she takes the decision to embrace this earthly paradise.

How important is taking a risk in someone's life? That depends on how you were raised and the situation you are facing. What about if the only risk you ever took is at a card game and everyone takes you for granted? Will you take what you consider a big risk just for the sake of proving independence to yourself? That is the dilemma a teacher faces in **Elizabeth Primamore**'s "Risk Taker" and his way to resolve this dilemma may surprise you.

Tony Reitano's "This is Sicily" places an Italian American, although someone would say Sicilian American to further identify the protagonist, in his family's motherland. How and why he ends up traveling to this beautiful island is the first part's theme, while the rest of the story is a lesson on dealing with the locals, with their good and sometimes pernicious ways. It is a very entertaining story, with lots of observations, descriptions and commentaries that make the dealings even wittier.

An unexpected turn makes Grandpa the star of the night when he casually replaces a philanthropist at a dinner. An event that could have been a stressful one suddenly changes into a magnificent occasion for him when a movie star appears as a guest and sits next to him. "Italian Gala' by **Michael Riccards** is a practical demonstration on how people perceive you and how humble some of the great names of the celluloid world may turn out to be.

A fictional account of a town in Northern Italy taken over by Nazi soldiers during War World Two, "The Devil's Pit" is a very convincing and thrilling story. **Aniello Russo**'s characters are well built even in such a short setting and the pace is rapid. One could find it very easy to be absorbed by the characters' impulses and notions and forget that the account is fictional.

Just as for "This is Sicily," the protagonists of **Paul Salsini**'s "Nonna's House" travel to Italy to inherit a house, but the situation here is very different. It's Tuscany, and guess what? Covid19 arrives! It's not the ideal circumstances for an American family, is it? Well, our heroes discover the resilience of Italians and of themselves when faced by the stress placed upon the community by this malignant and unfamiliar virus.

A very profound consideration of how death and the scourges of the modern world, cancer and AIDS, may influence our lives, one way or the other, make "The Presence of the Dead" a well-balanced story. In it, social commentary and acceptance of the inevitable are alternated by **Mark Spano** with an impressive grace.

"The Viewing" is not just another story about wakes and dead people. **Leo Vadalà** presents the innermost fears and mental acrobatics of a young man whose acquaintance, who everyone believes him to be his friend, passes away unexpectedly. The hilarious and incongruous reasoning of the boy is only matched in his comic effect by his astonishing actions. Mr. Vadalà seems to have found a way to laugh at death and I have to congratulate him for that.

Writing about mobsters is usually a bit of a minefield since there is always the danger of comparison, but **Anthony Valerio** sublimated his "Last Godfather" into a pseudo-spiritual although practical, astute, and harsh version of it; an actual thought-provoking concept.

INDEX

Birches

by Peter C. Alfieri

"Birches" is a story of a young teen-age boy,
who finds out for the first time about the vagaries
and callousness of unrequited love.

"There go Angela and Carla by the fence; catch Angela's hot pink outfit," Billy said. The girls had been at the rink for a while, or outside anyway because Carla had the blushed cheeks that she gets from being outdoors. They giggled and went inside to get hot chocolate. My feet hurt a bit as I was putting on my skates, but they always do from the cold, and I knew that once I got moving the pain would stop. We laced up our skates; Michael went rushing out to the ice and said, "Hey Tony, watch this short stop." Michael built up a burst of steam, screamed to the fence, and turned to a big rooster tail spray spooking two little girls and pelting the back fence with ice. We cracked up. I tried the rooster tail bit, but only got my spray half way up the fence. The little girls just skated on.

It was about that time of day when the sun and moon are both out and the leaves stop whistling. It was just right for starting out skating, a little cool, but I wished the sun would hurry up down. Michael told me that he was going to the dance next week with Linda Milano. "Who are you going with?" he asked, twisting his face because he already knew the answer to that question.

"Very funny," I said, "you know I'm not going, that I don't have a girlfriend."

"All in time, Tony boy, all in time," said Michael. In the same breathe he blurted, "The Yellow Rose of Texas, everyone skates to that." And sure enough, the rink was flooded with people skating in small circles, large circles, opposite directions, in and out the rink entrance. "Hey, there's Carla and Angela, let's skate after them," Michael said. Seeing Carla's long brown hair bouncing as she skated slid me back to cousin Theresa's wedding in July when I had to sit through four hours of all the adults and older cousins dancing and smiling the whole time. What were they all smiling at? It didn't look like any more fun than any other time seeing your relatives, only now people got to look at you flailing your arms around and seeing just how uncoordinated you really were.

Michael grabbed my hat and got in between Carla and Angela. He broke between them brushing Carla's shoulder, and threw the hat back over his head without looking. The throw was high and straight and steered perfectly to my outstretched arm. I flipped the hat back on my head. Carla looked back and caught her blade in a skate rut. Her arms only partially stopped her slide into the fence. We just kept skating without looking back and Michael had a big smile on his face.

"Let's get something to eat," Michael said. As we stepped up to the rail, Michael asked how I did on the Latin midterm.

"Ninety-five," I said, with my usual aplomb.

"Faggot," Michael said. "Mr. Donlin must have it in for me, I only got a seventy-eight."

"How do you like his sporty new glasses, and I have to find out who does his embalming," I quirked.

Michael said, "I think he died in the Gallic War, "Latin, what a waste of time."

"The drawbacks of a Jesuit education," I said. "It only gets worse, next year when we're juniors, we get to translate Cicero. I heard that's a lot of fun."

"What'll it be boys?" the counter man wanted to know. We both ordered pizza and Coke. We stayed at the counter awhile after we were served to watch some older girls putting on lipstick and looking in hand mirrors.

After we finished eating, we stomped over to the men's room. The light reflection hit the black slush from the other boys' skates. The wall at the entrance to the men's room read, "When you pee, remember me." *Remember me*, I thought, *who is there to remember?*

We went back on the ice, and skated in a big long circle. I didn't see anyone I knew, boy or girl, when a voice flew by me saying, "race you to the corner." It was Carla and she didn't seem mad at all about Michael's stunt. I tried with all my might to catch her, but couldn't. She stopped hard into the wall, but turned around to laugh, "I won." She had won all-right. I thought about asking her to race again to the next pole, but that would be a little corny even though I knew I could beat her. She asked, "Do you and Billy skate a lot?"

"Pretty much," I said, "up until about March, when it gets too warm and slushy. That's about when they close it down."

The music started again. It was an old carnival tune that I couldn't remember the name of. Carla and I started skating close to the rail. I had the greatest urge to stick out my right arm and reach for one of those prizes that you get from the man by the side of the merry-go-round, but of course, he wasn't there. Carla brought me back to the rink when she asked, "Are you going to the record hop next Friday?"

The record hop, I thought, *why doesn't she ask me what I got on Mr. Donlin's Latin test?* But she doesn't even know Mr. Donlin. She doesn't even go to the same school. Maybe I should just tell her what I got, why did she ask me about the dance? I laughed to myself that I get asked three questions all day and two of them have to be about that stupid dance. Looking away, I said, "I haven't decided yet."

I turned my face to hers and she said with the smallest, prettiest smile, "I haven't decided either." That was enough to crack all the ice in the rink. I noticed earlier that her skates weren't scuffed and I asked her if they were new.

I don't think I heard her answer or maybe I didn't even let her finish when we passed more trees. "The birches have buds again; they got faked out with the warm weather last week; are they in for a surprise. I hope that the weather is nice for the football game next Saturday. I've only been to one game all year, and it would be nice to see Prep win for a change." The music stopped, but sometimes they pick up another song right after one ends without a break, and I was hoping that would happen, but it didn't.

Carla said, "Angela's father is supposed to drive me home, but my feet are getting cold and I'd like to leave now. Would you mind walking me home?"

"No", I said, surprised and thinking that I sounded too eager.

Carla went over to Angela, and I saw both girls laugh a little bit after Carla stopped talking. I was pretending to read the skating schedule on the wall when I saw Carla out of the corner of my eye and turned to meet her voice and she said, "Well, let's go."

So off we went. It wasn't a very long walk, only about a mile or so, but I could see how a girl wouldn't want to walk alone. We got about half way and we had been talking about everything. Carla told me about her brother, who was coming home from the Navy, and I told her that maybe I would join ROTC when I got to college. She said that she wasn't sure if she was going to college; that she would decide by the end of next year or maybe the beginning of senior year. I said that college was a good thing, but not necessary if you got a good foundation in high school, that you could probably get just as good an education without college. Try telling that to my family, I couldn't help but think. We passed more birches, those stupid, stupid birches.

We were just walking with our arms swinging when, like magic, they touched. My body started to tingle. Without even thinking, I put my hand in hers. It fit so well, my fingers between hers, that I wondered why I hadn't held her hand sooner. We continued to talk as if nothing had happened, but her smile was brighter and her eyes glistened with newfound joy. I was so happy. I was savoring the moment like riding the last wave at the beach before going home when we turned the corner. About fifteen yards away, coming at us in the opposite direction, were two boys, seniors with varsity jackets. Carla quickly dropped my hand and smiled at them just as she had smiled at me.

"Hi Carla," they said in succession. They gave me an indiscriminate glance and kept on walking. I asked her who those guys were and she said that they were just some friends of her brother. We walked on only I kept my hands in my pockets the rest of the way, which was only a few minutes from her house anyway. We continued our conversation, but I can't honestly remember what we talked about.

When we got to her house she said, "Thanks for the walk," and gave me the faintest peck on the cheek and I stood motionless. When she got up the steps, I turned to walk home putting my face into the wind that had been at my back. I could feel the cold where Carla got my cheek.

Barely There

by Marilyn Antenucci

*Joey hears stories all day long, but when Frankie comes into his joint,
the bartender is appalled by the tale his paesano shares
after a visit with a grieving widow.*

Frankie shouldered open the door into *Joey's Place*. Sleigh bells
jingled when he slammed out the bitter Chicago wind. The bells were
Joey's only concession to the season, if a guy didn't count the aluminum
tree stuck in the corner of the joint. Decked out in sapphire balls, the
tree sprung to life a couple weeks in December when Joey plugged in
the revolving color wheel to illuminate the silver needles. At two in the
afternoon, the unlit tree kept a forlorn vigil. Joey looked up from behind
the bar. A mirror reflected his snowy head and the crisp white shirt
stretched across his beefy back. Joey greeted him with the predictable,
"*Eh, Paesano! Come stai?*"

Frankie just blew into his arthritic fingers and dropped on a worn leather bar stool. "Gimme a cup a coffee," he said. "I got this chill
I can't shake."

The bartender put down his knife, pushed the sliced limes
into a neat pile, and wiped his hands on the clean, white half-apron

tied around his ample girth. Joey filled the coffee grinder with beans. The aroma wafted the length of the bar, but Frankie seemed oblivious. Guys from the old days didn't come here to drink java, and he wondered what was eating his friend. Joey placed a steaming cup in front of Frankie and went about his business prepping for the hip Friday night crowd. They'd started drifting in a couple years ago from the renovated Hyde Park neighborhoods.

"OH! MY! GOD!" one of the young lawyers shrieked when she spotted the aluminum tree.

"Dude! That is so retro!" The savvy bartender played along, and the tree stayed up year round.

Hell, he didn't care how the six-figured crowd saw his rundown joint. As long as *Joey's Place* was another *awesome* discovery, maybe he could hang on until Social Security kicked in. He sliced lemon garnish then grabbed two white plastic buckets, filled them with mini ice cubes from the big freezer, and dumped them into chillers at the bar.

Frankie jerked up. "Remember Johnnie? Used to come in here few times a year with his old lady, Margie, and tell you how to make a bracciole like he invented it?"

"Yeah, tall guy, wore glasses. Gave me a recipe for broccoli and olive oil that was damned good on linguine. That's the guy who died, what a couple a weeks ago now?" asked Joey.

"Yeah, that's the guy I'm talkin' about. Johnnie and me go way back to when we was in school at St. Aloysius. Hammered each other pretty good on the playground. I seen him around once in a while, mostly run into him here drinking with Margie."

Joey opened a jar of stuffed jumbo green olives and spooned them into a stainless steel container next to the lemons and limes. He refilled Frankie's cup and twisted open the economy size jar of maraschino cherries.

"You know how I was in Florida seein' the grandkids?" Joey nodded and hoped Frankie wasn't going to start in about his Ex. "Well, anyways, I'm gone to Ft. Meyers and when I get back I'm glancin' through the obits from the papers stacked up and what do I see but Johnnie died and got himself cremated! So, today I figure it's cold as hell and maybe I'll take me a quick stroll over to pay my respects to the widow. Maybe I'll get a cup a coffee and some of those Polish cookies she bakes. Know how it is this time of year, Joey, no Christmas cookies in the house now the Ex is out the door."

The bartender rolled his eyes and wished he had a buck for every sad sack he'd listened to over the years. Frankie might head down that beaten path and be bawling when the paying customers started rolling in. Joey polished a beer glass and diverted the sob story. "So did you go to Johnnie's?"

"I'm dressed for payin' respects, ain't I?" Frankie said, glancing in the mirror and straightening his skewered tie. "So I knock on the door and before you know it I'm sittin' in Johnnie's kitchen, with no Johnnie, a mug of strong coffee and a plate loaded with goodies shoved in front of me."

"Margie pours out her heart to me, Joey. Tells me one day Johnnie's doing radiation for the Big C and the next day he's gone. "Breaks my heart," I tell her.

"Shame you and Johnnie didn't see more of each other," she says and walks out the room.

I'm thinkin' maybe it was time to get my hat and get outta there when she comes back with a couple old school pictures. She pours me more coffee and we stare at me and Johnnie and about thirty other delinquents lined up behind the nuns. Well, we're just sittin' there at the table cryin' like babies when she grabs my hand and pulls me into the bedroom."

Joey's shaggy brows arched over his wire rimmed glasses. He stopped chewing, and the maraschino stem came to a halt between his generous lips.

Frankie made a fluttering motion over his heart. "I'm tellin' you, pal, I was waitin' for my angina to come callin'!"

Geez, he'd never take Johnnie's wife for that type but doesn't interrupt Frankie's version of an old story.

"See, my mind is spinning about how I'm gonna get myself out of this mess when Margie points to the bed. "I still sleep with my Johnnie every night," she says to me.

"I'm lookin at the bed, and all I see is one of those Teddy bears with a heart stitched on his chest that says *Be Mine*. Kinda sweet, I'm thinkin', except this damned bear is wearin a big pair of glasses. "Johnnie's glasses," she says.

Joey tossed the bar towel over his shoulder and muttered, "No shit!"

"No shit!" repeats Frankie. "So, I'm calmin' down and thinkin' maybe it's kinda romantic that she cuddles up next to a Teddy bear in the middle of the night when I notice this bear's sittin' on top of a gray box, if you catch my drift."

Joey snorted. "Are you bulling me, Frankie?" and waited for the punch line to a bad joke.

Frankie ignored the interruption. "See, I'm just tryin' to figure if maybe it's OK for a bear to be wearin' a dead guy's glasses and sleep with his widow. Whatever works, ya know what I mean? Hell, I slept with my arms wrapped around Gina's pillow for months after she left. I'm just sayin'…"

"The bear's wearin' Johnnie's glasses and sittin' on his box of ashes?" confirms the skeptical bartender.

"I told you what I seen! I'm tellin' you, Joey, it was disturbin'! *What the hell goes on here*? I'm thinkin' to myself when she tells me how she sleeps like a baby every night and me, I'm pulling my tie loose so I can get some air!"

"You ain't makin' this up are you, Frankie? Cuz you know how I feel about bein' taken for a ride!"

Frankie's right hand shot toward the tin ceiling. "Swear on my mother's grave!"

An icy blast off Lake Michigan rattled the front door. A soft jingle pierced the silent room. Joey shook off a chill and walked over to the aluminum Christmas tree. He polished each pane of the color wheel and plugged it into the wall. The tree sprang to life as each tint washed over the metallic needles.

Frankie swiveled around on the bar stool while Joey poured them a shot. They stared as the miniature stained glass windows spun and the tree evolved into blue, then red, then green, then gold.

Joey lifted his drink. *"Salute, Giovanni!"*

"Riposi in pace!" echoed Frankie.

Joey poured another round and brushed away what he hoped was powdered sugar on Frankie's lapel.

Mr. Capri

by Lucia Antonucci

*Two friends spend a sun-drenched winter day in Manhattan
and experience an unexpected twist of fate! This light-hearted,
whimsical tale fills readers' hearts with joy and serendipity.*

It was a pleasure to find myself headed for Manhattan on this cold
but lovely morning, especially after spending so many days indoors due
to inclement weather. My friend had telephoned me the week before
and asked if I would like to meet her in the city. I immediately said yes.
She and I always had an enjoyable time together. A day in the city typ-
ically meant shopping and a great lunch. My friend always chose the
restaurant as she kept her finger on the pulse of the best restaurants in
the city.

I hopped on the train near my home and, at one particular stop,
a well-dressed man entered. He immediately went to look at the map.
He examined it closely and then turned to a passenger to ask some
directions. She shrugged her shoulders as if to say, 'I don't know.'
The man spoke with an Italian accent and his hand gestures confirmed my suspicions.

I got up and approached him. "May I help you? I speak Italian,"
I said.

The man's face lit up. "Thank you, Signora. I believe I am on the wrong train."

He told me where he needed to go. The location was on the west side of the city, although this train was headed east. I told him to get off with me and I would direct him with no problem. He was very grateful and, as we continued on the train, he introduced himself.

"My name is Renaldo Capri."

"Like the beautiful Isle of Capri?" I asked.

He laughed. "And you are?"

"My name is Lucía Cavalieri."

"A nice Irish name," he said. We both laughed.

We conversed further and I told him how much I loved Italy, particularly the southern part where I had spent much time visiting with family. He told me that his hobby and passion was photography. He explained that while traveling the country extensively, he had taken photos of many of Italy's cities, countryside and villages. He talked extensively about photography and expressed his view that photos, when taken correctly, capture the spirit of the subject.

The train stops went by quickly and I advised him that we would be getting off at the next stop. When we got to the street, I directed him to where he needed to go; he thanked me and went on his way.

I proceeded several blocks to where I was to meet my friend. As usual, she had the day planned and proceeded to share the day's itinerary with me. We started with shopping, spending time in a department store and several boutique shops. We then headed to a museum to view a photography exhibit my friend heard a great deal about. She had booked a tour of this exhibit for us and the docent was quite informative. We thoroughly enjoyed the exhibit and left there with a greater appreciation of photography.

It was late afternoon and my friend said it was time for lunch. She told me she had made a reservation at a new Italian restaurant that recently opened. She said all the reviews she had read were raving about this new place. That certainly was enough to wet my appetite. Besides, because of my adventurous spirit, I am always ready for new discoveries.

As we entered the restaurant and were shown to our table, I noticed it had a very Tuscan theme. But as we took in the restaurant, what really captured our attention were the walls covered with the most beautiful photography of Italy. There was color photography, as well as black and white, capturing Italy with so much expression and detail. Having just left the museum's photography exhibit, we began to comment much in the same way the docent did at the museum. We laughed that maybe we could give the tour here of these beautiful photos.

As the waiter approached with our menus, we remarked to him about how much we were admiring the photography. "Ah yes" he said. "In addition to having a chef who excels in the kitchen, he also has a passion for photography." He proceeded to tell us of the chef's specials and to take our drink order. After a few minutes he returned and we had made our selection from the menu, which represented the cuisine of Northern Italy.

My friend and I thoroughly enjoyed our entree, a delight to the palate. The wine was also wonderful. The espresso and pastries concluded a delightful meal. My friend had certainly done her homework on this restaurant. The reviews she mentioned were not exaggerated.

We sat and talked for a while. Surprisingly, the waiters did not disturb or rush us, even though the restaurant was quite crowded. After a while, I got the waiter's attention and asked for our check.

With an agreeable smile he said, "Everything has been taken care of, signora."

"It can't be," I said. "You made a mistake; please check again."

"No, everything is fine. We hope you enjoyed yourselves." With that, the waiter then pointed to the kitchen and out came the chef in uniform, with his chef's cap and white jacket. I was shocked. It was Signor Capri from the train.

"Signora Lucía!" he shouted. "I recognized you when you entered. It is my pleasure to serve you and once again thank you for your kindness towards me this morning."

My friend was in awe. During the day, I had briefly mentioned to her that I had met a fine gentleman on the train and that we had chatted about Italy, which she knew was my weak spot.

"Signor Capri," I said, "during our train ride you told me about your photography, which my friend and I have greatly admired. You failed to mention that you were a chef. Having enjoyed a wonderful meal, I now see that your cooking is just as expert as your photography".

"Ah Signora, you are ever so gracious," he replied.

We both thanked him and left with the promise that we would return another time and he agreed to join us for a drink. He hugged me, we said our good byes and left.

As my grandmother would always say, "Do good and forget it; do bad and remember it." It seems I did good that day. And it seems Signor Capri did not forget.

My friend said, "Lucy, the most unusual things happen to you; you should write a book."

Arrivederci, Mr. Capri!

The Wake

by Joseph L. Cacibauda

Where once family and friends joyfully celebrated church feast-days, birthdays, holidays, and weddings, they have now obligingly gathered in death. The sad occasion of a wake reunites the family and re-ignites flames of unresolved rifts, generational suspicions, and unrealistic expectations.

All of the children were there except Vinnie whose calls reassured them he was on his way. The brothers weren't surprised, but Annie was upset that the family had to go ahead and make a decision on the casket with one brother missing. Their mother was gone and she, the only girl, was now the family's matriarch. The role weighed heavily, this cloak of responsibility, and she wore it like a bulky Afghan, feeling it in her neck and shoulders, bearing the stress with a habituated stoicism, an accordance and homage to her mother. *Annie never stood still* is why everyone believed she was so wiry and never gained weight. She moved with a steady purpose, like a team captain picking players, standing off to one corner, quietly coddling folks in their misfortunes, smoothly massaging their fears and reassuring them with vivid news-story examples that they had valid reasons to be afraid. As she expected the worse, she was assuaged when it materialized, and perhaps in a dark crevice of her mind, she felt comfortable, able to keep her forebodings gathered around like fluffy kittens. In those times when outcomes tilted toward favorable ends, never mollified, she always had other catastrophes in waiting, those possibly worse than her last predictions. Annie believed God was out to get her. Forgoing relying on bounty-hunter dark angels, He personally was out to collect her soul for reasons she couldn't justify. Maybe a lustful thought entertained too long; or a perhaps a couple Masses missed, a skipped confession. She could have short-changed a collection once; or maybe it had to do with Original Sin, that sword of Damocles looming above everyone, but particularly her, its ominous shadow forever blocking out the light of God's blessings. She was convinced only a rosary and sign of the cross would keep His wrath at bay; afford her the time to dodge His vengeance. Granted, Vinnie's absence was a troubling happenstance, not altogether unexpected, but nonetheless troubling. Annie fretted, *The Triolo children should all gather at this sorrowful time to model family unity and to avoid relatives and friends wondering why Francesca's children were not all there.*

Francesca Triolo knew something was wrong. She had to triple her Maalox because her stomach was always burning; and, then she developed a cough. Airy, hissing spells. She held off going to the doctors. She didn't like them. *Those damned doctors always find something wrong with you* is what she would say. When her coughs persisted and she appeared to be in more pain, her son Jake demanded she go and drove her to all her appointments. Dr. Boudreaux was not long out of school (*So young, but real nice,* Francesca would say) and he hadn't experienced enough cases of such conditions to correctly diagnose her problem, nor had he the wisdom to seek a specialist's advice. He wrote prescriptions for stronger and longer lasting antacids. She trusted him, happily relieved that it wasn't anything more serious than *agita*. But it was more serious than heartburn. It was a large mass the size of a baseball in the lining of her stomach and was diagnosed as cancer by those with the knowledge and equipment to discover it. Annie immediately thought to get a second opinion, and even when the second and third doctors corroborated the diagnosis, Annie couldn't believe such a thing.

"We don't have cancer in our family. Italians don't get cancer," she told Vinnie on her phone call, her voice incredulous, a plea for some accord. "I don't understand how Momma could have that. She won't even say the word."

Francesca would not say the word, she was so afraid of the condition she would only call it "that." She had friends who died of cancer, ones she visited in their last days to witness their suffering. She would not say the word, so the children did not say the word after they learned the test results. Francesca knew what she had and that she would die from it. In the still moments, the children finishing the routines of her care, she laid in bed, her children thinking she was asleep, she stared at the ceiling. She couldn't tell them she knew without worrying them. She could not say what she knew without saying the word.

Fanno's Funeral Home was a large building on Magazine Street; its red bricks were painted a drab army green long ago, even before Francesca's husband Gino had been waked there. Sons Paulie, Calo, and Jake stood straight and solemn, arms hanging to the front with fingers interlocked, dutifully acknowledging guests at the front door as Annie moved through the viewing parlor, erect back, determined steps, like a nervous stage director on opening night, moving here, moving there, then setting flowers to be certain no giver's arrangement was set too far in the background or behind another's. Her husband Philip obediently followed her instructions to make certain the food was ready and enough; and, he watched over their two boys, Danny and Gino. He moved with the stodginess of an English butler, a stiffness that signaled his uneasiness in a suit that had ceased to fit. Like Annie, Philip was active, but unlike her, he took time to slow down and take care of himself. He was a bit overweight, not obese, but heavy. His short height caused his paunch to be more noticeable than taller men who perhaps ate and drank as much or even more than he. He was partially bald; his sides remained full enclosing a horseshoe bald spot like a leprechaun's. For the night, in deference to the event and respect for Annie's emotional condition, he was her compliant servant and readily carried out her wishes never needing clarifications.

Aunt Rosie, dressed in black, walked over to the casket. She was careful of her steps, her weight shifting from side to side as she lifted and placed each black laced shoe in a wide stance. She knew shoes could snag a carpet. Her best friend, Gustina, was now laid up in the hospital with a broken hip all because her shoes failed to slide over a carpet at the Mayfair buffet. A dark scarf covered Aunt Rosie's head nun-like as she quietly and reverently stood near the casket. It wasn't that long ago when she was the principal-aggrieved one standing and sobbing uncontrollably over Salvaturi, her husband of 60 years. It seemed to Rosie that these waning years were collapsing inwardly with the heaviness of others' illnesses and deaths, so much so that she needed new changes of funereal wear; and she had to make the conscious decision, for her own health, to temper the depth and length of her mourning for her friends' losses. And now, she stood over her sister Francesca, laying there, porcelain imaged, styled with an enigmatic grin that seemed foreign to those who knew and loved her in life. Aunt Rosie quickly reached out as Annie went by carrying a large floral arrangement.

"She looks so peaceful there, Antonia. Like she's sleeping. *Ahhh mischinu.* Where did the years go? Seems like we were just kids. She was the smart one, you know, Antonia. Of all of us, she was the smart one." Aunt Rosie quickly formed the sign of the cross and began to quietly weep. Annie repeated the gesture; and, she also began sobbing.

"You hear from Vinnie?" Uncle Vito asked Jake. His voice sounded like gravel in a tin plate and emanated from deep in his throat. Uncle Vito Colletti was married to Antoinette, Jake's paternal aunt, who the family called Ninetta. He was a small man, five-five, who spent his life cutting hair under the pedestrian ramp to the New Orleans-Algiers ferry on the end of Canal Street. Vito's lifetime of making other men look good was not wasted on himself. Even in his aging years, his hair was dark, evenly parted and doused with generous spritzes of Jerris Tonic. Stiff-starched pants and shirts, sharply creased, and mirror shined shoes were his trademark along with the ever-present smell of talcum powder and hair tonic, the same used to send customers on their way. A delicate face and pencil thin moustache seemingly sketched with a fine marker were evocative of Hollywood's leading men of his youth.

"Yes, we heard from him. He's supposed to be here any minute now. Probably got stuck in traffic somewhere. You know how the traffic is in the city these days. And you think they'll let you in when you're trying to get onto a street. No way. It's every man for himself anymore, Uncle Vito. Every man for himself," said Jake.

"What's he doing now?" asked Uncle Vito.

Aunt Ninetta walked up to the two, "She's got a good turnout Jake. God rest her soul. She had a lot of friends." Her subdued voice came through her nose in a slow singsong lament. Regardless of circumstances, Aunt Ninetta's frozen countenance always suggested sorrow, maybe pity, perhaps a tinge of disgust. She stood with a slight lean toward Jake, a head taller than Uncle Vito and much wider.

Jake looked toward the crowd, "Yeah, she did have friends, Aunt Ninetta. I'm not sure what Vinnie is up to now, Uncle Vito. Last time I talked to him he was selling air purifiers. Well, he wasn't just selling them; he was part owner of the company."

"Oh yeah, I know about that. I got some letters from him asking me to invest. That was quite a while ago. Is he still doing that?" said Uncle Vito.

"I think so. You hungry, Uncle Vito, Aunt Ninetta? There's food in the back there," said Jake.

"I'll eat later. Maybe after the rosary," Uncle Vito said.

"I guess I'll grab a bite before we pray," said Aunt Ninetta.

"I don't know when Father Donahue is going to be here. *Mangia'*, eat. I'll find out when he's coming from Annie," said Jake.

"I'm not hungry now, Jake. I've been having problems with my stomach lately. I gotta see the doctor, I guess."

"You worry too much, Vito, that's why. Jake, he's a worrywart. And you eat too fast," Aunt Ninetta said.

"Where the hell is Vinnie?" Annie whispered to Calo on her way to the backroom and the food.

"He'll be here, Annie. He'll be here." Calo leaned back, stretching with both hands on the lower part of his back.

"You still having trouble with your back?" asked Annie.

"Yeah. Guess I'm gonna have to get it looked at again. Who's got the time to see a doctor? I'll be all right," said Calo.

"Philip," Annie swallowed a shout to him as he went by, "Make sure the kids don't eat too much of those fatty lunch meats back there. And keep them away from the desserts. I don't need them getting diabetes from too much sugar. *Binidittu Diu*, that's all I need now."

Friends and relatives gradually filled the room dressed in mourning wear that held the scents of back closets and mothballs. The smells of warming food, cologne, heavy perfume, and flowers permeated the frigid air-conditioned rooms creating a pallid presence all their own. Men puffed pipes, cigars, and cigarettes in a smoking room to the back, their exhales wafting out toward the visitation parlor, hovering in fine wisps that trailed their own odors. The decor of thick carpet, heavy furniture, and gothic fixtures enfolded subdued murmurs. Relatives that once intimately shared lives in nascent years greeted one another with the awkwardness of those estranged by either circumstances or design. Where once they joyfully celebrated church feast-days, birthdays, holidays, and weddings, they now, each having been led to other places and lives through the whims of fate, were occasionally, yet obligingly, brought back together by death. Some family members stiffly greeted each other, struggling to be cordial beyond veneers of ill feelings from unresolved rifts, though belabored, their origins lost with age.

A few remembered. Cousins Lee and Sal viewed family gatherings as arenas to resume a long-standing grievance over land ownership in Sant'Anna, Sicily. One claimed the other's father secretly sold the property and pocketed the money. Neither knew where to find the small commune on the map much less any records to substantiate his claim. Their interaction had turned into a game of brinkmanship that in the end created a civil commonality, a purpose for interacting, however contentious, so that neither man would seriously ever wish to resolve the issue.

Uncles Vito Colletti and Tony Triolo, brothers-in-law, now well into their 70s had gradually learned to be cordial after years of accusing the other of digging up money the "old man" had buried in the pasture, or under the back stairs of the barn; no one knew for sure. In years past, the arguments usually exacerbated by homemade wine would go: "Only you knew where your Papa used to bury the money," Vito would say.

"That's a damned lie." Tony would counter.

"Alls I know," Vito would say, "is your sister Ninetta told me your Papa had $3000.00 saved from selling some cows and a wagon of hay. She said she seen him put it in a Prince Albert can with her own eyes."

"Then she saw him bury it too, right?" interrupted Tony.

"If she'da told me where the money was buried and I dug it up, why the hell would I be blaming you all these years, Tony? I'd just shut up and never bring up the subject."

With advancing age, their accusative tenors mellowed although neither man was inclined to ever trust the other about anything.

There was a slight atmospheric change in the room. The conversation level rose as people gathered toward the front door.

"Mama, Uncle Vinnie's here," Annie's son Gino said.

Annie headed toward the gathering and weaved through to greet Vinnie with a hug then a quick kiss on the lips.

"Glad you're here," she said and began weeping. Vinnie was turned this way and that as people grabbed his arm to shake his hand, or get set for a hug, or pat him on the back. He always rebounded by turning toward Annie.

Soon brothers Calo, Jake, and Paulie worked their way through the gathering to hug him and give him a quick kiss. Then the wives joined in and their kids, all hugging and kissing Vinnie.

"Danny, the last time I saw you, you were this tall," Vinnie said as he held on to the child's arm. Give me a hug."

Danny hugged his uncle but turned his face away when Vinnie kissed him. "Why does everybody kiss on the lips, Uncle Vinnie? We gotta kiss every relative here on the lips. Blahhh!"

"I understand, *paesano*," Vinnie said. "That's just the old Sicilian custom of greeting, but we can just shake hands," and he held out his hand. They shook hands giving each other a brisk wide pump and Danny looked down with a blushing smile.

"You hungry?" Annie said. "Philip, get Vinnie a plate. Go on, Vinnie, go get a plate and some wine. *Mangia.*"

"Wine would be nice," Vinnie said. He followed Philip to the back room.

Aunt Rosie held a paper plate to her chest and lifted a sandwich to her mouth between sentences. "I was sure your mom would pull through," she said to Jake. "She seemed to be strong when I visited her in the hospital."

Yeah, Aunt Rosie, we thought she was getting better too, but the doctors never gave us hope. They told us just after the operation that they couldn't get all of the cancer. I guess we didn't want to think the worst."

Aunt Rosie lifted a sandwich as if to take a bite. The ham poked out and limply flapped as she accentuated her talk with hand gestures. "She was a hard worker, you know, Calo. Worked hard every day of her life; even when we were kids Francesca had to work hard. Your Nannu Italiano would hire us out to work neighbors' fields. We would work all week chopping cotton, or hoeing weeds for 50 cents and at the end of the week, your Nannu Italiano would get the money from the neighbor and we would never see it. One time me and your momma decided we wanted our money and we both went to tell Papa we didn't want him to take our money next week. We wanted to buy some fingernail polish and a little pink plastic purse we could keep our polish in. The old man hit the ceiling when we told him we wanted our money. His face got all red and he threw buckets and tools against the cowshed. Come the end of the week he threw our money at us yelling in Italian, 'You want your money, so take the money. Here! That's the thanks I get for giving you food and a place to live. I would do better to raise a bunch of hogs. At least I could kill them and eat them. Go on take your money. *afanapole!'* He was a mean old man your grandpa Italiano, Calo. A real mean old man."

"Did you buy your fingernail polish and the purse?" asked Calo.

"We walked to this little old town that had a small drug store, a *farmacia,* and bought our things. When we got back, Papa wouldn't give us nothing to eat. My brothers Sal and Dominic sneaked food to us that night. That's how we ate."

"I remember when she was carrying you Calo. She was sick as dog. Sick as a dog, Calo, and worrying every minute that you wouldn't make it into this world."

"Really, Aunt Rosie. I never heard that before."

"Oh yeah. She'd say, 'Why did I get this way again, Rosie?' She meant carrying a baby. I'd tell her, the Lord would take care of her and you. And thanks to *lu Signuri ,*" she quickly crossed herself, "here you are."

Annie worked her way through the crowd and walked to Vinnie holding on to an elderly lady who struggled to keep pace. "This is my brother Vinnie, Miss Irene," she spoke loudly, leaning into the lady's ear. "Vinnie, you remember Miss Irene don't you? She lived next door to Momma."

"Oh, hello Miss Irene," Vinnie said and politely bowed. "Thanks for coming."

"Me and your momma were very good friends. I knew her when she met your daddy down in Jesuit Bend. Then me and my husband, Clarence, God rest his soul," she quickly made the sign of the cross, "moved to Oak Point, right next to them. Me and your momma used to make the St. Joseph cookies and bread for the altars whenever your daddy would make an altar. I ain't Italian, but I lived around Italians all my life and learned to cook like 'em."

"Well, it's nice to see you again. Thanks for coming." Vinnie bowed again, "Excuse me Miss Irene. I think I'm gonna try some of that pasta." Vinnie carefully backed away, still bowing as he moved.

Annie stood next to Jake. "You seen Father Donahue yet? We ought to get on with the rosary so we can have people who want to say something about momma speak."

"Not yet. I did call him at least three times last week to make sure he knew where to come and when we wanted him here. I hope he didn't forget. I wanted Father Mancuso, but he couldn't do it. Momma would have wanted Father Mancuso, I'm sure she would have."

"Let me get back to make sure everybody got something to eat," Annie said. "You think I should call the church?"

Jake shrugged, hands out slightly to his sides, palms up.

Father Donohue eventually arrived in a fluster.

"I got so lost coming across the river. I thought I was going toward Magazine and ended up on Canal Street. I don't get over here that often. Sorry I'm late."

"You're fine, Father. We were just worried you might have had an accident," Annie said. "I just read in the papers about a priest that was going to a wedding, I think it was some place in Brazil, and he took a wrong turn and ended driving into a large area of quicksand. They found his car a week later, but never his body. Good rest his soul." she made the sign of the cross, "Come on Father. Get something to eat before we begin the rosary."

Annie led Father Donohue to the back kitchen and gave him a plate stacked high with potato salad, a thick ham and cheese sandwich, and pickles and tomatoes that hung over the plate. As he balanced the food and the plate on his way to a table, he spoke to Annie. "I'm sorry Mrs. Brewer," he looked at his small black binder, "I've done very little in your parish so please help me with some information about your mother. It is pronounced Tree-0-lah yes?"

Annie peered into his binder and pointed at her mother's name. "No, Tree-o-low."

"Tree-o-low, he practiced. Francisco, correct?"

"Fran-cis-cah. But everybody knows her as Francis."

The priest took out a ballpoint pen and quickly clicked it to correct the spelling and make a note. "Thanks," he said. "So after we do the rosary, I will say a little something about your mom according to the information you gave me. And are we going to have people come up afterwards?"

"Oh yeah. My brothers and I will say something and whoever else wants to speak."

"You don't mind then, if I leave when my part is done because I have to be back at church to get ready for morning Mass. Since I got lost coming here, I want to be sure I have a lot of time to find my way back."

Annie shook her head "no." In the moment she could not think of a good reason why he should stay, except that she thought it was always pleasant and reassuring to be in the presence of a priest at these solemn and sacred occasions. "Will you be here tomorrow when we close the casket and go to the cemetery?"

"Oh, no I won't be here, but I think Father Mancuso will be able to be here for that and the burial."

"Good," Annie said. "Oh Father, here is a donation. Thanks for coming out."

The priest quickly traced his hand in a blessing over the envelope and put it in his pants pocket, under his cassock. He took a couple of bites from his sandwich, "Well I think we should begin, don't you?"

Annie walked around with a coffee cup in hand lightly clinking it with a spoon. She announced solemnly that the rosary was about to begin so everyone should gather around. She wanted to put everyone at ease by telling them there was no need to have beads in hand since the priest would keep track of the prayers on his own, as would Annie and a few older people who knew to bring rosaries. And so Father Donahue and the attendees began in chorus, "In the name of the Father, Son, and Holy Ghost..."

While everyone gathered for the rosary, Vinnie carefully eased out of the parlor. Humid night air rushed him, a refreshing change from the miasmic staleness of the funeral home. He walked toward the *Grey Albatross*, a gathering place of sailors and dockworkers, near the wharf where he had arranged to meet a high school buddy. He and his friend Wyatt Cox used to visit the bar even when they were under-age high school students. Up ahead, heavy drumbeats, blaring horns, loud tribal singing poured out onto the street like a pent up dragon stalking those leaving, nudging at their backs to clear a path for newcomers. As Vinnie walked through the crowd into the midst of strident chatter and the music, his eyes strained to see through the smoky orange light, its source a bright sign behind the bar. The light bathed everyone's face, their drinks transformed by the color. The sign said "Beer" is all. No brand or picture, just an orange neon statement of the mundane. Wyatt's face reflected the color as he sat between two burly longshoremen. Upon seeing Vinnie, he quickly stood up, big smile, opened arms, readying for a man-hug.

"Vinnie. Sorry to hear about your mom, man. I hadn't heard or saw anything in the paper. I would have been better prepared to come."

"That's cool Wyatt. Yeah, she had been sick for quite a while."

"I bet your brothers and sister are taking it hard, eh?"

"Well Annie sure is. She and Jake were the closest to mom. They did most of the caregiving."

"So when did you get in?" asked Wyatt.

"Just today. Had a heck of a time getting a flight at the last minute."

"You gonna stay for a while?"

"No, man; I can't stay. I got to get back to try to get something going.

Hell, nothing seems to be working for me. I get these leads on things and they turn out to be crap."

"Did you ever call that woman I told you about? My dad said she was looking for some place to invest some money. In fact he was talking you up a blue streak."

"No, I never got around to it. I got so involved in trying to find other ways to earn money just to pay bills. I got nothing left, Wyatt, nothing."

"Didn't I hear that you were working with a guy on that air purifier thing?"

"Yeah. I took him in as a partner; but he was a flake, man. I put in the little money I had and he blew it on crap that didn't work. He talked a good line, but he didn't have as much money or connections as I had, which was very puny at that."

"I don't want to bring up a sore subject, or maybe it isn't. Do you ever hear from Jamie?"

"That is a sore subject, Pal. Thanks for bringing it up."

"You know her brother got sent up to Angola for that robbery."

"Yeah. I know. Calo told me that."

"I'm sorry if it's a raw subject, Vinnie, it's just that I've heard from a few of our old buddies that she still goes by Jamie Triolo. They're always asking me if you guys are still married. You're not, are you?"

"Nope. I got an annulment when I found out she might have a husband at the time we were supposed to be married."

There was a dead pause then, "So what are you doing now?" Vinnie asked.

"Well, you know, I went back to community college and became a paralegal. I'm working with my old man. Looking up stuff. Doing research, you know?"

"You and Sarah still together?"

"Oh yeah."

"Marriage?"

"We don't talk about that much Vinnie, that is, we don't talk too seriously about that. We'll see."

Vinnie looked down at his watch, "They're saying the rosary now, so I ducked out. Glad you showed up man. Good to see you again. You gave me a good excuse to get out of there. Thanks."

"When was the last time you said the rosary, Vinnie?" Wyatt grinned.

"Oh hell. When was the last time *you* said the rosary?"

"I'm not Catholic, Vinnie. You know that. I'm an atheist."

"Let me think. Seems the last time I said a rosary must have been in catechism class, eighth grade, maybe?" Vinnie said, "I don't remember."

"Aside from them grieving for your mom, how are your brothers and sister doing?"

"They're fine. Everybody's trying to make a living and survive. So how's your family, your dad, mom. Your sister?"

"They're okay. You know my mom, always complaining. Could be raining gold coins, she'd bitch because no one gave her a bucket. Same old same. My old man fishes a lot, but he doesn't seem to catch a lot of fish."

Neither man seemed to have the will to rehash any of the past, or dredge up the names of old friends. The passage of time and the length of their separation had narrowed the range of their interest, their commonalities. Their conversation was slowly ambling to a dead stop. Now they talked about the *Grey Albatross*, the music, its people, Wyatt reminded him of some of the pathetic people they used to egg on at the bar, Vinnie feigned a sketchy recall; and then, rapid subject shifts served to fill the time of Vinnie's AWOL from the rosary. When there seemed to be nothing more to say and the men sat in an awkward silence, Vinnie snapped his wrist, "Well, friend, it looks like it's time to get back. You want to come over to say hello?"

"Vinnie. I hope you'll forgive me, but I don't think I would do anybody any good being there. I mean look at me, I'm not dressed. I know your brother Paulie a little. I've been in his shop getting some things fixed, but it's been a long time since I've talked to anybody else. I don't even know if they would remember me. I think it would kind of be a distraction. I hope you understand, buddy."

"I understand. Listen. I will call you before I leave town and we can get together one more time eh? Maybe have Sarah come along and invite some of the guys. You ever see them anymore?"

"Oh yeah, I see them all the time, but we don't hang out much anymore. I'm usually with Sarah or my family, you know?"

"Yep. I know."

The two embraced. Vinnie and Wyatt walked out together, each turned toward an opposite direction, giving a quick wave in parting.

Vinnie eased into the viewing parlor from the direction of the smoking room. His sister-in-law, Vickie, quickly met him as soon as he walked in and gently led him toward the food room.

"Where were you, Vinnie?" she whispered, "Annie and Paulie are all upset you weren't around for the rosary and they're really mad you weren't here to say something about your mom."

"I met a friend down the street. I had to get some air and get away from this gloomy place. I'm sorry, Vickie. I'll apologize to them."

"Don't do it now, Vinnie. Wait until everybody leaves. There're so pissed at you and if you say something now, they'll probably lose it and embarrass themselves in front of everybody. Then they'll be even madder at you for causing them to look like fools." She gave Vinnie a quick hug. "Poor baby," she said with a pitiable *what-are-we-going-to-do-with-you?* smirk.

The Triolo siblings were the last to leave the funeral home. Their spouses and children had gone home. The parlor now took on a very different atmosphere as all of the energies of the evening's condolences, the soft conversations, quiet tears, hovered silently, but palpably, as though pushing on the ceiling, invisible clouds gathering to form a weightiness that would have rushed out to mingle with the night's atmosphere if it could. Who knew what condolences, sorrows, and years of accumulated mournfulness were embedded in the carpet, the drapes, the walls, and the heavy furniture. For the moment, the family's grief had waned, their sadness overtaxed by the evening's event. It had been a long day for everyone. Tomorrow would be the burial.

"Mr. Rosen will handle everything," Annie said. He'll tell us what to do, where to stand, when to close the coffin. He's wonderful at this."

"Well, this is his business. It's good to let an expert handle the logistics," Paulie said. He looked at Vinnie. "Where did you go for the rosary? Were you here, or did you disappear again?"

"What do you mean, 'disappear again?'" Vinnie said.

"Well I mean you've been gone for two years. You kind of disappeared to us."

Vinnie held out his arms in the manner of *what are you talking about?* "I *disappeared?*"

"We were disappointed you didn't say something about Momma.

And, I'm really upset that even after I went over some things with Father Donohue he still mispronounced Momma's name," Annie said.

"I think he got his notes mixed up. Who was he talking about? Saying Momma had come over from Italy. And she was known for her wonderful meatballs, pasta and red gravy. We didn't write anything like that. I mean Momma would have never called *sugu* 'red gravy,'" Calo said.

"And Aunt Rosie is the one who can make meatballs," said Jake.

"I'm disappointed Father Mancuso couldn't have said Momma's rosary. We all spoke about her, even some of our kids. It would have been nice if you had said something," Annie said. "Everybody was wondering what happened to you."

"You guys covered everything, I'm sure. What else could I have said that you didn't say?" Vinnie said.

"That's not the point, Vinnie; it's just nice to have the whole family together at these times. I mean, we're all that's left," Annie said tearing up a bit.

"I'm sorry. I guess I didn't really think."

"How long you gonna stay around?" Jake asked.

"I'm thinking a day or two. I got to get back to Tennessee to try to get something done with my business."

"You can't stay longer? You know we've got some talking to do about the properties. Are we gonna hold on to them, sell them, lease them, or whatever. We're gonna need to talk," Paulie said.

"Whatever you guys decide is okay with me," Vinnie said.

"Well, that's well and good, Vinnie, but whatever we decide we got to make sure everybody signs off so none of us come back later wanting something else," said Calo.

"Of course, we're going to meet with the lawyer and sign papers to agree on what we all want to do. I don't mean to offend anybody, but it's like Daddy used to tell us, 'You can't even trust your relatives nowadays,'" said Jake.

"We're not going to argue over the land and money, are we? Even before Mamma's in the ground?" Annie said and burst into tears.

"Wasn't there some wine in the back?" asked Vinnie. "I'd like some wine. Anybody else?"

"Yeah, go ahead Vinnie. See if there's any left," said Jake. "I know it's not a pleasant thing to talk business with Momma laying in the next room, but sooner or later, we're going to have to get down to business."

"I'd rather wait until later to tell you the truth," said Paulie.

"I don't know how she got cancer. Dr. Boudreaux never saw anything like that when he examined her. I don't remember either Momma or Daddy telling us we had cancer in the family," Annie said. "Paulie, did Daddy ever mention that we had cancer in the family? I don't remember hearing that."

Vinnie came back with the bottle of Gallo Red and water glasses. "Who wants some?" he said waving the bottle.

Happily Even After

by Debbie DiGiacobbe

Independent and quirky, Isadora is more than content. She lives in the most perfect little community and has created a wonderful life for herself. There is nothing that can make Isadora happier until an accidental encounter at the dumpster turns everything upside down or right side up...for a moment.

Isadora lived in a small town called Neighborly. Like its name, everyone was, you might say, neighborly. They greeted you, asked how you were doing and even listened to you as you answered. They brought you soup if you were sick, and watched your dog, if you had one, when you went on vacation. Everyone knew everyone's name. They even knew the mail carrier, Larry, who was not too bad on the eyes.

Isadora didn't realize it at the time, as all things become clearer in retrospect, but she had discovered the most perfect place. Her tiny condominium was part of a building made up of four units, one at each corner, all with...that's right, neighborly people. As comes with condo living, there were many rules. Christmas lights MUST come down the day after New Year's, garden decorations were absolutely prohibited, and dogs must be walked in the street. That must be hard on their feet. Isadora was glad she didn't have a dog. They were so much work: feed them, walk them, pick up their… well, you get the picture. Isadora never liked rules, but everything else made up for their small inconvenience.

Isadora found balance by designating the inside of her home as a no rules zone. She even hung a sign on the interior of her front door saying, NO RULES. You guessed, it. Yes, signs on doors were prohibited too. It was quite simple. Isadora did what she wanted, how she wanted, when she wanted. If she felt like painting a giraffe on the wall, she did. If she wanted to hang her clothes up to dry in her living room, she did. If she felt like having macaroni for breakfast, she did. And she did all those things by the way…and more. In addition, Isadora surrounded herself with everything that made her happy: art, music, books and nature. What more could a girl ask for?

Her friends told Isadora that she could push the limits of her happiness by finding someone to love. But Isadora loved so many things already—especially her freedom. Plus, she was skeptical. She heard stories of love. If you were lucky to find the right person, you would be the object of their affection. They would do anything for you: ask you how you were doing and listen, make you soup even if you weren't sick, and…walk your dog. It would be…neighborly at the least! Silly, thought Isadora. I have all I need. I love my life just the way it is.

Isadora woke up every morning to a singing chicken; not a real one of course. She ate a bowl of Cocoa Puffs, grabbed her chocolate flavored coffee, and headed to work. She played all day with the children as she taught them eeeeeverything! She came home at night, decorated their papers with encouraging notes and smiley faces, made herself dinner, green eggs and ham (her favorite), read a good book, wrote about her day in her journal, and went to sleep. She had the perfect life.

The only thing Isadora wasn't fond of was taking out the trash, another rule of condo living, but she had gotten used to it. It was not that big of a deal unless she had to separate someone else's trash, like today. To the dumpster, she carried two heavy bags, one with trash and one with recycling: cans, bottles, paper, etc. What a pain! As she pried open the heavy lid of the one labeled Trash, she spied some beer bottles.

They were just sitting there, mingling with the trash as if they were at a party. Angrily, she stared them down—all twenty-four happy bottles of Coors Light to be exact. What's the difference between light and regular, she thought, when you consume all twenty-four? Really?!? She wondered why it was so hard to put them in the recycling bin, which was just a foot away. Not only did she have to recycle her own trash, she had to recycle everyone else's. This was the only rule that the town of Neighborly did not reinforce. Now, you tell me. How is that neighborly? Like I was saying, how hard could it be to recycle when the bin is just two feet away? One foot, two feet. What's the difference? Either way, the bin was RIGHT THERE! Isadora tried to understand what might make someone throw them in the trash. Perhaps they were drunk and got confused. After all there were twenty-four bottles. Could it be they didn't know how to read? Well, that didn't make sense. Everyone knows how to read. Even if that was the case, the dumpsters were clearly labeled with symbols: Food for Trash; Cans, Bottles and Paper for recycling. Plus, they were color coded. Teal for Trash, Red for Recycling. What's not to understand?? It was so easy. Isadora decided that whoever did this was defying the rules or just plain lazy. Probably the latter.

Recycling was the only rule Isadora didn't mind following. It was her civic duty. She vowed to leave the planet better than she found it starting with her community. She would fix this. So, standing on her toes, she threw her body over the rim of the dumpster stretching down into the bin, gingerly retrieving each bottle one at a time. Of course, they were more than halfway down, which did not make it an easy task. With each reach, she placated herself by thinking of it as a challenge. She tried to find the positive in everything. Still, it was gross her body hanging over a filthy dumpster filled with dog...well you know what, and other disgusting things. Finally, when she reached for the last bottle, the one at the very bottom, yes, you guessed it, she fell. Immediately, she panicked. She could see someone coming to the dumpster to throw out their trash and snatching her picture with their iPhone, which never seemed to leave their hand. They would post it all over social media. NEIGHBORLY NEIGHBOR FALLS INTO DUMPSTER TRYING

TO KEEP COMMUNITY NEIGHBORLY... or tidy or whatever. And, people would know it was not fake news because those who knew her, knew she was capable of the act.

After at least a dozen attempts to pull herself out, she began to whisper a scream. She struggled for what seemed like an hour when finally a tall, dark, handsome man with a wry smile came to her rescue. For real! Totally smelly and humiliated, she let him pull her out. And, as she brushed off a used tissue, banana peels and other disgusting slop, their eyes met, and it was...well, neighborly.

Jared and Isadora started dating. Every day, Jared asked Isadora how she was doing and listened to her answer, he made her soup even when she wasn't sick, and he walked her dog. Wait, she didn't have a dog, but he would have if she did. Isadora, too, reciprocated. It was a wonderful union as they fell madly in love and were more than neighborly to each other.

As you can imagine, Isadora and Jared, well you know the ending, they lived happily ever after...for a few months. As for Isadora, she lived happily even after.

A Conversation with a Stranger

Patricia (Rispoli) Edick

A quest for revenge born many centuries ago was now a plan in motion.
The answer was there all along, but the wait made victory
so much more succulently satisfying.
This is a story of how greed can lead us to a point of no return.

CHAPTER ONE

THE STRANGER
AND SO IT GROWS

Luke knew when to stop talking. Unlike the one they referred to as, "The Orange Man," he knew that more is usually not a good thing. He believed that it wasn't necessary to pound out a message at rallies filled with hysteria, or deliver loud rebel rousing speeches. He did not intend to use mass media or large gatherings to achieve success. One joyous convert would lead to another and so on and so on. Luke was not in a hurry. He, The Stranger, had waited this long and been a witness to the rise and fall of," The Gray One," "The Tan One" and "The White Haired Lady in the Big House." By his clandestine observations, Luke learned that brutality and strong arm tactics were not the floorplans that would help him to achieve success in his quest. Pitting man against man or creating a war between the, 'have and the have nots', didn't work. It is quite simple. Give them everything they need and want. Mass consumption in unlimited quantities until there simply was no more.

What he had been planned to do today was finished. He would watch and wait for the seed he planted to blossom into a burning bush of desire. He recalled a phrase from the Bible, "What you sow, so shall you reap." Over time, as Paul's wishes were fulfilled, the network would evolve and the message would grow. Paul's neighbors would be envious of his wealth, and they too would be ripe for picking. It didn't take the wisdom of a Profit or the skills of a Wizard to see the potential for enormous growth here in rural USA.

He turned his attention to another. It wasn't planned but it was too good to pass up on. Nate, who was seated on the right side of Luke, and the left of Paul, had taken it all in and although he had not uttered a word, his body language spoke volumes. Luke adjusted his chair so he could look directly into Nate's eyes; he knew that they are the key to one's soul. As soon as their eyes were locked, Nate felt a compulsion to speak; he had vowed to keep his mouth shut earlier, but the words were building up and needed to flow like a stream that swelled after a storm. His hands were shaking and his head felt like it was about to explode; he felt a tingling sensation throughout his entire body. He took several deep breaths but he could not calm himself. Nate let loose and screamed out the words, "I want in."

That was enough for The Stranger to accept the invitation and reel in this fish that had taken the bait. It didn't take long for Nate to make his desires known; "I have worked on this farm for as long as I can remember. I can't complain about the way Paul and his Family have treated me. They have always been kind to me and paid me a fairly decent wage and gave me a place to live. I have a shack I call home, and except for the really hot or extremely cold days it is comfortable. All I ever wanted was a roof over my head, a soft bed and food in my belly on a regular basis. I don't own much, but I don't have any debt so I always figured I was pretty well off. But, after listening to what took place here with you and Paul, I think I'm entitled to what he's getting. Paul will need my help with the livestock and besides which I have worked just as hard all these years as him and I should get my share of the reward."

He stopped speaking, but his mind was still whirling. Nate thought, *"I have lived in this County my whole life, never been to another State, let alone another Country. It's time I had some fun while I'm still young enough to enjoy it. What have I got to lose?"*

CHAPTER TWO

PAUL
FROM THE BEGINNING

It was very early in the morning of what promised to be a beautiful spring day. Paul Green sat alone in his kitchen on a rickety wood chair drinking strong black coffee. He heard the birds singing and the dogs barking but he didn't look to see what was going on outside. His mind was busy planning the day for him and the farm hand Nate. Paul's Father and Grandfather had always begun their days the same way, each of them sitting in this room at this table, drinking black coffee. This is the way men liked their coffee. Save the milk and cream for desserts and for the children.

There would be eggs to gather, livestock to feed, cows to milk, crops to tend and fences to mend. This was all in a day's work for Paul Green III.

He thought, *"The work has always been the same but now I have to do more of it. I'm supposed to be taking it easy at my age. It just ain't fair."*

His two boys had been conscripted into service by the Government to serve in a war in a Country that he had never even heard of.

That left him shorthanded. His feeling of discontent and even resentment for the powers to be was eating him alive, like a cancerous tumor in his gut gnawing away whenever he had to tackle a task without the help of his sons Jim and Mike. The Farm did not generate enough money to hire hands to replace them, so he had to manage with only Old Nate by his side. There were days when the two of them labored from sunrise to sunset and still didn't get everything done.

It was on mornings like this when his bones ached and he couldn't remember the last time he had gone fishing that the burning in his gut made him feel worse than ever. Paul wished that he had a regular job; one that paid a man steady wages for his efforts. He often daydreamed and pictured himself in a wool blend fitted suit like the ones he had seen in the catalogues. In these dreams he was all neat and clean, ready for his day at the office. He kissed his wife Kate and said, "I'll see you at suppertime," and then hopped into his shiny car for a short drive to his clean office. Farming was a dirty business and lately Paul never felt clean. It didn't matter how many showers he took, or how often Kate laundered his cloths, the stink of the farm was always with him.

Kate made her way into the kitchen. "Good morning Paul. What do you want for breakfast"? Paul looked up at his wife's face and a feeling of calm came over him.

He replied, "Don't matter, anything hot and filling will do. I probably won't be taking time out for a midday meal; lots of chores to do today."

Kate busied herself making breakfast and Paul went back to his coffee and his thoughts. A tapping sound from the outside door leading to the kitchen jolted Paul back to reality. He yelled out, "Come in Nate, breakfast is just about ready." Nate mumbled, "Morning," as he took his usual place across from Paul.

"Any news I should know about," Paul asked Nate.

"Well, as a matter of fact there is. I heard some talk that a Government Man is coming around telling people that Pigs carry disease, a virus, and it would be wise to kill them all before they make us sick."

Paul stopped drinking his coffee and looked up at Nate. He was bewildered by what he had just heard and shouted, "What... kill my pigs. That's crazy talk. What Government is this man from, Russia? Humans can't catch disease from animals. It's people who make animals sick. Nobody better come around here telling me to kill my pigs."

Nate didn't answer. He knew better. He didn't want to work all day with an angry boss at his side. He thought, "*Paul asks for the news and when he don't like what I tell him he takes it out on me. I got to learn to keep my mouth shut.*"

They finished their breakfast in silence. Kate sat next to Paul as she also ate in silence. The two men got up from their chairs, put on their coats and hats and exited through the kitchen door. As she watched them leave, Kate thought, "*Silence is golden.*"

The Stranger drove his car up to the barn, kicking up a cloud of dust in his wake. He thought, "*One more to go and my day is done. Today's subjects had proven to be especially easy to persuade. Isolation seems to make them more vulnerable.*" He took a quick look at himself in the rear-view mirror as he readied himself to exit the car. "Handsome as ever," he noted.

Paul and Nate were already approaching his vehicle.

Luke thought, "*It's time to raise the curtain and begin the show.*"

He stood beside his shiny vehicle and extended his hand to Paul, who had reached him a second ahead of Nate. Before Paul or Nate had a chance to utter a sound, the man said, "Good afternoon, Gentlemen; my name is Luke Wannamaker. Fine day we are having here on God's green earth. I would appreciate it if you could give me a moment of your time."

Paul shook the stingers' hand. He noticed the clean black wool blend suit the nicely groomed man was wearing. He wondered if this was the Government Man that Nate told him about. Paul liked the way the man looked directly into his eyes; that was a sign of honesty.

The man continued to speak to Paul: "Mind if we go inside your house to talk. I've come a long way. Sometimes I swear one might be tempted to sell his soul for a cold glass of water." The Greens never turned away a person who needed a drink of water. Water was the only thing they had enough of to be able to share with an outsider.

Paul led the group back towards the house. As they approached the house, the dogs that had been napping and enjoying the seasonably warm spring day, jumped up and began to bark vigorously, straining their leads. Just as Paul was about to yell at them to shut up, the dogs stopped barking and sat down in unison and appeared to cower in fear and to tremble as the three men passed by. This was not noticed by either Nate or Paul; they were just happy that the dogs were quiet. They were always barking at something.

Paul, Nate and the Stranger sat around the kitchen table. Kate served the men cold drinks and then she silently retreated to the adjoining room. Luke was the first to speak in his silky smooth voice, "Thank you for your hospitality and for inviting me into your home." He stopped for a moment to scan the men and the room, and then he continued. "I know how hard you work and that no one appreciates what good men like you need to do to keep food on your table and fill the pantries for everyone."

Paul and Nate shot a quick glance at one another. There was no need to speak. They both believed this to be true. The people living in this town, who didn't have to battle Mother Nature to earn a living, didn't appreciate what Paul and Nate did. Those ingrates took everything they had for granted. They had no idea, nor did they care what it took to stock the shelves of the grocery stores.

Luke continued, "Seems to me, Paul, that you should be better compensated for the dedication and hard work your Family has done for three generations on this farm."

Paul glanced at the pile of overdue bills on the desk in the corner. No matter how hard he worked there was very little left after satisfying the creditors to spend to buy the nice things he wanted to give to his wife and to his children. He couldn't remember the last time he bought Kate a new dress or he had money to spend on drinks at the local watering hole.

After a pause Luke continued, "I can make things right. You will have whatever you want, what you deserve. How does that sound to you, my friend?"

Paul looked closely at The Stranger sitting directly across from him and asked, "How is it you think that you know me well enough to call me friend?"

This didn't cause Luke to miss a beat in his presentation. He countered with, "Of course I know you Paul, I wouldn't have come out here to see you if I didn't know all about you. My goal is to help your Family get everything they need and want. I ask for very little in return, nothing difficult for you to do."

Paul's curiosity was stoked. He hesitated, and then in a lower than normal voice asked, "What do I have to do. I don't want any trouble with the Law."

Immediately Luke replied, "Don't worry about that, I am the Law. If you do what I ask I guarantee you'll be fine." He continued, "Paul I'm sure you heard by now about what they are calling the Swine Flu Virus. Funny thing is that people around here think that animals of the peccary or pig family cause the virus. How many pigs do you have on this farm?"

Paul shouted in anger, "Why are you asking about my pigs. I won't kill them if that's what you're asking me to do."

In his silky even tone, Luke answered, "Please listen to what I have to say. Remember I said that it would be easy. I won't ask you to do anything you don't want to do of your own free will. You invited me into your home; I didn't force my way in. What would you want for you and your family if there were no boundaries in the way?"

The Stranger was confident that in the end Paul's greed would overcome any doubts he harbored; sooner or later they all succumbed. There was no reason to believe that this subject was any different. The plan was simple enough. First the pigs, then the cows, the sheet, the goats, and so on and so on until there were no warm or cold blooded creatures left except for the humans. The second phase was the destruction of every plant, every flower, everything that could serve as a food source for mankind. Nothing would be left in the larders. Useless would be the tools to grind the wheat, butcher the meat, or fish in the seas. And when the humans realized that there was no more it would be too late to reverse the course that had been taken. The survivors would pray for death, an end to their suffering. The prophecy would be fulfilled, and man had destroyed himself.

CHAPTER THREE

AND THEN THERE WAS KATE

There was one more person in the house: Kate. But she was hardly worth investing any time in. Luke had sized her up and knew that this shell of a woman would do whatever Paul wanted. As The Stranger left, he glanced at Kate in the next room. She was sitting in a rocking chair as she stared wide eyed out the dirt-streaked window. This weathered chair with its tattered cushion and fading varnish gave her a temporary mental escape and brought a few moments of peace to her. As Kate rocked back and forth, the floor beneath the chair sang out in harmony. As the runners embraced the bare wooden floor it cried out, "They will return." Over and over the words were repeated as her eyes gazed out the window at the road that would bring Jim and Mike back to her.

Kate wasn't always like this. As a child she was filled with dreams and fantasies that helped her to deal with the sadness and the poverty that she was surrounded by. Believing that the Mom and Dad who raised her were not her 'real' parents, this very small and frail child drew upon her imagination to alter the reality of her life. She waited for her 'real' parents to find her, and when they rescued her, Kate would have all the joy and comforts that she longed for. There would be plenty of food and her only task would be to play with the multitude of presents that would be bestowed upon her. As an adolescent, Kate created a new dream. A rich and handsome man would come by and rescue her. They would live, "happily ever after" in their big clean home. But no one came. When Paul asked her to marry him, Kate accepted his offer. He wasn't bad looking and since he loved her, she was sure that he would be good to her. If her rich handsome man came by, she could easily leave Paul since she didn't really love him.

Kate tried to be good to Paul and did everything she believed that a good wife needed to do. Paul did provide for her and so she settled into a life that was happy enough and fulfilling enough and she no longer dreamed of escaping or of being rescued. She poured her heart and soul into loving and taking care of her family. Kate believed that she had found her real family. When her sons were taken from her by the Government, she was hurled back to the days of the unhappiness and longing of her youth. Only this time she was not waiting to be rescued from her fake family, she was waiting for the return of her real family. She coped by shedding herself of all the feelings that made the pain unbearable. An empty shell, her body going through the motions of living, her mind numbed to silence, Kate had given up the gift of free will that God had given her. She had nothing left to lose.

CHAPTER FOUR

AND SO IT WAS WRITTEN

The contracts that had been signed by the greedy ones and the saddened ones would be called in for satisfaction. It had been spelled out in language that was straightforward and simple: 'What was gifted to you at your Birth by God will become the property of the owner of the said contract at the moment of your demise. All tangible goods that have been obtained during your lifetime will be passed on to your heirs. No exceptions will be made to this, regardless of circumstances. However, this contract is subject to transfer of ownership upon receipt of something appraised by the owner of the contract to be of greater value than the collateral pledged at the signing of this agreement.'

It was written in such simple language that very few gave it much thought and signed without hesitation. They didn't think about what they were pledging as collateral; instead, they drew on the phrase they had heard so often, "I was born with nothing and I will die with nothing." So they believed that when they died they would have nothing left to give and while they lived there would be much to gain. This was true except for the intangible item referred to as, 'What was gifted to you at your Birth by God'. The gift was sometimes referred to as your essence, your spirit, or your soul. There is always something left to lose.

THE END

…OR IS IT JUST THE BEGINNING?

HE CAME UPON US…
HE HAD MUCH TO GIVE…
I INVITED HIM IN
AND DID WHAT HE ASKED.
HE GAVE ME SO MUCH
AND NOW I MUST PAY.

Alter Boys

by Fred L. Gardaphé

"Alter Boys" is a humorous look at the young boys who were entrusted with assisting in the administration of the Catholic Church's holy sacraments in the 1960s. Through their antics, they reveal the human side of spirituality...

When I was a boy, there were two permanent ambitions among my Catholic comrades in our village just west of Chicago. They were to be a priest or a gangster. The road to priesthood began early with becoming an altar boy; the road to perdition came shortly thereafter.

Being selected to serve mass at Sacred Heart Church was like being elected senator to Congress; it was even better than being a patrol boy, a singer in the choir, or a lunch helper, because you'd get out of school more often for events like funerals, you had immunity from suspicious acts for no nun would dare question the whereabouts of a boy who had just served mass, and priests would stand up for you if the occasion demanded; also, there was good money in in it, especially once you got to be the lead altar boy for baptisms, weddings and funerals.

You see, where I grew up, everyone believed in tipping. You never get something for nothing, and a tip here and there made for good service and friends everywhere. So, the custom continued beyond restaurants, bars, and deliveries, into the Church. Some of the priests hogged all the tips given out at special masses for weddings and funerals, just as the nuns took the tips for the choir, but a good lead altar boy knew to get to the families before the priest, and when he did, we'd walk out of church with at least a buck or two per server, more from the gangsters, who never carried singles and were the biggest tippers in town. That was pretty good money when you could still get real candy for a penny, a pack of baseball cards for a nickel, and a coke and fries for a quarter.

The everyday work for altar boys was serving daily Mass. Two masses every day at 6:00 and 8:15 in the mornings, and three on Sunday with the Italian mass in the church basement at 10 a.m., kept the thirty selected servers busy throughout the week in teams of two, posted every Friday in the principal's office. The 6 o'clock masses were for the workers and old people who rose early; the daily 8:15 was mandatory for all students in the elementary school from ages 7 to 13, and on Sundays, the 9:00 mass was for the fashionistas.

To fill the slots, nuns chose candidates from their 5th, 6th, 7th and 8th grade classes, and the priests made the final selections. They chose only those they considered to be the brightest and most likely to become priests one day. How they chose me, I'll never know, but for a while I took it pretty seriously and imagined we were pages in training to one day become knights. The priests were the knights of the church, the older altar boys the squires and the younger, pages.

The pages were usually the 5th and 6th graders. As rookies we had to do before, during and after a mass, and if you knew how to drag it out, you could miss a good portion of your first period class. We were the light janitors whenever there was a slight spill or a quick sweeping to be done; we were the go-fors whenever the priests forgot something in the rectory or their cars; we met deliveries, stocked the shelves with unconsecrated hosts, cases of mass wine, and fresh candles. We kept the cassocks and surplices in order, carrying the dirty ones to the convent for cleaning, returning with those clean and pressed to hang in the tall closets in the altar boy room, stage left of the altar. We helped the sisters prep the altar for mass; filling cruets with water and wine; and took Latin lessons with a priest during lunch or after school. Many of those tasks punched our tickets out of classes and brought us behind the scenes of the greatest drama in the hood: Holy Mass. What we saw and learned dispelled the mysteries we had been trained to imagine since first grade.

Promotion to a squire was granted once you passed the stressfully difficult test of correctly and audibly pronouncing the required Latin responsorials. The good guys always knew what the Latin words mean; I wouldn't understand those words until after I had left the Church and got deep into studying Latin in High School. The Squires were entrusted with lighting all the candles before mass, snuffing them out after. They were also the one who got to ring the chimes at key times during the mass. In the old days, the bells were handheld, but by the time I was an altar boy, Sacred Heart had three keys inserted into the face of the second of three steps that let up to the altar. Each key rang a different chime and the correct sound sequences were entrusted only to the squires.

As personal valets to the priests, squires would help them change into and out of the complicated array of vestments required for mass, consisting of the alb, amice, chasuble, a stole and the maniple, all donned in proper order.

The alb came first, always the same white garment fixed with a cincture placed over the black cassock the priest wore over his regular clothes; next came the amice, a linen neck cloth; the chasuble, the heaviest and most ornate (some even had solid gold or silver threads) would vary in style and color according to the liturgical season and the type of mass being offered, as would the stole that would hang over his neck: Shades of violet for Advent, Lent, and sometimes for funerals and Extreme Unction, the anointing of the sick; White for Easter, baptisms, weddings, and special feasts; Rose for special Sundays in Advent and Lent; Red for Pentecost, Palm Sunday, Good Friday and the sacrament of Confirmation; Black for All Souls day and funerals; and Green for normal Sundays. The silk stole hung like an unknotted necktie around the shoulders and a matching maniple draped over the priest's left arm.

Each priest had his own wardrobe and it was up to the squires to know which outfits went with each priest; the nuns would lay them out, and the squire handed them to him, witnessing the priest's required statements for each: like "Lord keep me from the temptation of the devil" when he put on the amice. Things could get pretty complicated when it came to special occasions like High Masses and Confirmation when guests like bishops and Cardinals would join the services, carrying all kinds of headgear like birettas and mitres, and gloves, and capes. And oh yeah, squires got to run errands for the priests and nuns.

A page was always paired with a squire for mass. In my early days as a page I mumbled as I mimicked the responses that the squire would say louder. The priest was director and leading actor for the mass; most would not proceed with their lines until we had clearly spoken ours. Father Freeman would think nothing of stopping mass if something went wrong, even if it was a big occasion, to correct our pronunciations and to chastise us for dropping lines.

While altar boys would be around for most of the seven sacraments, especially when they were administered through Holy Mass: Baptism, Communion, Confirmation, Extreme Unction, and Marriage, we weren't needed for Confession and Holy Orders—when other priests and seminarians would take over our jobs.

As soldiers of Christ, altar boys were trained to use two tools that I used to imagine were our weapons: the candle lighter with bell snuffer—our lance and the paten—our body sword, both of which could do some serious damage, like the time one of the boys accidently set fire to the lace curtains that hung behind the candle stands or when a parishioner took it in the Adam's apple, causing him to spit out the host at Communion.

Holding the paten between the consecrated host and the floor was one of our most important duties. The host, like the American flag, had to be burned if it touched the ground, and it was our duty to make sure that didn't happen. When it did, everything halted; the priest alone could pick it up and dispose of it by burning it somewhere in the sacristy after the Mass. Handling the paten could be painful during the larger masses for you had to move along the line of the communion rails that separated the main body of the church from the altar where the recipients kneeled, closed their eyes and stuck out their tongues.

As we moved along the inside of the rail with the priest, holding the paten just below their chins, we'd get to see people in close up, and as we'd move along I'd study faces, see things like dandruff, false eyelashes, women's make up, the hair in men's noses, and best of all the décolletage of the wild ones who dared to leave blouse buttons open just enough. Once Father Guistolise caught my glance down into a deep valley and smiled, then asked me to confess the act the next time he had me for confession.

Six o'clock mass was a drag, and usually given to the rookies. While I hated waking up to serve it, I loved the three-block walk that early in the morning, when no one was on the streets. In the warmer months, it was just me, the sunrise and the birds chirping in the cool morning air; in winter dark, I'd be alone with the streetlights, the crunching snow watching my breath lead the way to Church. The best job was the eight o'clock mass before classes started, which all students were expected to attend. There you'd be on display for the whole school. During communion we could check out all the girls, and play paten pranks on buddies, tapping their necks with the sharp edges startling them into the strangest faces.

High Masses, usually performed by three priests, and funeral masses, which demanded more than the usual two servers, were the most complicated and where things could more easily go wrong, so they were reserved for squires only. Once, during a funeral mass in the summer, after the older boys had graduated, Fr. Freeman had to rely on a few pages to fill out his group. It was the first time Danny had to light the incense used to anoint the coffin. We were told that incense would purify anything it touched, but this day, the coffin was anything but purified.

Fr. Freeman asked me to be the censer bearer, but Danny grabbed it out of my hands. He was a year older and so I gave in to his seniority. He dropped the round charcoal into the base of the censer, covered with the dried herbs, lit it and clouds of sweet smoke billowed out. All seemed fine until Father took the chains from Danny. It seems Danny had not properly dropped the cover, and so when Father went to swing the censer over the casket, the burning herbs and coal flew out, and smoldered the purple funeral spread that covered the coffin. Father dropped the censer and began beating the burning cloth with his bare hands. All of us did the same. When all the smoke had cleared, and the holy cloth pulled off the coffin, Father kicked the censer my way and under his breath told me to refill it, close it, and he picked up the ceremony as if nothing had happened. After the mass we were all given a warning and told that our tips that day would go toward a new coffin cover. Danny, despite his seniority, would never serve a funeral mass in Sacred Heart again.

In the 1960s, when Russia was our greatest enemy, the nuns would be sure we heard the stories of what communists did to Catholics. The best was the one where they marched into Cuban church in the middle of a mass, knocked the ciborium out of the priest's hands and began stomping on the hosts. They called it a miracle when blood started flowing out of the hosts.

One day Paulie said he was going to find out if that was true. No kid could say "Fuck you" better than Paulie the Pooch. The way he said it, you'd think he owned the phase. He'd say it when he was angry, "FUCK YOU;" happy "Fuuuck youuu;" calming someone down, "Fuckin eh you." You wouldn't think that anyone with that nickname could say it to anyone's face, but truth is that he used to be called Paulie Punch because his way of greeting people was to take a boxer's stanch and punch them. Mrs. Rossi once complained to the police that Paulie had terrorized her garden at ripe tomato time. When the cops asked her who did it, she yelled out, "Paulie che poonchoh." She was saying the American word for Italian *pugno*, but the cop wrote down pooch.

The cops in my neighborhood would take their evidence first to Rocky DiLegge before their captain. Rocky knew everyone in town and everything that happened. Going through Rocky was the quickest way to solving most street mysteries. When they told Rocky the suspect's name, he knew immediately who they were after, but wouldn't tell them; Paulie was son of his buddy, but from that day on Rocky called him Paulie Pooch, and so did everyone else.

Paulie Pooch will forever be remembered as the one who tested the blood in the host theory. Paulie, Louie "Lips" Lipari, and I were in the sacristy just after mass one morning. Paulie slipped a few hosts out of the box, dropped them and ground them into the carpet with his combat boots. Nothing but crumbs. I got to my knees to examine then evidence, crushing the crumbs in my fingertips. No blood. Father Freeman walked in and asked what we were doing on the ground. Louie and Paulie hid the crumbs with their feet and I said that I was just looking at their shoes. Father squinted his eyes with suspicion, shook his head, and as strolled toward the rectory calling out, "Paul, don't wear those boots when you serve my mass tomorrow."

When Father left, we picked up the crumbs as best we could. So, we had caught the nuns in a lie; that's when Lips smacked his forehead with open hand and said, "Dummies, it probably only comes out of consecrated hosts." Paulie's eyes moved to the ornate gold and silver tabernacle atop the altar that housed the leftover consecrated hosts behind tiny velvet curtains and a locked door.

"No way I'm breaking into that," I yelled. Only a priest could enter that holiest of holy places and touch the ciborium that held those potentially blood-filled hosts; none of us had the guts to do something that was probably worse than a mortal sin. Besides, sooner or later we would have to confess it and I wasn't up for that.

While Paulie never did get to test truth of the communist host story, he did steal a bottle of the wine used in Mass. That was when we were eighth grade squires and on Friday nights, Chico would host the pre-dance wine drinking where we'd all get a little buzz before coming to the church-sponsored dances. Each Friday, a different area church would hold a heavily chaperoned dance for Catholic eighth graders in the various towns. To gain entrance to Chico's garage you had to bring a bottle of wine; most of us stole it from our grandfather's but Paulie's grandfather didn't make wine, and he wasn't going to pay someone old enough to buy one for him, so slipped it off the sacristy shelf, and stuffed it into his leather jacket.

When it came time to open the bottles, Paulie didn't say where he had gotten the wine, but when Chico took the first sip, and spit "Where did you get this shit?" into his face, Paulie confessed that he had gotten it from the church. None of us had ever tasted the wine. Back then, it was only the priest who would drink it at Mass, and while we could smell it as it came out of the cruet, we never thought to bring it to our lips. A few others took short sips and then Chico grabbed the bottle and poured the rest of it over Paulie's head, laughing out, "I baptize thee..."

While many of us imagined becoming priests when we began our apprenticeships at the age of ten, most of us lost that urge once puberty called us to other places. I think just two of my gang went to the seminary, and none became priests. Hey, it was the 1960s, what do you expect from a time that brought free love, streaking, and birth control our way? As altar boys, we had seen the human side of the Church that taught us that a place we thought was perfect and sacred was run by ordinary humans with profane habits just like the rest of us mortal sinners.

Mia Slept Over

by Cecilia M. Gigliotti

A young woman reflects on a formative connection at the turn of adolescence.

Mia slept over one humid night in the seventh grade. Fresh from California. You'd been the first person to speak to her and she'd stuck by you the next five weeks. She didn't know much about you, and you didn't know much about the world. Your first canvas was the cafeteria. You two may not even have had anything in common, it occurs to you looking back, but boy, could you talk. For hours on end, you could fill that veiny fluorescent space, spill the contents of your brains, kill all the time you had and then some. In hindsight you think of it as joint fili-bustering, but in the moment you liked to think you transformed each other into artists of conversation. Conversation that burst at the seams with embellishment; conversation that wasn't conducive to the irregular nooks and crannies of a school day. Maybe that was why you took it to your basement in the wee small hours at the tail end of September. Out-fitted with sleeping bags and VHS tapes and flimsy silk pajama tops that hinted at beginning curves. Or yours were beginning: hers had already thoroughly begun. You never got around to the VHS tapes. No, you lay facing each other, bellies almost touching, the hum of the furnace behind the folding door. Your index finger eventually, hesitantly, resting on a freckle near her collarbone. Your mouth shaping her name until it forgot what shape meant. *Mia, Mia, Mia.* Italian for *mine*, you remembered later, after she was splayed out asleep.

Requiem for Guido

by Joe Giordano

A friend's passing brings back poignant memories.

I learned of Guido's death from a friend of a friend. He died last Christmas, the most depressing time of the year for me. Lonely nights stirred memories of my deceased parents and childhood scrambles from bed to discover toys laid under a tinseled tree they'd erected overnight. Mama and Papa played Santa Claus no matter the shambles of their finances. My thoughts returned to Guido, and I sighed. Now, I had another reason for tears.

I hadn't seen Guido in twenty years. When I was an archeology graduate student at the City College of New York, I was awarded a summer internship at the Naples, Herculaneum Villa of the Papyri, the only surviving library from antiquity. Multi-spectral imaging techniques had been discovered as a means to decipher script from the carbonized sticks that once had been rolled scrolls. As my plane landed in Naples, my heart raced in anticipation of being the first eyes in nearly two-thousand years to read the texts.

Waiting for my bag in the arrivals lounge at Capodichino Airport, my wallet was pickpocketed. Angst spiked in my gut when I discovered the loss sitting in a taxi on the way to the Ercolano Stelle Hotel.

The driver spoke no English, waved both hands, and honked incessant-ly as he zig-zagged through chaotic traffic. The seat belt was broken, and I clung to the vinyl hand-strap in the rear like a life preserver in a stormy sea. My mind cycled between panic over the theft, and the strong belief that I probably wouldn't survive the cab ride. When we arrived at the hotel, I unsuccessfully attempted to explain my dilemma to the driver who scratched his three-day-beard. Frustrated, I left the car without paying. He became so animated and angry that I thought I'd have a fist fight on my first day in Italy. He screamed at my shoulder all the way into the hotel. Guido was at the reception desk, and when I blurted out my story to him, he chuckled a *"Benvenuti a Napoli,"* and paid for the taxi.

After calming me and seating me in the lobby with a coffee, Gui-do contacted Professor Bartolo, the leader of the Herculaneum project. Guido convinced Dr. Bartolo to provide an advance on my stipend and arranged for me to share a small apartment with an Italian student near the Herculaneum Villa.

Until I was settled and developed a network of friends in Naples, Guido took me on weekends to his apartment in Positano with a view of the sea. Guido was divorced with two kids. His son was a doctor and his daughter an architect. Both worked in Milan near their mother and were rarely in contact with him. Guido had operated a small leather-working artisan shop before his hands became arthritic and was in semi-retire-ment, working part-time at the Ercolano Stelle Hotel. Guido tutored me in Italian culture. Through him, I learned how delicious tomatoes and pizza really tasted, and that the combination of spaghetti and meatballs was an American invention. Guido and I hiked the "Path of the Gods," and he treated me to the first *branzino* I'd ever eaten, baked in salt, served with lemon and olive oil, washed down with a Greco di Tufo wine.

My work at the Villa became intense, and my time with Guido lessened over the summer. Before I left Naples that September to return to CCNY, we agreed to stay in touch, but in the ensuing years my let-ters to him dribbled away to none. Life went on. My focus was my stu-dents and teaching at Queens College. I never married. Travel to Europe would've been a luxury. Guido wasn't one to sign-up for Facebook, so we lost touch completely.

Nonetheless, my experience with Guido on the Amalfi Coast was a refuge for my mind. I longed to walk with him again along the "Path of the Gods," view the isle of Capri, the sapphire-blue Bay of Naples, smell bright-yellow lemons, pick wildflowers, and eat bread-salad on my friend's balcony. I researched and found Professor Bartolo, since retired. I telephoned and asked him to contact Guido. I'd saved my pennies and imagined returning to Naples, hosting a reunion dinner for all our friends and acquaintances at a seaside restaurant that served *branzino* baked in salt. I had my toast-to-Guido-speech worked out. How Guido stepped in with an act of kindness when I was lost and afraid. How Guido had turned my first tragic hours in Naples into a triumph, a magical love affair with Italy and the Italian people. How I knew no way to repay Guido, but with a celebration recreating a moment from that wonderful time, telling his friends and family how much his gesture and Guido meant to me. When Dr. Bartolo told me that Guido had died, I slumped into a chair with a sense of loss and emptiness like the depths of an ocean trench. I'd never told Guido what his generosity meant to me. Now, I never would. I can only tell you.

The Sassafras Tree

by Sandra Marra Barile Jackson

*A little tree loved by God gets free will only to misuse it
and learns about humility.*

God had been very busy creating the world. As He finished His
work on one of the days, He noticed how barren the land looked.

"What the world needs is color." God thought, "I shall cover this
earth with several beautiful plants."

He formed flowers such as yellow daises, red roses and trees in
different sizes, colors and varieties. Loving this kind of work, He took
special care to plant each tree, sometimes an oak or a river birch or a
weeping willow until He started on the Sassafras tree.

Early on, God had planned how each tree would look, but the Sassafras, He decided, would have free will designing its own appearance
and purpose.

Standing there, a small structure in the grand forest, God asked
the Sassafras, "What kind of colorful leaves do you want on your branches, Little Tree?"

The hardwood looked around and answered, "Oh, Lord, first
I would like my bark to smell so sweet that the aroma would spread
throughout the forest."

The Lord who is all-powerful, granted the tree this small gift so that the bark had a root beer odor making the tree easy to identify in the forest.

Again, God spoke to the tree, "Now, Little Tree, what kind of leaves, do you wish?"

"Oh, Lord," the tree was grateful and filled with joy, "I love oblong, oval and elliptical shapes."

"Yes, Little Tree," God sat on the soft grass reaching for the golden dandelions, waiting patiently.

The tree could not decide. It looked at the Rosebud tree, then the Sarvis tree... but what kind of foliage should it select? It must be unique and very important.

Then, it looked at God's mighty hands. "God, your great hands." The tree started, "Maybe, my leaves can be shaped like your hands with long fingers; hands so enormous that the other trees in the forest would have to move because of my growth which would fill out the space. That's it! I want to be the most beautiful tree in the forest with all the other trees bowing down to me."

God tilted His head, as the tree continued to talk in circles unable to contain itself from being pompous.

"Silence! God stood shaking His finger. "You are putting yourself before others. I have created many marvelous trees each a beauty in its own right. You no longer have free will, for I will decide what your leaves shall be."

The timid Sassafras stood trembling as the wind blew through the forest whispering, "Little Tree, you have angered the Lord. Tisk! Tisk! You only thought of yourself and wanted to be the most important tree in the forest. You must learn to think of others. Loving and caring about others is one of God's Commandments"

The Sassafras tree stood quietly, as God laid His hands on the branches. Soon leaves shaped like mittens started to grow on the tree; sometimes there were more than one leaf on a single branch.

When the tree was covered, God said, "You are a beautiful tree; reach high to the sky. Be happy that I have selected you as one who stands as a jewel in my forest. Many will see you and love you."

In the woodlands, stands the Sassafras tree proudly knowing that once it had free will, but now humble and pleased that God had blessed it with the honor of growing in His Garden of Eden.

Arrivederci Oregano

by Mary Lou Amato Johnston

*An American travels to Sicily to connect with her grandfather's family
and brings a bit of the country home with her. Little did she know
that it would create a bit of drama for her at the airport.*

It was time to go home. Lina had spent three weeks with relatives
in Sicily and had gained six pounds to show for it. Ah, those juicy tomatoes from the garden, fruit from the village, pasta and bread made fresh
every day; it was all too good to leave anything on the table. Abbondan-
za! Behind her cousins' house, the hillside was covered with olive trees
and Lina gorged herself on them every day. In the shed, huge bunches of
oregano hung to dry, and the aroma stimulated the appetite even more.
Lina knew the smell of it would forever remind her of Sicily.

But now, she had to face the fact that this visit would soon end.
She cherished the time spent with cousins Rosario and Josefina and their
children Paola, Antonio, Nicola and Giuseppe. Their house was small
but lovely with its marble floors and mahogany wood. The dining table
was immense and the pasta bowl bigger than any she had ever seen. Lina
was treated like a celebrity there. Each evening, friends and neighbors
came by to meet the American cousin, and some extended family drove
from the surrounding area to join in. There was always an abundance

of food for all. These were lovely memories to take home, but now her vacation time was over.

When the day of departure arrived, Lina crammed her clothes and souvenirs into her suitcase. She said tearful goodbyes and wondered if she would ever see this branch of the family again. Josefina handed Lina a huge package. She said it was pastrami and cheese and olives to eat on the train to Rome and oregano for the family in America. Lina knew it was not possible that one person could eat that much food on the train in spite of the fact that it would be nearly an eight hour trip. But she was grateful and looked forward to sharing the fragrant oregano with the relatives back home.

Once on the train, Lina shared her abundant lunch with passengers seated around her until nearly all of the fresh food was consumed. She knew she could finish eating the last of it while she waited for her flight. But the oregano still made a large bulky package. She squished it down as best she could and stuffed it into her already overfilled suitcase, praying that it would not burst open along the way. She watched the last glimpses of Italy from her window.

At last the train pulled into Leonardo da Vinci International Airport. Lina suddenly felt quite alone as she made her way to the Customs and Immigration area where the lines were long. Security was very tight because of recent terrorist threats and guards with machine guns were stationed throughout the airport. At the inspection station a large German Shepherd stood quietly sniffing each piece of luggage as it passed through. Lina felt a bit tense but reassured herself that she had nothing to worry about. After all, what would an ordinary law-abiding American have to hide? Dirty clothes, a new pair of silk pants, a bottle of Acqua di Santa Maria Novella perfume, and a camera with hundreds of trip photos stored on it. It all seemed unremarkable. She remembered the olives and the last of the lunch and ate it as the line inched forward. All that was left was the oregano.

Lina would not have given it a second thought if it hadn't been for the men standing behind her in the line. They appeared to be American businessmen, experienced world travelers, she thought to herself.

They were chatting about airline customs inspections, inventive drug smugglers and the remarkable ability of the German Shepherds to sniff out drugs. She thought of the great help these animals are. Then one of the men mentioned that the drug carriers often used oregano to mask the smell of marijuana. OH GOD, HER OREGANO!

Lina froze and stared at the dog and his handler at the front of the long line ahead. She could not take her eyes off him. She was sure he was named Killer or Duke, this was obviously no Fifi. How could she get past that dog with her oregano? The dog was restless now. Lina sensed that his nose already knew there was an imminent discovery.

Lina felt beads of sweat forming on her forehead. It suddenly seemed as if the line was moving forward more rapidly now. She knew she faced a moment of truth as she visualized this vicious canine ripping open her luggage and scattering dirty laundry in plain view of spectators from all nations. She imagined her new silk slacks torn to shreds, and that was more than she could bear. Something must be done immediately as there were now only a handful of people in front of her.

Quickly evaluating the limited resources available to her, Lina took out her new bottle of perfume. Trying to be as inconspicuous as possible, she sprayed herself lavishly making sure that the mist drifted down to her luggage. Then, without raising her eyes, she quickly unzipped her suitcase and let fly with several large blasts of Acqua di Santa Maria Novella onto the package of oregano.

The two gentlemen stepped back and turned away from her. Maintaining the most innocent look she could manage, Lina glanced up to see Killer and his handler walking down the line straight toward her. Her heart was pounding. She could not have uttered a sound if her life depended on it. As the dog approached, her mouth went dry and she froze, unwilling and unable to move. The moment was at hand and there was no escape.

Lina is positive to this day that Killer paused beside her although no one else seemed to notice. The magnificent creature pointed his muzzle in her direction. He sniffed and emitted a strange little half sneeze that sounded more like a horse whinny than a canine sound.

Then, man and beast continued on, exiting through a door marked EMPLOYEES ONLY.

Lina dared to breathe again. The line moved ahead. When it was her turn, she handed over her papers. It took less than two minutes before she was waved through and her bag was never opened. She returned to the US with her perfumed flavored oregano intact and her criminal record unblemished.

But every time she cooks spaghetti sauce, she notices a slightly different flavor and she smiles remembering her visit to the land of her roots.

Responses

by Thomas Locicero

*In "Responses," the main character, "You," reacts to an unexpected event
while at his most vulnerable. He counts on the very flaw
that gets him into trouble to get himself out of it.*

You are sitting on the toilet reading "Bullet in the Brain." So engrossed are you in the story that you neglect to extend to yourself a very necessary mercy flush. You are three hundred and fifty pounds—at least that is what you choose to believe—and, at that weight, a mercy flush is more refreshing than a cool glass of water. You are frightened for Anders. You tell him to shut up, but Tobias Wolff tells you that Anders continues to talk, and you are afraid that the title refers to Anders' fate. You wonder if you feel for Anders because your last name is Anderson. Your bathroom has no windows. Sweat makes tracks in your doughy skin from your scalp to your chin; some beads settle on the corners of your mouth. Your tongue instinctively snatches them. You taste salt and you think of fried chicken. Anders's sarcasm reminds you of your own. You want him to shut his mouth so that he might live to insult again. You also want him to keep talking because that is what you think you would do.

You remember your first intelligent insult. You were nine. A boy had said, "God, are you heavy!"

"My name's not God," you had responded. "Besides, Joe didn't complain about my weight last night."

"Joe who?" the boy had said.

"Joe Mama."

You remember your classmates' laughter. You had single-handedly brought back to popularity the "mama" joke, a hand grenade in sweaty palms, infallible in eliciting a response. You'd thought it meant that you'd be accepted. You might have been. But you also remember something else, a tidbit you wish you could forget: the boy punched you in your stomach, dislodging a nugget from your bowels. You would spend the remainder of your academic career known as Stain.

You read the word *Capiche* and you understand. You hold your breath and the room is suddenly silent. You hear Fodder growl. You let your breath out, then hold it again. A floorboard creaks. In your apartment, all the floorboards creak, some even moan, but they require weight to speak. You hear your curio door open. Fodder's growl has a catlike tone to it. You've never heard her make a sound like that. You hear, Shush! Fodder obeys. Stupid dog. You know she's too fat to jump the gate, and you know why: you let her eat your considerable crumbs. You're too afraid to stand. You use a piece of toilet paper as a bookmark and place the book on the vanity. You hate your fear. You're sure you outweigh the intruder. You could tell by his creaks that he weighs less than Fodder. But you consider the odds that he doesn't have a weapon on him. Even if he doesn't, you figure he has access to steak knives, butcher knives, a blender, a frozen honey-baked ham. You survey your cache: a hairdryer, toenail clippers, the book. Then you remember that you are as naked as a Donskoy. Yesterday's towel hangs over the shower rod. It is too small to fit around you. No, you are too large.

You manage to stand. The wind from your ass rides an unfortunate current to your nose. You gag. You know that flushing will give away your position. You pinch your nostrils and lower the toilet bowl lid. The creaks approach. You step into the tub and stand behind the liner. You consider wearing it, a potluck toga. You can't help but think that it looks like something Marlon Brando would wear. Then you notice patches of soap scum, and you think to yourself, "had I known I was having company, I would have cleaned." You want to laugh. The doorknob jiggles and Fodder barks. You pass wind. Fodder's barking ceases before your farting does. You clench. Your eyes follow the echo, and you wince.

"Is somebody in there?"

The voice is deep. You are convinced that he is bigger than your initial estimate. The funny response would be to say, "No." But that would be as obvious as a 'mama' joke. And look where that got you, you think. You say nothing. The intruder tries the door again.

"Don't make me break down the door."

You imagine him crashing through the door, passing out from the smell, and coming to to find a fat, naked man sitting on his ribcage.

"This is your last chance!"

"Hello," you say, not knowing why.

The intruder speaks at the same time your stomach—and Fodder—growl. You think you hear the word "alone."

"Yes," you say, "I'm alone."

"I said, 'Do you have a phone?'"

"It's in the kitchen. It's tethered to the wall. I've been meaning to get a cordless. I'm sorry." You cannot believe you just apologized to a man who broke into you apartment. You realize that he didn't actually break in. You have an unusual habit of locking the door to your bathroom even though you live alone, yet leaving the door to your apartment unlocked. In more than a decade, no one entered your apartment without your invitation, and the one time somebody does, you're on the toilet without a stitch of clothing in sight. A canned hunt.

"In the bathroom," he yells. "I'm not gonna ask you again." But he does. "Do you have a phone in the bathroom?"

You want to say, "Who do I look like to you? Rockefeller?" Then you remember that he hasn't seen you yet. The word "yet" makes your head swim. You think of your decomposing carcass and of the people you hope find it. You compose yourself. You can't believe the words that pass your lips: "Sir, if I were gonna have any appliance in my bathroom, it would be a refrigerator or a microwave. Something sensible. Maybe a nice toaster oven."

"A cell phone," he shouts.

He is pounding on the door. You realize that what he wants to know is whether or not you've called the police. But you figure this out too late: you already said, "No, I swear on my mother."

"You better not be lying to me, Fat Boy."

You think of Anders. The man he encountered called him Bright Boy. Anders was given a sarcastic name because of his sarcastic behavior. You appreciate sarcasm. Your intruder, you think, is mean. Then you wonder how he knows that you're fat. You purposely don't have any photographs of yourself around the house because you're diligent about avoiding anything that causes you to lose your appetite. What few mirrors you have are there for you to check for food between your teeth and for wild nose hairs before your "masseuse" visits.

"How do you know I'm fat?"

There is a pause. "You have a throaty, phlegmy sound to your voice," he says. "And from the echo. Didn't you ever hear of Kegel's exercises?"

You put your hands on your hips. You didn't know you had a fat voice. You want to tell him that you're insulted. You want to tell him about a mousy-voiced masseuse who visited you last month. She turned out to be so rotund that in a playful moment you wore her bra as shoulder pads and said, "Hut hut."

"Well, I know you're white," you say. There is another pause. You want to add, "And uneducated." But you know that if you do, there's a good chance you might wind up like Anders. You're not even sure of Anders's portion yet, but the title of the story must have some significance, you think. Then you think, "If he's uneducated, how come he knows what Kegel's exercises are?" Your immediate follow-up thought is, "Who's Kegel?"

"How do you know I'm white?"

"From your voice."

"You better stay in there." You think you hear him mutter, "Racist."

"Body-shamer," you whisper.

You listen. He opens the door to your bedroom. It is filled with worthless clutter, much of which you would have thrown out had it not been for your separation issues. You know he will be busy for a bit. You figure it is an opportune time to wipe your ass.

As you step out of the tub and onto the floor, the tiles click like rock candy falling from a piñata.

"I better not hear you move again, you hear?"

You look in the mirror and do The Twist. You realize that your stomach hangs over your incidentals and that from the front you are G-rated. You continue to twist as you turn your back to the mirror. You look over your shoulder like a pouting model and you find your cavernous crack, which you are convinced could conceal a warren of rabbits. You flounder for air. Fresh air. You've been warned innumerable times that your maligning manner would get you killed one day. You imagine a chalk outline of yourself: arms and legs akimbo, head tilted, elbows out, shoulders high. Cause of death: heart attack due to contemptuous dancing. Or worse: the detectives would miss the bullet—it, the hole, and the blood vacuumed into a layer of flab. Suddenly, you fear that sarcasm might not cause your demise after all.

You understand the possibilities that this might come down to a life and death struggle. You reason that it could have but two outcomes: you could win and tour the talk show circuit, a hero to the heavyset; or you could lose, in which case you would be too dead to be concerned about an insignificant thing like dignity. Either way, you are quite confident that the word "naked" will be in the first paragraph of your obituary. Perhaps the first sentence.

As you clean yourself up, you ruminate on the events and non-events of your life. You never had anyone who thoroughly befriended you, you were never intimate with a woman you didn't first pay, you were expelled from college, fired from jobs, all because of your unquenchable desire to outwit and outlast others. You mother said your sarcasm stems from insecurity. You dismiss her obvious theory. You are sure that you were insecure long before you were sarcastic. To you, it is verbal chess: you are the King and everyone else is a Queen on the run. Your mother is the one who recommended 'Bullet in the Brain.' You said, "Wouldn't sleeping pills be less messy?" You decided not to tell her that your masseuse friend is almost as large as you and is very secure.

You decide to do something strange, as if doing so is out of the ordinary for you. You lift the toilet lid, sit and read. A moment passes and you begin to wish that you had a father like Anders. He seems to be a man who is sure of his place on this planet. You could learn from him, and there are few people who you believe could teach you anything. Another moment passes and you're mourning Anders as inconsolably as a man like Anders would have mourned himself. Then another moment passes and you think that you might be mourning your passing. You pass more gas. You think it sounds like an old deaf man yelling, "What?" You giggle.

"What are you doing in there?"

"Nothing, I swear."

"You shouldn't swear so much, you know."

You think, *This coming from my robber, the bastion of morality. What the hell? What the hell?*

"I'll try to work on that," you say.

"Are you being sarcastic with me?"

You say, "No." And then you mouth, "I swear," because you simply cannot help yourself.

You reread the part where Anders went too far, and you think 'subjective' is an appropriate word. Then you realize that your own story doesn't have a warning title and that your wit might determine the outcome. You touch your stomach. It is processing again. You're not built for physical confrontation. Your father used to say, "You might be heavy, but at least you're slow." You didn't understand the joke until you were ten.

Then, before your thought is complete, you speak: "Is there anything I can help you find?"

"You don't have anything worth taking," he says. "You don't even have any money in your wallet."

"Take the dog."

"Too fat. Hey, you know any fat jokes? You're so fat…" he leads.

You whisper, "You're so stupid, you think the Horn of Africa is a trumpet." You need a moment to compose yourself. "No."

"Really? Not even one?" He sounds disappointed.

"You picked a good time to rob me," you say, changing the subject.

"Yeah? Why's that?"

"I'm moving to Tulsa."

"Where, exactly?"

Idiot, you think. "I don't know yet. Anyway, I was gonna have a garage sale."

"What were you planning on selling?"

"Everything except for a few things that are valuable to me, you say. If I tell you what they are, do you swear…I mean, promise not to take them?"

"Promise?" Your intruder is insulted. "Just because I help myself to a few items doesn't mean I'm completely immoral. You don't have to get self-righteous with me, Fat Boy."

"My sincerest apologies," you say. "And please, whatever you do, don't take my figurine."

"What figurine?"

"The one in the living room."

"Where?"

"On the mantle of the fake fireplace. The one with the nurse tending to the boy."

The portly masseuse gave it to you. It was meant to represent her sacrificing herself for you. You remember thinking, *The world's first four-hundred-pound love martyr. She bought it with your credit card. You hate it.*

"Did you find it?"

"Yeah, I found it."

"Don't take it."

You hear the rustle of a plastic bag.

"Don't worry."

"And don't take my baseball card collection."

"I won't," the intruder promises. "Where is it?"

"Under my bed."

You hear the intruder rummaging underneath your bed.

"And don't take the bagpipes, either."

Both the baseball card collection and the bagpipes were gifts from your father. He always pushed his interests on you. You knew he took the valuable cards and kept them in his house, in a fireproof case underneath a floorboard that you loosened when you slipped on ice cream. One day you'll inherit your own cards and you could pretend to appreciate their value. You never primed your spittle out of the bagpipes. They smell like morning breath.

After more of your admonishments, you listen as the intruder pretends not to be stealing the radio that gave you such a shock that the crescent moon of your thumbnail turned black, the noisy portable fan, the travel alarm clock that only has one volume—piercing—the high protein bars that taste like wallpaper glue, and three scary novels.

"Anything else I should avoid?"

"I think that's everything." You are surprised by the joviality in your voice. Fat voice, indeed!

"Before I go, I feel like I need to say something to you."

"Sorry?" You mean it to sound like, Excuse me?

"No, I'm not apologizing. I feel as if this was a divine appointment, like I was here for a higher purpose than just to rob you."

You cross your legs. Suddenly, you can't wait for your intruder to lecture you.

"It takes some discipline to be rich. It takes some discipline to be thin. But it takes a lot of discipline to be both rich and thin."

"I'm not following you, you say. Does this have something to do with us?"

"Us? There is no us?" You've angered your philosopher.

You wince. "Me, then?"

"Being poor doesn't necessarily make one lazy. Being fat doesn't necessarily make one lazy. But what kind of lazy excuse for a human being do you have to be to be poor and fat? That's all I have for you."

"Thanks for that, Socrates," you mutter under your breath. Then you remember. "And don't take my Play-Doh. It's on my dresser. You won't miss it." You only use it for a stress ball. It smells like hard margarine.

You hear him struggle with his booty. You think you hear him whisper, "Goodbye, doggy." The front door clicks. You wait several minutes before slithering out of the bathroom. You remember that you are too large to slither. You tiptoe into your bedroom. You try to put on a pair of boxer shorts too quickly. You fall. The bed breaks your fall. The bed breaks. Fodder barks. You tell her to shut up. You barricade the front door with a chair, the seat of which resembles the distensible pouch of skin pelicans use to hold fish, and lock all the windows. You pick up the telephone and dial 9-1. Then you place the phone back in its cradle. You're not sure what to do. You go back in the bathroom and flush. You pick up the book and go into the kitchen, where Fodder is so excited that she piddles on the floor. You take her gate and break it over your thigh. You whimper. You let Fodder out on the fire escape and, as you stand guard, you read the end of the story. You, again, dial a 9 and a 1, and, again, you hang up. You let Fodder in. A church bell chimes. You recognize it to be from St. John the Baptist Baptist Church. You've always wanted to visit it just to ask someone, Why the redundancy? You locate the church's phone number in the Yellow Pages and you call.

"St. John the Baptist *Baptist*," a young woman's voice shrills. "How may I direct your call?"

"Why two Baptists?" you ask.

"So people will know we're a Baptist church as opposed to a Catholic church."

"Why not St. John the Baptizer Baptist Church?"

"I'm just a receptionist, sir. Is there something I can do for you?"

"Yes, I was wondering if you have any patron saints of the morbidly obese and the sarcastic."

"Again, sir, we're Baptist. I think you might need to call St. John the Baptist Catholic Church. But I doubt they can help you."

"Why not?"

"I imagine it would be hard for someone to reach sainthood without some self-discipline."

You change the subject: Have you ever read 'Bullet in the Brain' by Tobias Wolff?

"No, sir, I haven't."

"Well, Anders dies."

"Don't tell me—bullet in the brain."

Her sarcasm delights you. You want to tell her about your near death experience. You want to tell her that you had an epiphany. Well, half an epiphany. You want to tell her you want to change. A little. But your strongest inclination at the moment is to ask her out. You've never been on a date before, and you're certain she doesn't moonlight as a masseuse. *What the hell?* you think. *You just got robbed in the middle of the day. You might have died. What have you got to lose?*

"Would you like to go out with me some time?"

You hear a noise. Maybe a grunt. It sounded like hmmm. A hopeful response.

"Did you just say "hmmm?"" you ask.

"No."

"Oh."

"No."

"I heard you. No hmmm."

"No. The first no was for the hmmm. The second was for the date."

Of course, you can't, you think to say. *I'm a stranger. You were raised right. Maybe I could just call you again.* But you actually say, "May I ask why not?"

"Well, for starters you're morbidly obese and sarcastic."

"Hmmm."

You hang up and dial 911.

Throughout the night, you think of Anders more than you do your intruder.

As you lay in bed, your Play-Doh stress ball in your hands and Fodder at your feet, you think that there are measures you must take to minimize your sarcasm. You can't sleep. You're too afraid. You take a deep, throaty, phlegmy, lung-rattling breath—a very fat man's breath—and you slowly exhale. You check the lock for the twentieth time. Maybe the thirtieth. Great, you think, now I'm morbidly obese, sarcastic, *and* I have OCD. A real catch! Your fear is now enormous. It approaches you like a dark shroud, too large even for you. You're not afraid of your intruder returning. You imagine him in some home in the suburbs lecturing the elderly for being old. You've had bad things return to you before. Mostly weight, but still. No, you're afraid of the police officers' response to your response at their returning to you a portion of all that you deem to be worthless.

Diana's Storia Segreta
(Diana's Secret Story)

by C.J. Martello

*During WWII, as an enemy alien, Ciro, the father in a
successful Italian American immigrant family is out past curfew,
arrested and placed in an internment camp.
His daughter, Diana, feels responsible for the family's tragedy
as her father is never the same. Diana's life is forever changed
until one fateful night . . .*

Working in publishing has always been just what Diana wanted
to do ever since she was a little girl. At this point in her life, living in
New York and working at a major publishing house, Diana was living
her dream life. It wasn't that her life was incomplete. She was definitely
satisfied with where she was in her life, but she always had an anguished
side to her that kept her from being the fully loving person everyone
thought she was.

She was beautiful with jet black hair and aquamarine blue eyes
and a smile that radiated warmth—that was everyone's mistake. They
saw her and assumed her personality went with her appearance.
A beauty carrying on her Italian roots in a style reminiscent of the

Renaissance, Diana's personality was more reminiscent of a representative of Dante's Inferno.

She was known for immediately belittling those that made errors or a simple social mistake. An intern once walked over to her asking if she could watch her work. The immediate reply was "What makes you think you already know enough to even begin learning from me to add to your shallow basic knowledge?" The intern welled up in tears and transferred to another department within the hour.

It was amazing to everyone that David Santodoro worked well with Diana. Some said it was because David had an Italian sensibility about him which Diana Terzapiano admired and felt she shared with him. David's parents had come over from Italy when he was three years old.

Her parents had come over from Italy before Diana was born and David was the only one who had heard her story. Occasionally, when the two of them had to work late, at Diana's suggestion, they would go for dinner and drinks at Covolo's Steak House. It was Diana's favorite restaurant and David enjoyed the Italian atmosphere as much as she did.

They would eat and drink and talk about their families. They would exchange stories of what Italian life was like according to the stories their parents told of the old country. Diana had an older brother and David had an older sister so they would share their siblings stories, which always made for good conversation.

Diana's parents Ciro and Angela had come from a town outside of Rome called Genzano. Both of their parent's families owned floral farms going back for generations. Ciro and Angela had known each other since they were babies playing in the courtyard while their families celebrated their floral harvest.

Their town of Genzano was known for one thing: the *Genzano Infiorata*. Each year since 1778, the town would hold the *Infiorata* to celebrate the feast of Corpus Christi and as a sign of gratitude for the end of the plague. The townspeople would lay out carpets of flower petals in designs in keeping with a specific theme. The petals would cover

2,000 square meters of Via Italo Belardi with portraits ranging from saints to royalty.

When Ciro Terzapiano was sixteen years old, he decided to show how much he cared for Angela Panevino. He was finally old enough to have input for the design of the family *Infiorata*. He eagerly lay out the design with the assistance of his parents and siblings. The theme for the year was the celebration of Mary, the mother of Jesus. The design would be simple and forthright: the Madonna ascending into heaven on a cloud of white rose petals on a blue sky.

As the feast approached, Ciro devised a simple plan to show his love for Angela. As the artist in his family, it fell to him to draw the layout that would be used as a stencil for the family's portrait. He skillfully hid the full extent of his plan from his family.

Once the family had gone to Via Italo Belardi to begin the process, Ciro laid out his surprise. The Madonna was just as the family had instructed Ciro; however, he had drawn Angela's face as the Madonna's face.

When the Panevino family arrived to help the Terzapianos add the finishing touches, they all had their areas to work on. Ciro made sure that he was the only one to work on the face of the Madonna. In the meantime, Angela worked, at a distance, on the outline border of the entire portrait.

A cheer broke out as the last flower petal borders were laid out at the top of the design by Angela, giving her an upside down view of the Infiorata. As Angela made her way to the bottom of the portrait, her family joined her with smiles on their faces. Finally, Angela was able to see what everyone else had been looking at the entire time—her face on the Madonna. She smiled and broke into tears as it was finally acknowledged by everyone that she and Ciro was a couple.

As the years went by, Ciro and Angela saved every cent they could. Their families had agreed that Ciro and Angela would be the first of their families to go to America. The plan was for them to begin a floral business that would allow them to pay back a loan from their families and offer funds for other family members to immigrate to the United States.

Ciro and Angela were very fortunate when they arrived at Ellis Island after their ocean-crossing trip. Their cousin Amadeo had suggested they head straight to San Francisco, where he had lived for eight years. He told them there was a large Italian community and there were quite a few people from Genzano.

As they waited for their train to San Francisco, they were trying to buy food when a kindly Italian gentleman came to their rescue. Amadeo Giannini sat with them and talked about Italy and how he had come to America many years before. He gave them his card and told them to look him up if they needed anything once they got to San Francisco. Ciro and Angela knew God was smiling down on them since their cousin who was going to meet them in San Francisco was also named Amadeo.

When they arrived in San Francisco, their cousin was waiting for them. He had arranged for them to rent an apartment and he even found Ciro a job at a local florist. That weekend was the Feast of Corpus Christi and their fellow Italians from Genzano celebrated with a dinner and to honor their arrival. They even introduced them to the local priest, Father Angelo di Domenico from Sts. Peter and Paul Catholic Church, which was around the corner from where they lived.

Ciro and Angela were very happy as they began their lives in America. Life was beautiful in San Francisco's Little Italy. They were able to speak Italian and shop Italian. They learned enough "American" to get along, whether speaking to customers or out in the community. Ciro worked at the flower shop for years and learned the business. They saved and were able to send money back to their families to pay off their loan.

Ciro learned where the wholesalers were, how to get the best prices, how to charge the customers, and how to run the shop. Eventually, Ciro was given the opportunity to buy the shop when the owner decided to retire. That was when he remembered the Italian man he and Angela had met when they were waiting for the train in New York.

Ciro had met the man and spoken to him through the years and decided to call him. A.P. turned out to be A.P. Giannini, the President of the Bank of America and yes, he would be happy to meet with Ciro and Angela. It was thanks to that first chance meeting in New York that the Bank of America gave Ciro and Angela the loan they needed to buy the building and the business.

It was a glorious day as Ciro and Angela's friends and families joined them in the opening of "Sara Rosa" Flower Shop. Ciro's close friend Rudolpho, a carpenter from Genzano, designed and built a display case for the front window of the shop. Another friend, Antonio, was the artist who painted the sign for the shop. It seemed that Ciro and Angela may have gone far from Genzano, but brought its friendliness with them.

Ciro and Angela felt that once they had the shop they could begin their family. Sara Rosa Flower Shop had been open for two years when Angela became pregnant with her first baby. Since the shop was named after Angela's mother, Sara Rosa, they decided to name their first born, a son, after Ciro's father Carlo, but they called him by the American version Charlie.

The years seemed to fly by and Sara Rosa became the most popular flower shop in the neighborhood. Located on the corner of Columbus and Union Streets and directly across from Washington Square Park, Sara Rosa was at one of San Francisco's busiest corners. It was a glorious time for the Terzapiano family. They lived in an apartment above Sara Rosa and the neighborhood had so many Italians that it was like being in Italy.

There were Italian food stores and restaurants throughout the neighborhood. Even Joe DiMaggio, the "Yankee Clipper," had a family restaurant a few blocks away. They were active members in the Sts. Peter and Paul parish where daily Mass was at 8:30 and the 9:00 a.m. Mass was on Sunday, and both Masses were in Italian.

Many of the Italian feast days were celebrated just like they had been in Italy. Of course, there was no Infiorata as there had been in Genzano. However, their Sara Rosa Flower Shop always provided the flowers for the many church celebrations and they always donated the flowers that filled the church on the Feast of the Ascension. This gave

Ciro and Angela great pride as that was a reminder of the Infiorata when Ciro first showed his love for Angela.

Four years after Carlo was born, Angela became pregnant once again. They were so excited because they had been trying to have another child ever since Carlo was born. As the pregnancy progressed, Angela began to have problems. By the time she was six months pregnant, Angela had to be hospitalized and lost the baby. It was a very sad occasion made only more heartfelt when they were told the baby had been a girl. Before they buried her, they gave the baby the name Regina in honor of Mary Queen of Heaven.

Within the year, Angela became pregnant again. Ciro made sure that Angela didn't do any work in the shop. He was going to pay one of the neighborhood girls to help Angela, but Mariastella, Rudolpho's wife, insisted on helping no matter how much Angela protested. Since Mariastella did all the usual chores including cooking, Angela made use of her time by studying for her citizenship. She always felt she wanted to be more American and now that she had time on her hands; it was perfect.

It was a beautiful but sunny San Francisco day that May 12, 1934, when Diana Angelina Terzapiano was born. She was the perfect baby with a head full of raven black hair and the bluest aqua eyes anyone had ever seen. She was as beautiful as her smile and it was difficult to decide who they would choose to be her Godparents as everyone got in line for the honor.

When the christening day arrived, Ciro and Angela and Carlo stood next to the proud Godparents: Rudolpho and Mariastella. The couple had done so much for them since they arrived in America that there was no question, in their mind, that they should be Diana's Godparents.

Life was beautiful as Charlie helped Angela take care of his little sister. Being six years old Charlie began kindergarten at Sts. Peter and Paul School. Of course, Angela was back at work in Sara Rosa and brought baby Diana with her.

She was a good baby and laughed easily when the customers spoke with her or about her. Even though both Angela and Ciro loved Diana and showered her with attention: Ciro and Diana had a special connection. Whenever Ciro came near Diana, the baby would smile and look at her father with adoring eyes. He called her his "principessa," and that was just the first loving nickname he called her.

As she grew older, reading came very easily to her. She and her father would sit and she would take one of her books and help her father pronounce words. They were children's books and very short, but they were just what Ciro and Diana liked because they could both understand the words in them.

One day, Ciro returned from making a flower delivery and, to Angela's surprise he had Charlie help him bring in a large overstuffed chair. They placed the chair in a corner of the shop where it wouldn't be in anyone's way. This corner became Diana and Ciro's school room. Now, whenever the time was available, they would sit in their "study seat" and study English together by reading her books.

Ciro started to call her "maestra," meaning teacher in Italian. Diana made everyone laugh when she decided as the "maestra" to give Ciro homework. Ciro began teaching her flower arranging and bought her a simple child's book on flowers. Much to everyone's surprise, Diana wrote her own little book to describe the different jobs everyone did that made the Sara Rosa Flower Shop such a happy place.

Angela wasn't left out because when they were in the apartment, the "maestra" would help her with studying her citizenship books. It wasn't long before Angela was able to go to the courthouse with Mariastella to finally become a citizen. Ciro still didn't want to bother since he was always busy with the flower shop. He felt having Angela become a citizen was good enough for the two of them.

Diana began kindergarten at Sts. Peter and Paul School just as Charlie had. The teachers adored her because she was so smart and such a beautiful child. Diana had no problem being the first in her group to finish reading a book or in writing her homework. She was especially proud to write her own stories, which she shared with her teacher. From a very early age, Diana was always helping out her classmates when they had problems writing their assignments.

Diana made many friends and everyone lived in the neighbor-hood, so they would play at each other's houses. Their neighborhood was like all the other Italian neighborhoods where everyone looked out for each other's children. The kids were always eating at each other's house. The meals were the same Italian food no matter whose house you ate at. It was always a treat when one of the kids' mother would make a grilled cheese or a peanut butter and jelly sandwich just like the Americans did.

One of Diana's best friends was Judy Belavanti, whose mom was born in America but her dad was Italian. The house they lived in was at the other end of the block from where Sara Rosa was. Judy's house was a lot of fun to visit because she had a lot of dolls. Her mom had saved her own dolls from when she was a baby and now Judy had a collection of seventeen different dolls. Diana thought that was special because every-one else she knew only had one doll.

In May of 1942, Diana was going to be turning seven years old. Ciro wanted to give her a special gift since she would be in first grade. His old country friend and Diana's Godfather, the carpenter Rudolpho, had become very successful and had opened his own shop doing custom work for many of San Francisco's wealthy citizens. Knowing how busy Rudolpho was, Ciro went to see Rudolpho in September of 1941.

Over a good bottle of Italian wine, Ciro and Rudolpho talked over the good times they had shared growing up in Genzano. They recalled going "al cinema" with their girlfriends. They had all been good friends since they were teenagers and understood each other.

Ciro told Rudolpho the real reason for his visit was that he want-ed his principessa to have the most beautiful dollhouse for the new dolls she would be getting for her seventh birthday. They laughed as Ciro told him all Diana could talk about was her best friend having seventeen dolls while she only had one. He couldn't give her seventeen dolls, but he could give her a beautiful dollhouse.

One thing Ciro made clear was that he had come to Rudolpho early enough so that Rudolpho would have plenty of time to complete and design the project. His one other request was that he deliver it on her birthday, May 12 or as close as possible. Rudolpho was excited to take on the project for his godchild and refused to accept any payment from Ciro. Ciro felt humbled and honored that his friend would show him such kindness.

As the holidays approached, Sara Rosa Flower Shop became very busy and Diana did her part to help out when she wasn't studying. Charlie, almost being a teenager, helped make deliveries while Diana learned to work the cash register and help out at the front of the shop. Angela had a couple of women from Sts. Peter and Paul who she could call on to help her do the flower arranging in the back of the shop.

As Christmas drew near, the holiday season had a tinge of desperation as there was a war going on in Europe. There was a lot of talk in the neighborhood about Mussolini and whether he was really doing the right thing for Italy by joining forces with Germany. The United States refused to enter the war, which made most people happy. With Italy becoming an ally of the Germans, the Italian-American organizations like the Ex-Combattenti that collected money for the widows and orphans of veterans of Italy from WWI became concerned over what might happen.

On December 7, 1941 the Japanese bombed Pearl Harbor and on December 8th America entered the war on the side of the Allies. This meant that Germany, Japan, and Italy were now the enemy of America. This action immediately created problems for all Italian Americans who had not previously sought citizenship and were labeled enemy aliens and this, unfortunately, included Ciro.

By the end of December the draft had been enacted and many of the young men from the neighborhood had either registered for the draft or enlisted on their own. Groups of young Italian-American men that used to hang out together since they were kids playing baseball signed up together to protect America.

As January 1942 approached, the government became concerned that a risk existed of Japanese-American, German-American, and Italian-American enemy aliens might try to attack the U.S. from inside the country.

On February 2nd of 1942, President Roosevelt signed Executive Order 9066 into law. This law resulted in giving the U.S. Army the authority to arrest and remove any enemy aliens amongst those three groups. Of course, the Japanese were all declared enemy aliens, whether they were citizens or not.

Those of German extraction were considered less of a problem because there weren't enough of them in California to worry about. However, when it came to the Italian-Americans, it was another story, especially in San Francisco and other areas near the coast.

All enemy aliens were told to register and it wasn't long before the Army began to force people to move to other "zones" than where their houses were located and to towns that were twenty-five miles or more from San Francisco.

Ciro and Angela's problem was compounded by the fact that Angela was a naturalized citizen and their children were born in the United States and were automatically citizens. However, Ciro had never felt the need to obtain citizenship. "What was the need?" he had always said. They lived in America, they owned a home, they owned a business, and they supported their neighborhood and their church. They were as American as could be as far as Ciro was concerned.

However, the law limited where those who had not become citizens, and were therefore enemy aliens, could work and even walk. Many people couldn't even go to their businesses just because they lived on the wrong side of a dividing line.

For Ciro, the laws were very confusing and as an enemy alien he was very worried if he would have to leave his family and San Francisco to live in another town. Once again, Ciro called upon his friend A.P. Giannini for advice. A.P. told Ciro to come to his office and together they would see what they could do with the help of one of the bank's lawyers.

After looking over Ciro's documents and considering his options, the lawyer made a suggestion. If A.P. could contact a certain politician that was on the bank's board, they might able to get an exception for Ciro so he wouldn't have to move. A.P. picked up the phone and called his friend the politician and explained the situation. His friend told him he would call him back shortly after making a few phone calls.

A.P. and Ciro talked about Italy, the war, the good old days, and how terribly many Italian Americans were suffering. After all, fishermen had their boats confiscated for the Navy's use as patrol boats but were forced to find other work or fish elsewhere away from San Francisco.

Finally, after twenty minutes A.P.'s friend called back. He had spoken to a few members of the examination board and had gotten them to give Ciro a favorable ruling. Under a hardship exception he was allowed to stay in their apartment above the Sara Rosa Flower Shop.

However, there were rules he had to follow to maintain this exception. One was that he had to stay in the house from a curfew of 8 p.m. until 6 a.m. every day. He could only drive to the wholesalers to buy his flowers and return directly to his shop. To enforce these rules, Ciro was subject to being watched and the mileage on his truck would be checked at random. Ciro told A.P. he had no problem with these rules and was very thankful. He insisted that he wanted to send a bouquet of roses to A.P.'s wife. A.P. said it wasn't necessary and he was happy to help his friend.

Ciro was relieved to tell Angela and the children the good news that he would not have to leave. Later that night, he explained the rules for maintaining the exception to Angela. He didn't want Charlie and Diana to worry any more than necessary.

Ciro returned to being his happy self and paid attention to the rules. He had to get used to the curfew and staying home, but he knew other Italian-Americans who had a more difficult time. Some of his old friends had even been picked up and sent away to be held and interviewed.

Sara Rosa Flower Shop had been visited twice within a month by investigators who checked the mileage on his truck through the window in the morning. They returned past 8 p.m. in the evening to make sure Ciro was home and also to have him open his truck so they could check the evening mileage to be certain he had only gone to his flower wholesaler.

Ciro thought to himself that he couldn't understand why America had turned on him. He had been a good person and built the American dream. He and Angela had paid back their family loan within two years of moving to America. They'd even bought Sara Rosa and the building it was in without missing a single payment. They had also sponsored several of their relatives so they could come to America and also have the opportunity to live the American dream.

It saddened him to know that his adopted country would turn on him simply because he didn't have his citizenship papers. He made sure that Angela, Charlie and Diana did not know of these thoughts. He kept up his joyful personality when he was with them, but it was difficult to keep up that personality when he was alone in his truck.

The first two months flew by and before anyone realized it, they were enjoying a warm April. The children playing outside after school was like a breath of fresh air after the stresses the war brought on. Diana spent her after school evenings playing with her best friend Judy who had all the dolls. She was always at home for supper so there was no worry about her being out after curfew, even though the days were getting longer.

Ciro still let Diana be the "maestra" as they sat in their special chair in the corner. Diana was getting older and her seventh birthday would be coming up soon. That was a special occasion that Ciro was looking forward to. At least then there would be happiness in the gloom he was suffering through in his private moments.

One day, Diana begged to stay at Judy's house for supper after they got through playing with their dolls. Judy's mother had said it would be okay. Angela reminded her that there was a curfew and she had to be home before that time. Diana smiled as she agreed that she'd be home by curfew. Ciro hadn't yet returned from the wholesaler and so Angela decided to let Diana have supper with the Belavanti family.

On Ciro's trip back from the Wholesaler, he was delayed in returning because there had been a problem with some investigators stopping vehicles on the highway. By the time Ciro got home, it was 7:45 p.m. He worked as fast he could to empty the truck so he could go to the end of the block to get Diana, who hadn't yet returned home.

Ciro walked down the block as fast as he could since he didn't finish unloading the truck until ten past 8. Diana was ready in a minute or two and they left to walk the block back to Sara Rosa. They were halfway up the block when a big black car pulled up next to them and four men hurried out. Diana was scared and began to softly cry while the men questioned her father.

They walked them the rest of the way to Sara Rosa and when Angela came to the door, they explained that Ciro was out after curfew. He had broken the rules and it was their duty to arrest him. They gave Angela and Charlie and Diana a few minutes to say good-bye to Ciro and took him away. Diana could not stop crying and neither could Angela. It was all so sudden.

For more than a week they didn't have any word on where Ciro had been taken. Finally, they were told by some investigators that stopped by that Ciro had been sent away to a camp for enemy aliens. They had no idea when he would be returning, but they would stop by if they got any news.

Diana was inconsolable and cried for days. It was her fault for not coming home before curfew. She was busy having a good time and it had caused her father to be taken away. Angela tried to explain that it wasn't her fault and that investigators had stopped her father on his way home and that made him late. Diana was inconsolable and refused to believe her mother.

In early May, while her father hadn't yet been released from the camp he had been sent to, there was a visitor to Sara Rosa Flower Shop. It was Rudolpho with the dollhouse Ciro had asked him to make for Diana. Without Ciro's presence, instead of a happy occasion, everyone was saddened at the sight of the beautiful dollhouse gift Diana was given.

On her birthday, Angela presented Diana with the two dolls Ciro had picked out to go with the one doll she already had. Diana just couldn't act happy like she used to. She missed her father too much and she still felt it was all her fault.

Finally, one month after her birthday when her father had been gone for eight weeks, the family received word that Ciro would be allowed to return home in one week. That was the best news they had received on a long time. They made plans to have all the things Ciro liked waiting for him: his bistecca in padella, his favorite Tiramisu dessert and his favorite Vino Toscano.

When Ciro was dropped off the next week, he was a different person. Gone was his instant smile. Gone was his easy manner of greeting everyone. It was as though the life had gone out of him. Everyone noticed the change, and no one and nothing could change him back to how he used to be. Ciro eventually relaxed but he lost forever the outgoing personality he'd had before. Unfortunately, his wasn't the only personality that changed.

Ciro's little principessa Diana lost her smile and her friendliness just as her father had. It never returned, even as she grew into a beautiful woman with raven black hair, aquamarine eyes, and a smile that seemed to radiate warmth.

This was the person David Santodoro knew and dealt with. Being privy to her background gave him some understanding. Diana never mentioned that she had spent her entire life feeling responsible for her father's being taken away. She always felt responsible for her father changing into a person without the laughter, humor, love and friendliness he had before being taken away due to her foolishness.

After their meal at Covolo's that night, Diana and David had a pressing deadline that meant they had to get back to the office. The few drinks they'd had lightened their spirits and made them more open to working late. Through the three years they'd worked together, this had become their pattern and it suited their work style just fine. Deadlines always made them focused and helped them achieve a state of "flow" where nothing else but focusing on the job at hand mattered.

David and Diana had been back at the office by 8 p.m. and gotten right into focusing their attention on getting things done. Suddenly, their focused silence was broken as the office phone rang. This was unusual because everyone knew the office was closed by 6 p.m. The phone rang three times and Diana decided to head to the outer office to take the call. Their families, including Diana's brother Charlie, were the only ones that had the number for the after-hour's line for emergencies.

After about ten minutes Diana returned from the phone call, clutching a Kleenex and with tears in her eyes. She approached David and, as she did, she shocked him by giving him a hug and deeply crying into his shoulder. The call was from Betty, the daughter in a family that had lived on the same block and two doors over from the Sara Rosa Flower Shop.

She had been trying to get a hold of Diana for the past two weeks. It wasn't until she remembered Diana's best friend as a child, Judy Belavanti, that Betty got some information. Judy told Betty that she didn't know how to get a hold of Diana, but she knew that Charlie lived in Daly City, just outside of San Francisco.

That was when Betty found Charlie's number. When they spoke, he felt it was so important for her to contact Diana that he gave Betty the emergency office phone number. Charlie insisted that she immediately call Diana that very night.

Diana cried softly as David followed her into her private office. She opened a desk drawer and took out two glasses and her special occasion bottle of Scotch. She motioned David over to the office couch and continued her story.

Betty's mother Joan had suffered for many years with Alzheimer's but had moments of clarity. She had early onset Alzheimer's and the doctors felt that she had suffered some kind of psychological trauma in her life. They felt this trauma is what brought on the early stages of dementia.

Betty related that occasionally her mom would slip into some nonsensical rambling about the Washington Square Park neighborhood and Sara Rosa Flower Shop and "that" Italian family who owned it. She never said enough to put together any kind of cohesive story and Betty just accepted it as part of her mom's dementia. However, that wasn't the case.

As Joan's mother got closer to dying, Joan's suddenly had more moments of clarity. Finally, her ramblings made sense. She told a story and made Betty promise to contact Diana. It was a death bed promise and Betty was going through with it. It was the psychological trauma the doctors had wondered about.

Joan was sorry and had been haunted her entire life by what she did that altered the lives of the entire Terzapiano family. She had thought that nothing would happen of any consequence.

She wanted to teach Ciro a lesson. She was jealous of the entire family for their success in owning a business and not suffering financially while she had to struggle as a single mother. She had meant no harm.

Back in 1942, Joan saw Ciro as he headed up the block to the Belavanti's house. She knew it was past 8 p.m. and past curfew. It was Joan who had called the investigators and reported Ciro. As she spoke with the investigators, she urged them to hurry.

Her entire life had been burdened with the knowledge that her action had changed the Terzapiano family. When they moved to San Diego, she couldn't bring herself to talk to them. She couldn't find it in her heart to apologize during her entire life. Now, on her deathbed, she made Betty promise to find Diana and tell her how sorry she was and had been throughout her life.

When Diana finished telling the story to David, they hugged each other and as their tears flowed, kissed as Diana smiled with her heart for the first time since she was seven.

Alberto's First Date

by Edward Albert Maruggi, Ph. D.

*Alberto Bianco is a shy thirty-year-old and getting his own dates
is still difficult. His best friend, Vincenzo, arranges a blind date for him
with Maria Centine and it becomes the best date that he's ever had.*

He was standing in the shade leaning against a square wooden
pillar just off the wide boardwalk that ran in front of Tito's Trattoria.
With his hands in his front pockets, he scanned the crowd while waiting
for her. He looked at all the young women passing by for matches with
the brief description he'd been given. Waiting brought back memories
of other arranged dates. Although he was nearly thirty years old, getting
his own dates was still difficult. He had always relied on close friends to
arrange for them, due to shyness. Consequently, many of his dates were
less than desirable companions: not very pretty, sloppy dressers, too old
or much too young, some even with crooked teeth, bad breath, or body
odor. If at first glance a girl seemed attractive, she would be melancholy
or vain or snobbish, talk incessantly, or not at all.

His shyness had lessened over the years, but it was still an issue.
How shy did he used to be? While a senior at the Leonardo Da Vinci

Technical High school, it took him ten weeks to ask blue-eyed, blond-haired, Lucrezia Barone, who sat across the aisle from him in History class, to attend the final social function of the school year. He hesitated for days before he had enough gumption to ask her. And when she replied, "Yes, I'd like that," he almost fell over with complete surprise. The caption under his photo in the senior yearbook said it all, "Alberto is handsome and he's a nice guy, but wow is he shy."

Alberto pondered what an American girl might think of the fact that he still lived at home in a modest apartment with his mother, father, sister Pia and her family, back home in the southern city of Matera. Sometimes he felt overly coddled. But this is the norm for young Italian men. Why leave the comfortable lifestyle that he's known since birth? Someone to clean his room, make his bed, wash and iron his clothes, cook his food, and loan him the family Fiat Punto?

Alberto wondered if the young lady would be punctual, being as he had read that Americans were obsessive about time. In his experience, Italian women were seldom on time for a date, whether due to a general Italian polite agreement that you couldn't expect your host to be ready just on the appointed time, so it would be rude to appear on the dot, or due to some shared perception that keeping a man waiting made him more eager.

Renee, his friend Vincenzo Amoroso's girlfriend, was the exception. But she had never dated anyone other than Vincenzo since early high school, and had never shown any coyness about her enjoyment of his company. Mr. and Mrs. Bianco had grown less fond of Vincenzo over the years since high school because he and Renee lived together, which according to them was "living in sin." Mamma Bianco, especially, considered Renee to be a "loose woman."

But then, they would not have approved of Vincenzo back in high school, had they known that he lured Alberto into skipping classes to go joy riding in Mr. Amoroso's steel gray, eight-cylinder, 230 HP, 1998 Alfa Romeo Giulietta, diesel. About twice a month they set out on these great rides through the grape-pocked Aglianico del Vulture vineyards, traversing massive olive groves and winding through the small towns of Venosa and Rappolla. Only once in a great while did they drive to Matera's burlesque theater, and then only on a day near the weekend, when many students called in sick. Mondays, not Fridays because most workers at the Fiat Punto assembly plant failed to show up for work on Fridays and therefore the boys might be in danger that one of their relatives who worked at Fiat would see them at the theater on Friday. As an extra precaution, they always sat in the front row at the burlesque performance, slouched so far down in their seats, the top of heads barely visible. They couldn't allow themselves to be seen by anyone who would report back to their parents

Alberto's parents were, he had to admit, more than devout Catholics. Mamma recited the rosary each and every weekday and twice on Sunday. She also attended Mass on nine first Fridays of each month. She made a Novena as often as possible to pray that her only son would get married someday. She is very respectful, to a fault. Daily, for the past fourteen years, she has worn black—shoes, stockings, underwear, dresses, hats -- since her mother died. His parents insisted on Alberto becoming an altar server at the age of eight, in addition to attendance at Mass every Sunday, at their parish Church of Santa Lucia where Papà Bianco, an avid gardener, took voluntary care of the Church's landscaping, including the flower and vegetable gardens, often with Alberto's help.

Several years ago, the Biancos had purchased the apartment next door to their current residence. It was a two-bedroom rental at this point, but was intended for Alberto when he finally married, so all members of the family would remain "insieme," together.

The Bianco family dwelling itself was a three-story walk up. Daughter Pia and her family occupied the third floor. Alberto's bedroom was on the second level directly above the kitchen. Mamma served as his alarm clock. To wake him each morning, she tapped loudly on the kitchen ceiling with a broomstick, then yelled, "*Alberto, è tempo di alzarti.*" Time to get up. It always took a while for him to respond to her calling, so she would continue to tap every five minutes until she heard the squeaks in the bedroom floor; the signal that he was up.

He'd often oversleep on Sunday morning and arrive late for the very crowded 10:00 a.m. Mass, which meant standing at the rear of this very small church, usually close to the exit. When Vincenzo was also late for Mass, Alberto would be led astray.

"Alberto," Vincenzo would rationalize with a serious frown, "we are not going to benefit from attending Mass at the very back of the church; only those Catholics who occupy a pew and put money in the collection go to heaven. Why don't we go to the bar at the corner of Viale Verdi and XXX Aprile for a cappuccino and a panino, instead?"

It was the very same mischievous Vincenzo who had arranged this date with a distant cousin of Renee's. Vincenzo had said, "You'd be in Rimini on vacation and the beach at Rivabella is beautiful. She is an American girl alone in Rimini. For goodness sake," he said with hands outstretched. "Neither of you know anyone your age there. Mamma isn't there to disapprove. Do yourself a favor and spice up her vacation. If she looks anything like Renee, you should be in luck." While watching the street for his date, Alberto thought back to some of the prank dates Vincenzo had played on him and shuddered. It was true that Renee came from a family of lookers with brains, but you could never tell what that would mean in a "distant cousin." And then again, if she was like Renee, there was the Mamma factor. If Mamma found fault with smart, beautiful Renee, what might she think of an American cousin who might lead her baby astray? Maybe even steal him overseas?

Forget Mamma's disapproval. Alberto longed to meet someone who would suit his own tastes. This beach vacation was perhaps his last chance to relax thoroughly, before he had to find a way to put his recent education to work. Private Investigation was not a line of work where you were likely to meet the kinds of girls Alberto would find appealing, much less anyone who might gain Mamma's approval.

At almost precisely 17:30, the crowded boardwalk traffic in front of Tito's was beginning to ease. Turning slightly to his left he spotted the form of a young woman emerge between two elderly couples.

• • • • • • • • • • • • • • • •

HIS EYES WIDENED. *I hope this is my date,* he thought, grinning, then checked himself. "What if it isn't?" He realized he was staring and blushed. *I'll be terribly embarrassed if it's not her.* About two meters to his left, a beautiful young woman scanned the crowd. She had long, straight black hair that flowed down the middle of her back. She was slim, a little shorter than he, with large sparkling brown eyes. No makeup covered her high cheekbones, straight nose and full pink lips. Her smile was wide and genuine and her teeth were pearly white and straight, like maybe she'd worn braces as a teenager. There were no rings on her fingers but a set of small white gold balls for earrings with a matching gold chain with a cross hanging from her neck. She was casually dressed; tight off-white shorts with a medium blue Tee shirt with orange trim that read "New York Mets" as an accent to her shapely, full, breasts. Her legs were also slim with great calves. He hoped this was she.

Catching his eye and walking towards him, this young woman announced softly, "You must be Alberto because what I see fits the description I was given."

She introduced herself as Maria Centine. Centine was the name of a wine produced by Banfi Vineyards in Montalcino, a pleasant medium-priced red wine that Alberto regularly enjoyed. Was this a sign?

Her handshake was soft and moist, as was to be expected on first meeting. They smiled and immediately began strolling along the beach. She removed her sandals. He followed as they inched closer to where the warm sand met the Adriatic's aqua clarity, dodging bathers on the way. Because it was a late summer's day, the beach was crowded, with several colorful beach umbrellas popping up as late afternoon sun worshippers came from work to take advantage of the sun's final rays. Maria was quiet, so Alberto initiated the conversation.

"Where are you from?"

"I live in the New York City area. My parents were both born in the province of Basilicata. In Melfi, actually. I'm here to visit relatives and friends," she submitted while brushing her hair from those big brown eyes.

"Where around New York City? New Jersey, Connecticut, West-chester?" He wanted her to know that he was worldly.

"I live with my parents in Queens, one of the five boroughs of New York City, in a neighborhood that was heavily populated with Italian immigrants years ago. It's now a mixed blend of ethnic groups, mostly Puerto Rican." She looked at him shyly.

"How long will you be here?" he continued, as he tripped over an errant beach ball.

"I return four weeks from yesterday."

"Are you employed in the New York area?" Alberto winced inwardly. *Did that sound like an interrogation?* Fortunately she answered without missing a beat.

"I'm an Administrative Assistant for Alitalia Airlines in their downtown Manhattan office. I began working there after graduating from NYU's Travel and Tourism program. My main responsibility includes booking large tour groups to worldwide destinations that Alitalia serves. I really like my job." They continued glancing at one another, being careful not to step on any seaweed that had washed ashore during the day.

Shading her eyes from the sun she glanced back at the Rivabella condominiums dotting the shoreline.

"How about you?" She smiled. "Renee's cousin, Monica, told me that you live in Matera." Alberto was never big on details when answering questions about himself, so he glossed over most of it. He wasn't proud of the fact that he didn't end up in the top ten percent of his high school graduating class. In fact he was in the lower third. *Put up a good front, Alberto.* But as a senior in high school he had registered for an elective course in Basic Forensics because of his interest in chain reading mystery novels, especially those with crime scene investigations. The course was worth five credits and he needed all five to graduate with his senior class. His mother and father would have been embarrassed if he hadn't graduated with his friends.

"I'm a private investigator, just getting set up at the moment," he answered almost sheepishly. "Not long after high school, while apprenticed to my father as an ironworker, I saw an ad in the *Giornale del Popolo di Matera* about a program that immediately excited my brain cells. As a result, I enrolled in a full-time program entitled *Become a Certified Private Investigator in Twenty-four Months.* A private company on contract to the Matera Police Department offered it. The purpose of the program was to encourage young men and women to eventually apply to take the Police department's *L'esame per i Servizi Civili*, their regional Civil Service examination.

"As the two-year program progressed, although I enjoyed—and learned a lot from—my internships within the police department—I realized that my goal was to become an *Investigatore Privato*, and choose my cases. I graduated near the top of my class. After completing the program, I apprenticed for eighteen months with two different professional private investigators. Now I'm hoping for an opportunity to officially begin my career and to handle my own cases."

"What were some of the courses in the curriculum?" Maria asked, eyebrows raised, while sinking her feet into the warm beach sand.

Counting on extended fingers he named off: "Ethics; surveillance strategies; interrogation and interview techniques and recording; report writing; cybercrime and white collar crime; evidence collection; data processing, spreadsheets, and computer research; dealing with various government agencies; courtroom conduct. Things like that. I also took a couple of electives, Advanced Tae Kwan Do and Small Arms Proficiency."

He didn't share with Maria that one of the courses in the program was called "Mannerisms." It looked at processes used by interrogators for determining if a suspect was being completely truthful by analyzing their physical movements and vocal responses to questions. It is a technique Alberto tried to refrain from using with friends or family, but it was useful as he watched Maria, who responded to his brief resume with a genuine smile that almost knocked his socks off.

She wanted more information about him and he was interested in learning more about her. Their mouths moved in sync as they both asked, "how old are...?" They hesitated and decided that it was not a relevant question. Both laughed at their embarrassment. Looking at him directly, she smiled.

"What brings you to the Rimini area?"

They dodged a couple of children darting across their path, throwing handfuls of beach sand at one another as two teenagers on beach bicycles raced past.

"I worked various odd jobs all summer, so I thought I would take some time off during August like the rest of the natives. Rimini is the area where many Italians go for sea and sun, the food is excellent, and the people are friendly and helpful. You won't find many tour buses filled with Germans, Americans or English here!" He said with a sweeping motion of his arm. "It's considered off the beaten path, a well-kept secret."

She happily accepted when he reached for her hand as they walked for about half an hour, talking mostly about how Italian Americans retained or shed various aspects of their Italian culture over the years. They moved away from the water toward the boardwalk and a row of restaurants while Maria breathed in the cool, salty air blowing in lightly from across the Adriatic. Before them, waterfowl and gulls were swooping down picking up scraps of food that picnickers accidentally lost from their meals. A dozen or so brown and white sandpipers digging around in the sand quickly skittered away from them as they approached them.

Alberto didn't believe he was thinking only of hunger pangs when he turned to her.

"Are you hungry?" When she immediately responded, "Yes," he asked if she was familiar with any of the restaurants here on the beach or in town.

"No, I have never visited Rimini or Rivabella before. My family visited Portonuovo, near Ancona, a few years ago, but I wasn't with them. The only other time I've been to Italy was for two weeks when I was six or seven years old."

"I know of another trattoria about a ten minute walk further up the beach with a terrific menu. The format is family style dining. I think you would enjoy the food," he suggested.

Being they were both hungry, they hastened their step hand in hand, passing several eateries on the beach, each with their own colored beach lounges and colorful cabanas. The black and reddish-orange colored cabanas looked like a group of *coccinelle*: ladybugs huddled together.

They found the waiting time at Angela's Trattoria to be fifteen minutes. Alberto was surprised that diners had chosen to eat *la cena* so early, at only 18:30.

Painted on the arched bricked inside walls of the restaurant were colorful murals of Italian scenes; the Bay of Naples, a panorama of Florence from Michelangelo Park, the Vatican Dome, the Amalfi Coast and the narrow gauge railway that runs through the Centovalli into Switzerland.

While waiting, Maria could see the glow of the wood-fired oven behind the counter at the rear of the dining room, where waiters were collecting pizza orders for other customers. The waiter arrived just as they were seated at a table for two near the trattoria's front window. It was a typical old-fashioned restaurant that had never gotten rid of the red and white-checkered tablecloth with a Chianti bottle in the middle of the table and a well-used candle in its neck. A basket of fresh-crusted bread was immediately placed before them along with a wine list and a menu.

The waiter asked if they wanted water. Alberto said "Si" when Maria nodded.

"*Gassata* o *Naturale?*" he asked.

"No bubbles," Maria said.

Alberto followed Maria's lead by not having a *primo*, only a *secondo* and *contorno* from the list of vegetables. At this point, he didn't want her to know how much he indulged himself with food and wine. With dinner, Maria ordered a glass of white "*Vino da Tavola*," and he preferred a glass of Primitivo, a red wine from the Province of Puglia, in Italy's heel.

"I enjoy mostly white wines, but will have a glass or two of red, occasionally," Maria offered while placing her napkin in her lap. "My brother and father like Italian wines. We have friends who own a wine and liquor store in Brooklyn, who give them a deal on wine by the case."

"Do they prefer red or white?"

"Red wine, by far. Their everyday wine is usually Chianti from the Ricasoli Winery, in Tuscany. For holidays, they buy premium wines from the provinces of Piemonte and Lombardia, like Barbera D'Asti, Amarone, and Gaja's Barbaresco."

"If I ever settle down, I'd like to make wine. My father has all the necessary equipment; barrels, grape press and crusher, all handed down from my grandfather Giovanni Bianco."

"Do you mind if we ask the waiter for butter for my bread?" Maria asked with a quizzical look.

"I will, but I can't guarantee that he will bring it," Alberto said, pointing at the nearby tables. "Notice that they all have bread, but no butter. For some reason, Italians generally do not use butter on bread. It is the same in our home."

"I guess I don't really need it," Maria said apologetically. After Alberto made repeated requests, the waiter, reluctantly, brought a single, small pat of butter. Maria smiled at Alberto and said, "Thanks."

The noise level rose a few decibels as the trattoria became crowded with late diners, and wine flowed freely. A table of twelve was having a loud and rowdy pizza party while a large family was celebrating an anniversary a few tables away.

Earlier, Alberto had silenced his cell phone in deference to his lovely date. As he glanced at it for the first time, he saw that he had a call from an unfamiliar number.

"Shall we walk the beach again?" he asked Maria. Outside the window, the boardwalk lights had come on. Whoever had phoned would have to wait.

•   •   •   •   •   •   •   •   •   •   •   •   •   •

BY THE TIME THEY HIT THE BEACH for a digestive stroll it was almost 20:00. The early evening was beginning to cool, so Alberto helped Maria slip on a tight, lightweight short-sleeved black knit sweater. It accented her curvy body. Still on the topic of food, she said that she preferred "slow food," so very different from the "fast food" so popular in the United States.

Turning toward him, she asked, "Have you heard of McDonald's, Wendy's, Kentucky Fried Chicken, Burger King, Tim Horton's and Taco Bell, all fast food restaurants in the U.S.?"

"Yes," he responded with a laugh, "we have them all here in Italy and probably a few more you didn't mention. There is one exception, however, there are no Starbucks in Italy; probably Italians feel that Starbucks would infringe upon the espresso, cappuccino, and latte trade."

"Do you like pizza?"

"Mmm, absolutely, my mother makes the best thick pizza in all of Italy. She makes her own dough and pizza sauce and buys buffalo mozzarella from a nearby farmer. At home we have pizza once a week. When I'm out with friends, however, I really prefer a thin and crispy pizza, but only from a wood fired oven."

The winds had died, as they often do when the sun begins to fade toward sunset. During their stroll, again at the water's edge, Alberto explained to Maria that over the years he had collected a substantial amount of sea glass, maybe four thousand pieces. With hands on her hips, she looked at him with eyebrows raised, head tilted and a puzzled look.

"Sea glass? There is such a thing as sea glass?"

"Yes there certainly is. Since I was a toddler, my family would often vacation on one of the beaches near Taormina, Sicily. I enjoyed strolling on the beach with them after dinner and became fascinated with sea glass that I would find. Even today, with each piece of found sea glass or shard, I ask myself, "How did this piece end up it in the water? How old is it? How long has it been in the water? What kind of a container was it? Was it tossed overboard? What is the history of this piece?"

"I can see how you became an investigator." Maria smiled. "Tell me more."

"As I grew older, my father, who was a very skilled ironworker, and whose work is displayed in many countries around the world before his retirement, would invite me to go along with him on several of his installations. He explained to his clients that I was his helper. An example of his work in Italy is the gate to the main entrance of the Vatican Museum. It is a doublewide gate with an ornate religious work of bronze incorporated into the design. Each hinged gate is 2 meters wide and 4 meters high." Maria looked impressed as Alberto continued.

"The Queen of England is a lover of dogs. Her staff cares for more than a dozen. At her summer castle in Balmoral, Scotland, stands a black wrought iron fence that took my father four months to complete, surrounding the dog pen. It measures a half-hectare. I personally think it is a monstrosity, but apparently the queen likes it. After the installation was completed, he took me to Brighton Beach. There I found several pieces of colored sea glass including water beaten ceramic and pottery shards, very different from off the coast of Italy. This was the beginning of my quest to collect pieces from all over."

"Many believe the seashell collecting capital of the world is on the west coast of Florida near Sanibel Island. It's also is an excellent place for finding sea glass in the shallow beach water of the Gulf of Mexico. Because of these travels with my father I've been able to collect sea glass from many countries when his work took us near large bodies of water.

The very best area that I found for collecting sea glass is in Bermuda just outside of its capital, Hamilton. A specific beach, which is probably three hundred meters long, is completely covered with sea glass. There's not a place that one can step without stepping on sea glass. When the waves come ashore, one can hear the tinkle, tinkle, tinkle of colliding sea glass as the water strikes. Natives say that several years ago there was a factory that produced various sizes of colored glassware, including bottles."

At this remark, Alberto bent down to the water's edge with his feet in a few centimeters of the Adriatic. He quickly located a piece of brown colored glass about the size of a two-euro coin that had sharp edges around its periphery. With a strong heave, he flung it out to sea.

"Why did you do that? I thought you would have shown me my very first piece of sea glass." Maria exclaimed with hands on hips and an impatient glare.

He smiled. "The piece I picked up had very sharp edges; it had been in the water for only a short time. Collector's sea glass has softer projections at the edges, smooth and slightly frosted. It most likely receives this appearance from being tumbled and weathered by sand and water and time. I sent it back far enough so no one would be able to step on it, and maybe it will get the proper tumbling before it returns to shore."

Alberto reached into the water, again, this time picking up an acceptable shard. It provided Maria with a visualization of what he had just described. Holding this piece between his thumb and forefinger, he raised it to eye level toward the west, for better viewing. He knew what it was because, as a child, his favorite soft drink had been Coca Cola. His mother did not appreciate his drinking bubbly soft drinks. "It's not good for you," she would bark. So when he was away from the house, Papà would buy Alberto a Coke, the same color glass as the piece he was examining.

"At one time, this was probably the bottom of an early Coca Cola bottle," he declared.

"Okay, detective. What's your clue?"

Alberto liked her curiosity. "It is nearly clear with a trace of a light green. Also, it appears to be thicker than either a beer bottle or a wine bottle. There is a set of raised numbers on the outside, see?" Maria examined it closely.

During the next hour or so, they collected about twenty-five sea glass pieces of various colors. Alberto especially enjoyed the view each time Maria bent over to reach for a piece of glass.

Almost all of the collection was a medium to dark green or a medium to dark shade of brown, most likely from wine and beer bottles. He had hoped that they would find a few of the more elusive colors, variants of blue or red, or milk glass, or—even more unusual—ceramic pieces. Because his collection was already so extensive, he tried to restrict himself to collecting odd pieces, only.

Alberto held the collection in his outstretched hand, and to his delight, Maria asked. "Can I have them?"

• • • • • • • • • • • • • • •

ONE BY ONE THE NEON RESTAURANT LIGHTS along the beach were beginning to dim, like dying embers of a campfire. Several other couples of various ages strolled the wide weather beaten boardwalk on this balmy evening. Under the boardwalk's brighter lights a few children were playfully scurrying about in all directions. The beach games had ceased, however. The sky was filled with thousands of twinkling stars and on the east horizon a large deep orange colored moon was starting its several hours' trip over the Adriatic and across the heavens to the west.

In the summer, dining establishments in Rimini close at 22:00, but Alberto knew that shops offering gelati and dolci would certainly be open until 23:00, since so many Italians enjoyed a *passeggiata*, an after-dinner stroll, stopping to chat with friends or for their favorite sweets.

"Maria, I know we had a dolce at dinner. How about a gelato, now?"

"I'm not sure. I don't usually eat between meals."

"I know a place that serves the absolute best gelato in all of Emilia-Romagna."

After consideration, she conceded. "If you think it's that good, I'll give it a try."

It was a short walk to Roberto's *Gelato è Dolce*, just off the boardwalk toward the edge of town. Two lines had formed at the outdoor service windows, each with eight to ten patrons. The full-length glass door that led inside allowed them to see the display cases filled with tiramisu, almond paste cookies, tiny cream and chocolate filled puffs, brioche, elephant ears, cannoli, and several other pastries that Alberto recognized but could not name.

"I'd like the smallest cup of *caffè gelato* and a glass of water please," Maria requested when it was their turn.

"The medium cup with pistachio and chocolate scoops, and a double espresso, please."

Maria frowned. "Alberto, doesn't caffeine interfere with your sleeping at night?"

"Apparently, it doesn't, at least not the caffeine in an espresso. Recently, I met a friend at a bar for *caffè* and we discussed this very topic. According to him, a study of hot beverages conducted by researchers at the University of Bologna a few years ago indicated that espresso has less caffeine than regular coffee. It may have something to do with the way that the water presses down through the espresso coffee while being heated. True or not, I'm not sure. But, *cioccolata calda*, hot chocolate, with all its caffeine would certainly keep me awake."

They finished their gelati and deposited the empty paper cups, napkins and plastic spoons in the proper colored containers. Maria commented: "Italian recycling is much better organized than ours."

"Welcome to Italia. We've been recycling ancient buildings since before Rome ruled the world," Alberto quipped.

As they walked down the street hand in hand, he could see Maria trying to conceal a yawn. He detected a slightly tired look in those previous sparkling big brown eyes. It was then Alberto realized that she had arrived from the United States just two days ago and must still be feeling the effects of jet lag.

"Are you staying on the beach or at a hotel near here?"

"I'm staying at a family friend's two-bedroom apartment one block from the beach. The husband and wife are currently on an archeological dig in Egypt and won't be back until the middle of next month. They live here year round."

He looked at her hesitantly, and then took the initiative. "Do you mind if I walk you back to your apartment?"

"I'd like that. The apartment is located on a *strada* that's not well lit at night. I would feel much safer if you did."

Their stroll led off the beach a short block west and two blocks north, past closed shops and a few bars that remained open until midnight. On a narrow, treeless street of square and rectangular pavers stood three buildings of yellow and gray stone, four stories high, with square windows. Maria guided him to the middle unit and to a brown double door, one step up from the street. She slowly turned her back to the door, faced Alberto, held his hands in hers and smiled.

"I enjoyed meeting you. Thank you so much for a wonderful evening," she said with a broad smile. "You are my first blind date and I enjoyed it very much."

He slipped his hands down to her waist. "I enjoyed your company as well. You are, by far, the best blind date I've ever had." With this exchange, he thought, *finally I don't feel that I need to say arrivederci but rather "ciao e buona notte."* He gave her an Italian hug that included a peck on each cheek, and with eyebrows raised, asked, "May I see you again? Like, tomorrow?"

"I'd like that," she replied without hesitating, "though I need to go shopping. There are several things I forgot to bring with me on this trip, including a bathing suit. I'd also like to begin shopping for gifts for some of my friends and relatives in the U.S."

"Being that you intend to purchase a bathing suit," he said enthusiastically, "could we meet at the beach, say, about 15:00? The beach should be very crowded because the weather forecast for tomorrow calls for mostly sunny skies with a few wispy clouds and a temperature of around 26 to 28 degrees Centigrade. Not bad for late summer. Shall we look for each other near the bath house?"

She smiled. "Sounds like a plan."

· · · · · · · · · · · · · · ·

THE BEACH APARTMENT Alberto rented was several minutes on foot from Maria's location, a narrow bricked *strada* that dead-ended at the beach. With his arms swinging side to side, head high, Alberto smiled and whistled as he strolled happily back to his room. The night was still balmy and moonlit. Shutters were up; apartment windows on both sides of the *strada* were wide open to cool off the upper floors.

From one of the third level apartments, strains of Louie Prima's, "Oh Marie," drifted down to the *strada* level. He stopped, sat on a concrete step and listened to the lyrics. How appropriate, he thought.

Oh Marie, Oh Marie
In your arms I'm longin' to be
Mmm, Baby
Tell me you love me
Kiss me once while the stars shine above me
Hey Marie
Oh Marie!

A few autos, a couple of noisy motorcycles and three mopeds sped past, one beeping its horn for some unexplained reason. Alberto dodged a young man on a bicycle when he accidentally stepped off the curb.

He'd just spent several hours with a date that he actually appreciated. He was elated! He must contact Vincenzo tomorrow to thank him for "evening up the score," so to speak, after some dreadful prank dates Vincenzo had recently set up to tease him.

New Corners

by Maria Massimi

As Richie drives out to Long Island on a sunny summer day,
we travel back to his past with him. He recalls his old neighborhood,
and the move his family made to the suburbs.
We learn how he feels about his memories and the role his past
has played in his life.

As I sped down the Thruway and over the Throgs Neck Bridge, I was aware of being part of a caravan of other summer sun-seekers who had braved the exigencies of the week, and who were heading to the Island for a day of reprieve from the grueling week. I knew I was already late for the annual family barbeque out at Mikie's house in Hempstead. *"Oh, gee, I'm about forty-five minutes late already,"* I thought, and never seemed to break that record. At least I would arrive long before desserts were put out, probably after everyone had had the first round of hot dogs, before some serious eating. Everyone else would have already arrived, including friends coming from farther away in Westchester. Even though there would always be cake and ice cream and summer ices, it was always assigned to me to pick up the cannoli and other pastries along with some pignoli biscotti and crunchy chocolate cookies for dessert. The bonus of working in the neighborhood of Einstein Research Center near Morris Park Avenue, Bronx, is that it is the haven of Italian pastry shops and bakeries. It feels good arriving each morning to work, to a neighborhood that despite having morphed over the ages, still resembles enough the one of my early years in Brooklyn before we moved out to the Island. Here one could find relatively unknown restaurants with uninspiring décor and paper placemats, but where the food was consistently good and where on a Friday night it would be difficult to find a free table. You could dream of the bakeries of the old neighborhood whose shop windows were laid out with cream-filled cakes and cherry-topped wares, or some displaying freshly baked breads in circles and oblongs and raisin-filled squares. Here it still housed fresh fruit and vegetable stands out on sidewalks, and fish mongers on almost every block. The neighborhood for me was the comfort of the familiar.

· · · · · · · · · · · · · · · ·

Mikie had called me that morning to remind me of our usual annual game to which the whole family always looked forward, young and old alike. "And don't forget to bring your mitt, Richie, for our game of softball." With that I ran back upstairs to grab the gear to throw into the trunk of the car before setting out. In these final days of August, his words brought me back to our last day on the block where most of the tenants of our building had come out onto the sidewalk to bid us farewell. Grandma held her handkerchief tightly in her hand, others held back their tears. The last cardboard box had been finally loaded onto the roof of our wooden-sided station wagon, the motor running. "Come on, Richie, hurry up, and don't forget your mitt." The bats and mask had already been loaded into the car.

· · · · · · · · · · · · · · · ·

Those were the last words I remember, which closed the first chapter of my life. My brothers, Jimmy, who was the youngest, and

Mikie in the middle and I, the oldest, along with our parents, said our last good-byes to Aunt Mary, to Grandma and to Poppi, to Mr. Gibbons, our upstairs neighbor, and to my best friend, Paulie, who stood statuesque on the edge of the curb still not believing that we were really leaving. We turned over our share of ownership of Cracker, who was the building's dog, adopted by all of us who lived at 16 Melbourne Street. We closed the trunk and finally jumped into the car, and Dad turned the corner to set out for shiny new beginnings. Now with the sun shining over my visor I conjured up vivid images of that sun-shiny day of my youth, the day that had the biggest impact on my early years.

Our last minute regrets were overshadowed by the expectation of new beginnings, and we looked forward to our new life, that is, everyone but Jimmy who cried all the way out until we reached the Expressway. It took him only as long as the first night sleeping in his new bed and in his own room to stop complaining. We spoke of a sprawled out neighborhood in the suburbs where each family lived twenty feet from each other by law! There, sprawled-out lawns hugged newly painted white houses with mailboxes standing out by the road like proud sentinels lining sidewalked streets. Houses were all identified with characteristic emblems of individuality stamping their own square plot of proud ownership on the globe. I recall one house which sported a brown cement deer with black and white glazed eyes sitting comfortably erect on the corner of the property; another, with a porcelain orange and brown cat deftly climbing the wall next to the front door; some had happy red geraniums dancing in stylized cement planters which emulated those pots adorning wealthy villas. One or two houses were guarded by stone lions flanking the front entry, and still others had humble Madonnas that lit up at night. Almost all had bright new American flags of varying sizes gleefully swaying from front porches or facades. Front walks were impeccably clean, and lawns were part of a competition that was uniquely American.

And thus a new home lured our parents into the suburbs of Long Island, where we kids could safely ride bikes, where Dad might spare some time shooting baskets with us on our own driveway, and where Mom would now drive to PTA meetings instead of taking a bus even if it were raining. She could drive to the hairdresser, dry cleaners and food market instead of carrying heavy bags of groceries for six blocks. Gas was not cheap, but a necessary commodity of new entry. Ballparks and playgrounds were within walking distance.

For sure our parents sacrificed for us, with mortgage payments, taxes and worries about unforeseen bills. These worries inevitably found a way into the recesses of their mind during daily activities, even when they pushed them back in order to enjoy their shiny dreams, to enjoy a piece of the pie that they had finally cut out for themselves. Neighborhood moms would take turns before school each morning, to wait with us for our shiny yellow school bus to turn the corner and come to a screeching stop, scooping us up within the big metal doors that reached out to us like familiar arms. In the fifties, most of us kids in the neighborhood were Italian, Irish or Polish and were shipped off to Our Lady of Fatima Elementary School for safekeeping, for the formation of our mind, body and soul. As we climbed into the cavernous vehicle we would wave to Gary, whom we learned years later was half Jewish, and who remained at the corner to wait for the city bus that sped him off to the public elementary school. We would meet up with Gary again after school, though, because every day after most of the homework was done, there would be a game of "catch" down in the empty field next to the parkway. In those morning minutes waiting for the bus before school, we had time to snatch conversations about new baseball cards that had been recently issued, kid around with each other, tease the girls, check on the homework, ask questions like, "Did you get #16 of the math homework last night?"

No longer would we have to fall asleep watching the blinking light at the corner, which no matter how we pulled the curtains closed, still flashed across our room at night, posting grey irregular figures that danced across our walls, begging to share our dreams. We would no longer need to share our bedroom, or negotiate among the five of us our allotted time in the bathroom each morning. Nothing woke us before we needed to get up on Saturday mornings, as there were none of the sputtering noises of busses, trucks, and motorcycles, those vehicles that could be heard through our window as they raced off to get an edge on the morning traffic.

And so, as a caterpillar that takes months to transform into a butterfly for its next stage of life, we, too, slowly self-transformed into other beings of ourselves. We left behind the "city kids" persona, children of the first generation. We stopped chewing gum for the most part. We sported new 50's brown and white saddle shoes on the first day of school like all the other kids who were not wearing brown leather penny-loafers. Keds sneakers were solely for gym. We could no longer just run downstairs to Grandma's and Poppi's whenever we needed a hug or were lured by the aroma of fresh-baked bread or of unmistakable tomato sauce simmering on the stove, the tantalizing aroma that circled up the stairs and found its way into our apartment on Sunday mornings after Mass. Grandma would save a fried meatball for us right out of the pan before adding it to the bubbling gravy. It would have a distinct savory taste that exploded in your mouth and made all things right again. For sure, we believed, that we would be able to drive to visit on Sunday afternoons to "catch up" on the week's news. We looked forward to seeing our cousins who used to live right upstairs from us across from gnarly Mr. Gibbons, and with whom we were bonded like siblings, until the day we were separated by highways, parishes and zip codes. We began to somehow look different, feel different, and to think differently, with new horizons in our focus that went beyond the corner of our block.

Like broken pieces of a glass that had slipped through our fingers and had fallen to the floor, the memories of the anecdotes of a life that had been good to us, were ultimately slipping away. We came away with unmistakable values, traditions, and warm memories, some inevitably eroded with the rust of time. We left behind the fun of walking home together in groups. We would stop by Penny Candy or look for loose change in our pockets to slip into the bakery and buy a fresh donut before reaching home. We knew when we heard Nicky's mom call him in for supper each evening that it was time to stop doing our homework and start helping in the kitchen. You could set your watch by when she would raise the window and call his name. He would hear her around the corner where he and his friends would be playing hardball against the only solid brick wall without windows or door on the block. The walls within our own pre-war apartment held our earliest experiences of life, our earliest thoughts and fears, disappointments and dreams. There we learned to form a consensus of which evening program we would all watch together, how to navigate among the needs and wants of those who lived, breathed, and shared the space so close to ours, above a lobby where the mosaic floor was inscribed with the first words we learned in Latin, "Cave Canem."

In our new life, when mom and dad had to go out together at night, we were old enough to be left alone. But if we heard scary noises or thought we heard creaky creatures crawling in the attic, we no longer had the luxury of knowing that Aunt Mary was just downstairs to hear our screams. We were on our own. If we finished our schoolwork early there was no one to sit around with us on our front porch waiting for friends to join us or to pass the last half hour of the afternoon looking for Dad to turn the corner coming home from work, carrying lunchbox in one hand, newspaper in the other as he walked back from the subway stop. There was no one to share a laugh, to count the cars with two instead of four doors, or to tell funny stories. One was the day our itinerant Friday afternoons art teacher, Mrs. Hershey, wore two different black shoes, and did not know it until Hank undiplomatically alerted her to the fact in the middle of the lesson. The rest of us held our heads down hoping to not let out a titter of laughter. I suppose he wanted to even the playing field since she made it unmistakably clear that he had not been dealt the genes of an artist.

No familiar friends walked by our sidewalk to whom we could call from our window and exchange a wave. There would be no passing parades in front of our house with uniformed firemen, school bands, politicians and policemen in all their glory, or boy and girl and cub scouts waving to parents and younger siblings licking ice cream cones dripping down their shirts, and on Memorial Day waving crepe paper poppies and flags in front of our steps as the crowds passed by. We always dreamed that one day we would be able to reach out and touch one of the passing floats from our apartment window. We had heard the story of a kid who had tried it once, and was nearly killed from falling out the window. We never knew if it were a true story or not. We missed Mr. Gibbons, who took daily walks around the block, who stored Tootsie Rolls in his pocket to dispense to us kids if we could tell him one new thing we learned that day. In our old neighborhood someone's mom or dad was always miraculously nearby to save us from a stranger or from ourselves. The front stoop heard all our stories, our jokes, complaints or longings. It was there that we learned if Mary's dad was still hung over, if Paulie's mother had her baby yet, if Mary Ann's sister was really going to go to college.

• • • • • • • • • • • • • • • •

For a while we continued to hear about news from the old block. Anthony and his family would also be moving to a different town, farther out on the Island to Patchogue. We would never again vie for Margaret's attention as we had in the cafeteria in those days of sixth grade. And we could only hold onto sepia memories of playing kickball with Sr. Therese on the school playground. Our most thrilling memory of the nuns in all those years was seeing Sr. Therese rolling up her sleeves and playing kickball with us on the concrete court, her black and white habit undulating around her head like penguins dancing happily and freely in the breeze.

It was a world within a world. We had traded more than a neighborhood, a front door stoop for neatly shuttered houses. We traded human drama as it unfolded for isolated verdant plots of home ownership. We were not to realize until years later that we would miss the sights, smells, sounds and sentimentality of familiar haunts, or the companionship and theatre of everyday life. Of course we appreciated and enjoyed the luxury and privacy of washed down streets, of refuse-cleared front walks, tidy rows of gardens, and razor-edged lawns that embraced our new life. But little did we know that what we had left behind was already part of our DNA that would remain tucked under the surface of our psyche, tugging at our heart strings, hoping never to be totally erased. Those city-stoop conversations, late-night muffled car motors, and hushed voices outside the glass windows of our rooms as we fell off to sleep, never quite vanished altogether. They had formed the first molecules of our conscious being. They were the roots of who we were, and who we were to become.

Driving alone now on this summer day, I let my thoughts wander where they may. Past memories found a comfortable place to collect in my mind. I yearned for what we had lost: community, companionship, daily theatre on the block. Yet I knew what we had gained: the song of birds outside our windows, trees that changed color in our yard, bigger skies, and new corners. I was now looking forward to that game of "catch" later on, and as I turned the corner and pulled into Mikie's driveway, I realized that I was a patchwork of my past and present, and was all the richer for both. I stepped out of my car, with worn mitt and fresh desserts in hand. I would look forward to the future, to a life that was beckoning, offering promises of the unknown, and of transforming new corners.

The Sister Left Behind

by Suzanna Rosa Molino

Pietrina was going to America—so much to visualize!
How tall is the Statue of Liberty? How would she learn English?
Yet the nightmarish scene at the Naples port on that sorrowful day
in 1929 was a scene she and her husband Mario never would have imagined.

Pietrina's emotions swirled–she was going to America! Absolutely giddy with excitement, she fluttered around the bedroom, her hand lightly swatting a small collection of dresses hanging in the wardrobe, her eyes scanning the three modest pairs of shoes lined up neatly on the floor. One at a time, she picked up several frames of family photographs from the dresser and stared into the brown eyes watching her. She peeked inside of a small wooden jewelry box, imagining it–and all of her belongings–packed efficiently in one *valigia*, the new piece of luggage purchased for the voyage. She never before had owned a suitcase–where could she and her humble family possibly afford to go?

But now...onto America. *Two more weeks.* Too early to pack.

Butterflies took flight in her stomach. Mostly, excitement ruled over her fear, feeling as thrilled as she ever had about anything in her 26 years. (Perhaps not more than her beautiful wedding day to her beloved Mario two years prior.) When the fear crept in, so did doubt... *No-no-no, how can I leave Mamma e Babbo? What if I never see them again? Dio mio, America is SO very far from our beautiful Sardegna. What are we doing?? Is this truly the right thing??*

Yet as the Mossa family's plans unfolded during those months in 1929, Pietrina's elation won as she listened to the stimulating details, living arrangements, and ship information. She and Mario would travel by boat to *Napoli* on the mainland, with her sister Antonica, and husband Giovanni, Mario's brother. They had purchased passage to America aboard the *Conte Biancamano*. *Zia* Amelia and *cugina* Olga–an aunt and cousin who lived along the same cobblestoned street in the village of Luras–also would be in their entourage.

Pietrina's mind skipped ahead to departure day... *What would the ship be like? Would the journey be demanding? Is New York City as grand as they've heard? Just how tall is the Statue of Liberty? How will I learn English?* So many mysteries...so much to visualize.

Once in Brooklyn, New York, the Sardinian Mossas would reunite with another Mossa brother who had emigrated two years before. Amelia's husband Antonio had worked long hours as a carpenter to save enough money to send for his precious wife and 10-year-old daughter.

By airmail, the family had received decent reports from Antonio and his *paesani* who boldly had crossed the ocean and settled into American life. *Antonio's letters were encouraging. Certainly, Italians would not continue to migrate if not for having found the riches and opportunities expected in the United States, sì?* Pietrina's thoughts flooded her uneasy mind. She could scarcely sleep.

Gazing into a small mirror into her large brown eyes, brushing the curly black hair from her smooth face, Pietrina stood in the third-floor bedroom of her parents' home and wished–for the hundredth time–that her parents were going, too. But that hopeless idea was crushed. Stubborn *Mamma* Rosa refused to discuss the topic with her daughters. *Oh, that woman was as stubborn as their farm mule Lupini, when he didn't want to walk a step further!*

"Non io," the sturdy five-foot Rosa firmly answered, as Antonica and Pietrina repeatedly pleaded. *Per favore, reconsider, Mamma... per favore?*

"Non io." Rosa's words echoed through the kitchen in every conversation that erupted about the subject, adding nothing more to each discussion besides, *"Sono nata su quest'isola e morirò qui!"*... I was born on this island and I will die here.

The sisters knew it was hopeless. *Mamma* and *Babbo* would never change their minds. Their lives were entrenched in this crumbling antique village, toiling fields on their nearby farm, tending to the old house, barn, and animals; they existed to provide for the family. No grander dreams, no desire to upend their lives, not even for the grandiose land of America. The life they know and understand is *qui*–right here. At the ages of 68 and 72, they were not exactly primed to begin again in a strange country, finding work, adapting to another culture, and learning a new language. *No.*

Yet deep down, *Mamma* Rosa's heart was torn in two. Her daughters were leaving her? Leaving their village, giving up this beautiful island? Leaving Italy! How could she possibly bear it when the time came? She *wanted* to understand her children, wanted to offer support. But she did not comprehend this yearning to flee. Was theirs a hard life here? *Sì.* Was it flawless? *No.* Yet did they not also have some pleasures: music, food, faith, surrounded by stunning panoramic views of mountains and clear azure seas. *Sardegna* is one of the most beautiful islands in *Italia...nel mondo...*in the world. Most importantly, the Mossa and Cabras families experienced together the key and vital part of life... *la famiglia.* Family.

Miserably, Rosa knew she could not prevent her daughters' departures. They are married women; her sons-in-law had the final say. *Yes, they were leaving for America–a continent away. Our family will be divided...possibly forever. God comfort me.*

• • • • • • • • • • • • • •

Pietrina examined her third-class ticket behind black-framed eyeglasses she didn't actually need. Her shoulders were covered with a black cape, her suitcase at her feet, the strap of a worn leather satchel hitched over a shoulder. A white scarf covered her black curls. In line to be examined by health officials before embarking, Pietrina's nerves were frayed. A week earlier, an infection had developed in her left eye, now bloodshot. Further proof disclosed the problematic eye by swelling underneath, a reality of its soreness. *No! Why this week, why now?*

"*Non preoccuparti, cara,*" Mario assured his wife. "Don't worry, my darling. It will be okay. The inspectors are checking for major health problems: noticeable illnesses, coughs, symptoms, and other signs of diseases. They will not stop you for this, not for only a small eye infection."

Her sister's and brother-in-law's tickets had been already stamped *visto al controllo* by an immigration inspector–seen at the check. They had been cleared of any health issues, indicated by the words on their documents: *Ha espletato le operazioni sanitarie* (has completed the health care operations). Amelia and Olga had not yet been processed, waiting eagerly behind Mario and Pietrina.

Her turn. She wanted to vomit. The stomach butterflies were in flight, but for a different reason...not elation now–*fear.* She could barely look at the health inspector as she clutched her ticket, passport, and ship documents. Mario stood behind his wife. He watched as a small light was shone into her eyes. The lids were pulled up, down, sideways. He could see Pietrina trying not to flinch in discomfort.

What unfolded next was nightmarish. *CHE...WHAT?* Had she heard the Italian inspector correctly? *They were not allowing her through? How can that be possible??? Twelve months of planning, saving, deciding, uncertainty. Being willing to uproot their lives in Italy...for niente...nothing? America, the land of hope and promise, was not to be? No, No, Nooooo!*

Infection or no infection, thick tears pooled in the young Italian's eyes. Her vision blurred. She couldn't see, she couldn't hear. Only the words, "*Mi dispiace, Signora...mi dispiace,*" drummed repeatedly in her head. She felt dizzy, nauseous. She needed to sit down before she fell over. She half-heard her husband's rapid Italian pleading with the inspector, asking questions, explaining, convincing. But the port employee shooed him away impatiently, motioning with his hand for the next in line to step forward.

Mario caught his wife as her legs collapsed. Pietrina allowed him to guide her away from the mass of people, his arm wrapped around her waist, as he struggled with their luggage. He pointed her in the opposite direction from where Antonica and Giovanni waited on the other side of the inspector's stand. But not before he caught his brother's widened frightened eyes.

Mario's face was stone. At home, rumors had found their way into the village–countless Italians had been turned away at the ports of departure during processing: some were too old, others too infirm, and in some cases, people were merely the victim of an irritable immigration processing clerk. *Is this man one of them?* Those poor villagers who had finally made the wrenching choice to escape Italy for improved opportunities in "the promised land," then abruptly turned away like pieces of cargo set to the side ... *a horrible fate! And now it is happening with my wife. Dio mio, this cannot be real.*

Against a wall, the Mossas stood motionless, stunned, in shock. Activity and noise swirled around them as hundreds of other passengers moved through the line, laden with luggage, babies, trunks, and satchels; mothers clutched small children's hands. Mario had no idea what to do next; this was completely unbelievable.

What of our lives now? Please, Dio, do not let this be happening–God, hear me. Let someone tell us this is an enormous mistake. We need to, we MUST, get on that ship! We are going to America! Help us.

· · · · · · · · · · · · · · · ·

Morning sun sliced across Pietrina's face, her cheeks streaked with tears from days of crying. Unwillingly, she opened them and automatically reached to the empty side of the bed where Mario normally laid. The realization hit her again, like a punch in the stomach.

My husband truly left without me? He left without me. They all did: Antonica, Giovanni, Amelia, Olga–all of them left me! What will I do now?

Fresh tears flowed. Profound disappointment pinned her body to the bed. She was literally unable to lift herself up, nor did she have the will. This outrageous situation was beyond comprehension.

Mamma Rosa and *Papà Giacomo* were as completely shocked as anyone when their daughter returned to Luras the following day, led delicately into the house by neighbors who had accompanied their families to Naples; they had taken over the care of Pietrina after the ship left the port. Barely able to extract the details from Pietrina, they merely watched helplessly as she hid in her room grieving day after day. She was inconsolable.

Was there an iota of relief, Mamma Rosa wondered, for her daughter not to leave the only life she knew? She was so young. But oh Mario. How could her son-in-law have had the willpower and strength to depart without her? What kind of journey would it be for him, for Antonica, for the rest, after the despair of parting ways during that horrible port scene?

It was unfathomable to Pietrina's parents how difficult it must have been. The well-organized plan had been ruined, not only for their daughter–for all of them. She had been deserted. Surely, the situation was insufferable for her. It felt that way for Rosa, without having witnessed it.

That day at the port was the last Pietrina saw of her family. They were on their way to their new lives in America.

• • • • • • • • • • • • • • • •

Mario never gave up the vision of bringing his wife to the States. He worked long hard hours in the Brooklyn restaurant, a job he had arranged prior to leaving Italy–which was the reason he was forced to leave his wife behind. The decision had to be made quickly. Mario could barely process the situation–there wasn't time to think. He and Giovanni had discussed it hurriedly and privately away from the women, agreeing on the inevitable–Mario *had* to go without Pietrina. He could not surpass a job opportunity when many Italians had great difficulty finding work once in America. He *had* to begin. There was nothing in Luras for him, for any of them, to secure a brighter future. He would send for Pietrina later.

Leaving behind his wife was the single hardest thing he ever had to do in his 37 years. He promised her over and over–and over again–he would send for her as quickly as possible. He encouraged her to be patient, assured her they would be reunited again in no time.

Oh, but for the terror in his bride's eyes...the frightening sound of her wailing...he could not shake it. It haunted him while awake; it spooked his sleep. *Stupido controllore!! Idiota!!* (Stupid inspector. Idiot.) What should have been a thrilling voyage had been replaced by anguish. He could hardly get out of bed. His family felt the same and were quiet during the sixteen-day passage. Their sorrow was unlimited; the journey tainted.

. . . .

Mario kept his promise. How could he possibly be happy living in another country without his dear Pietrina? He did not want to only *send* for her, to force his sweet wife to make the journey without him, *no*. He returned to Sardinia to accompany Pietrina to America himself. *Sono il suo marito! I am her husband and we will do this together. This time it will be okay. I will fix this for her–I will help my wife forget that dreadful day on the port last year.*

Yet fate has other ideas for us sometimes, *sì*? The best plans are interrupted, postponed, some never to reach fruition. This time, by the happiest of news. Mario reunited in Luras with his wife, yes–*and* their daughter Tina, a beautiful chubby *bambina*. His first sweet child!

The talk of returning to America faded more and more as the Mossas settled into life, with Mario accepting what he considered temporary work as Pietrina became pregnant again...then again...and eventually bearing four children. Their days broke into routine with the small children and work. The vision of America seemed further and further away. *It is almost impossible now. I cannot afford six passages.*

As much as was doable in those days of slow communication, the separated family stayed connected across the ocean through letters and static-heavy phone conversations. Pietrina wanted to feel happy hearing about Antonica's life in America, and yet the dread of "that day" haunted her, and probably would forever. Brooklyn babies were born, apartments were rented, houses were bought, money was earned, English words and phrases were learned. Tidbits of news slowly drifted between New York and Sardinia.

And that was the way it remained. Pietrina never recovered from the abandonment. Dying too young of heart complications, this time it was *she* who left behind her beloved Mario. This time...forever. Perhaps on that terrible day at the Naples port, Pietrina's heart had actually broken in half and was unable to mend itself.

A broken heart...along with her broken dream...a dream of living in America.

From Train to Tradition

by Sharon Nikosey

John, a farm boy, takes up running after he returns home from WWII.
But who runs if they don't have to in the 1940s? A young farmer trying
to capture the attention of a certain woman on the train, that's who.
The decision John makes to try to save money, turns in to a real life-changer.

Bright and early on a Monday in the fall of 1946, former Army Sargent Johnny Santamaria gets up to feed the chickens and gather eggs. He picks some tomatoes and chives in the garden and brings them in to his *Mamma*. The breakfast he will soon enjoy sure beats the food in the mess halls by about a mile! He is proud of the time he served his country. His parents Stefano and Maria, are immigrants to Massachusetts from Filagudi, Italy. They are very proud of all three of their sons who served. What they are most happy about is that they all came home safely and joined their sister Rosalie back at the farm north of Boston.

After breakfast, Johnny and Rosalie hurry off to catch the train to work. Rosalie is a clerk at a clothing store in Boston. It doesn't pay well, but it is much more pleasant than making tires at the rubber factory where she used to work. Johnny was lucky to land a job doing construction. Winters are tough because the work often stops. However, the reward of seeing something he worked on become a completed building makes it worthwhile.

Johnny has taken extra care with his appearance today. There is a certain young woman he sees on the train each morning. He has decided today is the day he will speak to her. Or, he will ask Rosalie to strike up a conversation with her. Or, he will become overcome with shyness, again, and not do a thing. How is it he can travel all over the world, live with troops of men he's never met before, fight for his country, but cannot say hello to a beautiful girl?

They get on the train, and "she" is there. Johnny picks a seat across from her. If only she would drop something, and he could pick it up for her. Should he compliment her on her hat? No! He could ask her for the time. No again. He just boarded the 7:10 train, so it's probably no later than 7:12 by now. Stop the presses, did he catch her looking at him? He waits a few minutes until he thinks he feels her eyes on him. Yes, she *is* looking at him! He gives her his most sincere smile. She smiles shyly back. His heart beats as fast as it did when he ran a six-minute mile at boot camp. He smiles to himself until, too quickly, it is his stop. He wishes Rosalie a pleasant day, ventures another smile at the most beautiful girl on the train, and departs. He didn't speak with her with words, but at least they managed to communicate...*something.*

After a long day at work, Johnny is full of happy energy. He decides to walk the 10 miles home. At least he starts out walking. It's a beautiful day, and his abundance of energy makes him start running. He runs until he gets a pebble in his shoe. After he gets rid of it, he walks and jogs the rest of the way home. To add to his pleasure, he realizes he has an extra fifty cents in his pocket that he didn't use on train fare.

This routine continues for the rest of the week. On Friday morning, he again takes his seat across from her. Today, not only do they smile at each other, but she says "Excuse me, did I see you running to Wakefield last night?"

"Well, yes" Johnny replies, "I decided I would run home from work instead of riding the train for a change." (Two dollars and fifty cents in change, that is!)

"Wow, that seems kind of far." she says. Johnny feels himself turning red.

"Oh, it's not too bad. I love the fall. And I always enjoyed running when I was in the service."

At this point Rosalie has had enough.

"Ciao" she says, "I'm Rosalie, and this is my brother Johnny. We live in Wakefield."

"Ciao. I'm Kay. I live in Reading and work at our family restaurant in the North End. Have you heard of Cappy's?"

Johnny and Rosalie shake their heads. "We don't eat out very often."

"Oh, you should come by sometime." replies Kay looking at Johnny. "You should meet my father. He is in the BAA." Johnny looks confused, but likes the idea of meeting her father. "The Boston Athletic Association" clarifies Kay. "They organize the annual Boston Marathon each April." Johnny is still confused, but thrilled that they have actually spoken, and he knows her name!

That weekend, while Johnny is working on the farm with his brothers Basil and Steve, he asks if they ever heard of the Boston Marathon. "Sure," Basil replies. "That is where a bunch of guys try to run from Hopkinton to Boston, all in one day. I think it is about 25 miles!"

Steve chimes in "Well, that sounds about as fun as cleaning up after the chickens."

They all chuckle, but Johnny becomes thoughtful. He has been running about 10 miles a day all week. He enjoys it, but could he run more than double that distance?

Johnny couldn't be happier when Monday rolls around. He is looking forward to seeing Kay, especially now that they have broken the ice. Rosalie seems to enjoy chatting with her also. The daily ride to town goes by quickly. Although Johnny is tempted to take the train home so maybe he can see more of Kay, he enjoys his long run and saving train fare.

By Friday morning, Kay again mentions coming to the family restaurant and meeting her father. "To talk about the Boston Marathon," she says.

Johnny has a feeling that she has another reason for wanting him to visit the restaurant. He has dated a few girls after returning from the war, but there is something special about Kay.

"I will try to stop by on Saturday afternoon" Johnny promises.

On Saturday, Johnny whistles through his farming chores. His brothers are curious about his cheery mood, and ask what is going on. Rosalie smiles knowingly. Johnny has checked the train schedule, which runs less frequently on the weekends. If he finishes everything by noon, he can clean up, shave and make the 1:30 train.

He is about to leave when Maria stops him.

"Johnny, can you take three chickens down to Mrs. Rando? And bring back some extra fish they have."

"Oh Mamma, can't Basil or Steven bring the chickens? I was going ...somewhere."

"No honey, they are still busy working in the field. And I'd really like to get the fish soon, so I can begin preparing it for Sunday dinner. Now, where do you have to be on a Saturday afternoon, all spiffed up?"

"Nowhere, Mamma" says Johnny sadly. "I will go to Mrs. Rando's."

"Kay, I am sorry I didn't make it to Cappy's on Saturday. My family needed me around the farm" said Johnny apologetically the next Monday on the train.

As disappointed as Kay was, she appreciated his loyalty to his family.

"That's alright, Johnny. You can come after work if that is better. On Thursday nights, I work until 9."

"Yes" said Johnny cheering up. "I will try to come Thursday after work." As soon as he says it, he thinks with dismay of how dirty he is after a day of construction. He probably wouldn't make a very good first impression. But he doesn't want to let her down again. He will just have to bring a clean shirt and a comb.

On Thursday, Johnny manages to roll up a t-shirt and store it in his lunch bag to change into after work. He follows the directions Kay shared with him that morning. As much as he would like to run there and arrive quickly, he decides to walk as to not get his clean t-shirt full of sweat.

Kay's face lights up when she sees him enter the restaurant. "You made it" she says happily. "Come meet my Papa. I've told him about you...your running." *She told him about me*, Johnny thinks giddily. Maybe it is time he told his Mamma and Pa about Kay.

"Papa, I would like to introduce you to Johnny Santamaria from Wakefield. He is the man I told you about. Johnny, this is my Papa, Anthony Cappadona."

"Please to meet you, Sir" said Johnny respectfully.

"Well, Johnny, I am pleased to meet you. Kay told you that I help organize The Boston Marathon?" Johnny nodded. "Well then, if you like running so much, I bet you could run 26.2 miles. What are you doing next Patriots' Day?"

Through the rest of the fall, the winter, and into the spring, Johnny continues to meet Kay on the train. He also continues running home from work most days and saving a little money. Some weeks when there isn't any construction work, he disappears for a couple of hours and runs around Wakefield. He hasn't told his family, other than Rosalie, thinking they won't understand about running. One day Stefano asks him how his shoes wear out so quickly. Another day Maria scolds Johnny when she notices he cut the legs off a pair of pants and made them into shorts. In the laundry, she wonders whose sock has blood stains at the toes. And Johnny's appetite–well she cannot keep up with that.

"Mamma, you make the best spaghetti in the world" Johnny praises her.

• • • • • • • • • • • • •

Patriots' Day arrives at last. Mr. Cappadona has offered to give Johnny and a couple of other runners a ride to Hopkinton to the start of the Marathon. The drive seems to take forever. Johnny tries to calculate how many hours it will take him to run back, and that makes him rather nervous. But Kay has come along for the ride and puts a reassuring hand on his. When she says Good-bye, she hands him a small Italian flag and a pin so he can attach it to his shirt for luck. Johnny is now determined to make both her and Mr. Cappadona proud of him.

Johnny lines up at the start with about 100 other men. They shake hands and joke around a bit. The other runners seem like real decent guys. Some have run the Marathon before and offer advice. Others, like Johnny, are feeling somewhat overwhelmed at what looms ahead. He will just keep thinking of how much he likes running, and how Kay will be at the finish line handing out bowls of clam chowder to the runners. The starting gun sounds, and they are off. Through Hopkinton, Ashland, Framingham, Natick, Wellesley, Newton, Brookline and finally Boston.

That night at home, Johnny is walking like a stiff, old man. His body feels beat up, but his heart is soaring. He ran 26.2 miles in one day. Kay and Mr. Cappadona were proud of him. And he is in love.

The next day, Stefano opens the Sports section of the Boston Sunday Post. There is his own son Johnny in a photo! He is wearing an Italian flag pinned to his shirt, and running with some other men in the Boston Marathon!

"Johnny" he calls out, "I want to show you something." Fortunately, it is a day off from work, because Johnny isn't moving very quickly.

"Is there something you want to tell me about yesterday?" Stefano asks showing him the photo. "Actually, yes Papa. I met a wonderful girl named Kay Cappadona, and I want you and Mamma to meet her. I want to ask her to marry me."

• • • • • • • • • • • • • •

It's Patriots' Day 1996 and the temperature is in the 50s. Some would say perfect running weather. Johnny and Kay's daughter Sharon and her husband Don are on the starting line of the 100th running of the Boston Marathon–along with 38,000 other male and female runners, wheelchair contestants and walkers. They are feeling a little overwhelmed about what they are going to attempt. But they love running. They know Johnny and Kay will be in Framingham, with their children Eric and Marlena, to cheer them on. Sharon's brother John Jr. and wife Ginny will be in Newton with a cold drink for them. And cousin Emily will be at the finish line to drive them home. It's going to be a very special day, and a new family tradition.

White Mountains

by Marge Pellegrino

When a young family escapes their suburban apartment for a cabin by a lake,
they bring along more than just supplies.

We've never stayed in cabin #3 before. It's pretty much like #7, but I'm not planning on spending much time inside, so what the hell. The view of the lake is all right, but it's gonna be tough going to get down to the water before sunrise. There's this steep grade with rocks jutting out like shooters in a deserted game of giant's marbles. Green, gold, gray and bluish splotches of lichen splattered on them like somebody painted the sky just before sunset without a drop cloth.

Chucky's already down at the shore, one foot wet and muddy. He's teasing the ducks, throwing sticks and leaves into the water. My folks say he's a lot like I was at four. Loud and non-stop locomotion. A real boy.

We took this cabin because DeeDee can keep her eye on the jungle gym from the kitchen window.

"Chucky, lower your voice," she whispers with a force that makes her hiss, while he's trying to tell her to come check out some acorn caps he found around the other side of the cabin. Why bring a kid along if you can't let him get a little loud? Five minutes don't go by without her telling him to "get off that tree," "keep it down," "put those logs back where you found them." I can see her worrying about bugging the neighbors back home in the apartment, but I wish she'd give it a rest up here.

Stokesie and his brood just pulled into #4. He's driving the same beat-up Ford for the last 11 years. You'd think with his promotion to manager, he could afford more, or at least pretend to. DeeDee hates the way Stokesie and Carol live, but because he has it over me at the store, she's all sweetness and light to them to their faces.

With the bags and groceries stowed, I settle onto the wooden bench on the front porch. A coupla nail heads stick out from the boards on the railing.

I'll have to remember to bang them in later so nobody gets caught.

DeeDee is inside getting the wood ready for tonight.

"Chucky, stop hitting those weeds," she yells. How the hell can she see him from there?

Suddenly I can't wait to get out onto the lake. When she gets going like this, I know she's not mad at Chucky—she's mad at me, and I'll be damned if I can figure out why this time.

Well, maybe I can.

"Meet you at the dock," I yell to Stokesie.

In town everyone rakes their leaves into neat little piles, then stuffs them into plastic bags. On a Monday in the fall when the trees finally get good and naked, the sidewalk looks like it's wearing a string of black plastic pearls with all those bags lined up for pick-up. But here, the dry beige, red and orange leaves cover the top of my boots. Nobody'd think of raking 'em up. Mixed in with pine needles the leaves give a crunch that bites under the foot. I make enough noise so that I can't hear the rhythm of the boats slapping against the dock until I get right up to it.

I check the wooden marker attached to the boat key, Number 8, moored on the far side of the dock. The color of the dock and

A FEAST OF NARRATIVE

boathouse is past forgotten. The only readable line on the list of "do's and don'ts" is to put a life vest on kids under 9.

Chucky's gonna love it if DeeDee will let him come out in the boat with me alone this year.

"Drop that stick," DeeDee's voice echoes as I put the tackle box down and head to the boathouse for oars. The wood groans under my feet. Some of the straps of the beat-up life preservers hanging from the nails on the north wall are so frayed that it looks like they're growing white hair.

Did I mention that DeeDee's blond hair hangs down to the middle of her rear end? It pisses me off when she forks over $25 for some jerk to trim the dead ends every coupla months. She goes to Casas Adobes because somebody in-the-know told her it's the best place in town. I always offer to do it for free, but she never lets me. She says she needs the time for herself. Picked up that little gem at parenting class no doubt. At least she gets something out of those classes. Which, by the way, is time she has just for herself. I get the feeling she doesn't trust me with the scissors.

The last time we were up here at the lake she started in on how much she hated spending every fall fishing. At least we could try some place other than these drafty, dingy old log cabins over and over, she was saying. This cracks me up because before we got married, she loved sneaking out of town to come up here.

Well, anyway, they've finally all made it down here. She has one leg on the dock and one on the boat, suspended there just a split second, still running from the mouth. The line holding the boat steady slips through my fingers.

So she gets a little wet. Only Stokesie and Carol and the kids are around to see her looking like a drowned rat, so it shouldn't be such a big deal, but she's playing it like she's performing to a packed house. I'll guarantee she won't speak to me for quite some time.

But the look on her face, that surprise just before she hits the water, that will get me by.

Befana

by Annadora Perillo

*Prior to her impending wedding, a trick of fate finds Elena at a farmhouse
outside of Florence, where her experience with this charming place
and its proprietor will, perhaps, change her life forever.
As Elena sleeps, the old woman weaves magic into her dreams
like a lace-maker, and she awakens to a whole new world of possibility.*

There was an old woman tossed up in a basket
Seventeen times as high as the moon;
Where she was going I couldn't but ask it,
For in her hand she carried a broom.

Old woman, old woman, old woman, quoth I,
Where are you going to up so high?
To brush the cobwebs off the sky!
May I go with you? Aye, by-and-by.
— Mother Goose

The old broom whispers over stone swept smooth, secrets in
sunbaked tiles of terra-cotta; lifetimes of footsteps like rain on red-clay

rooftops, the pattern of drops falling *pianissimo*, quickens and mounts toward thunder, hushed now as when a baby sleeps. The house sighs, stirs with its breathing, resonant with laughter, first steps dampened, a moist spot. Children dart between raindrops; barefoot rhythms of childhood linger; elusive rhymes. A man's bootsteps tread (traces of soil, sun caked bits of earth, antediluvian dust, a wisp of field), and stop in a soft pool of sunlight where a woman sits plaiting her hair. He strokes her head; his fingers tangle in twists of flax. At the door latch he hesitates as she pins up the braid, and with a handful of straw from the sheaf beside her, takes up the golden rhythm of daylight, ties rush to broom.

The broom responds, sensing the familiar feel of the old fingers, distracted, fitting itself to the floor, its brush broken now and bent, slants to corners, carries her weightless. "*Switch, switch, switch,*" it whispers like a spell. A slip of down evades it, lifts in to the air, settles in the sunlight with a sprinkling of dust as they sweep out over the terrace of wide flat stones softened with moss and trailing vines tanged up lichen-stained walls of the cottage where she'll pitch the broom stick against a ledge.

In her eyes clouds tumble, wisps of white curl, sweep over the sky's grey-blue reflection. She pulls hairpins from her apron pocket, and holding them in her teeth, takes them quickly in turn to secure the thick coil of her hair.

"Something's coming," she says, distracted by a bird's distant pitch.

"Witch!" whispers the broom.

The old woman cackles, scattering seed for the birds. The stone crackles beneath the falling seed, the step and pecking of hens, tip of wings. The last handful spatters like rain.

Her heel sticks in a soft patch of moss; pebbles roll beneath the thin leather soles of her shoes and catch Elena breathless. Her bright blouse fills with wind, flutters papery and light, like a scarlet poppy in the distance, sprinkled among the high corn. Wispy spirals of her hair, loosely caught, pull free, as she sets a small leather suitcase down beside her, brushes away the strands of brilliant auburn that blow in her face, and takes out a sheet of paper that strains to fly as it unfolds in the wind.

She shields her eyes from the sunlight that dazzles, warms the top of her head. It catches the curve of a sickle as it slices the bright heat, rushes through golden shafts of wheat. On the narrow terrace between the lines of vine-supporting turkey-oaks and olive trees, slants on the bare skin, blond hair of the young reaper; his body arched with the rhythmic motion of the blades. Bound bundles of the severed stalks, in triple, lay evenly spaced on the fields, like pyramids tilting toward the sky.

She thinks over the sketchy map; her finger traces the broken-arrow-line to where it intersects, boldly written and highlighted in pink, the words "Shepherd's House." She breaths them softly into the wind as it brushes through the fields of tobacco, winter-wheat; beats against the wings of honey-bees, dizzily droning from the fruit trees and wildflowers, following the path of her finger to their wooden hives on the terrace above the house.

"*Pronto?* Alessandro? *Sono io*—It's me. *Si, sono qui. Appena arrivata*—I'm here. Just. *Si, bene, benissimo*—fine, fine. *Senta*, Alessandro...." She sighs in to the receiver, smiling at the old woman in way of explanation, edging herself out of the way, apologetic.

The old woman smiles, pleased with this pretty girl: words rushing from her lips, forced through straight white teeth, her whispered lines splintered. She nods her head and smiles with an aspect of infinite tolerance. "*Pazienza*," it seems to say. "*Pian piano*—go slow." As she moves through the cool dark kitchen, the air stirs, scented with herbs, tobacco leaves, and violet-honey. She lays transparent slivers of pink prosciutto across pink and peach slices of summer-melon; slits open fresh figs. A salami is produced from the broad beams of the pantry, a flour-dusted dome of bread is lifted and laid outside on the terrace table with white plates and a liter of wine. The clean white edges of the cloth fly in the windy sunlight.

"Listen, Alessandro," she says, lapsing in to the lisp, affected "h" of their native Florentine, straining to suppress her spirit, superlatives. "This place—it's perfect—I think, it's what I'd hoped," she says through his muffled asides, sounds of paper-sorting, restless arrangements. "The *Signora*—*molto gentile*—has been so nice. She says I can stay tonight, since something's happened to Lean—Lena, the real estate agent. She won't--can't be here until tomorrow."

"*Come no?*"

"Some sort of incident—with the car and the Via Aurelia—The *Signora* says—it's a miracle she's not killed."

"*Cazzo*," he says, swearing an oath against the infamous ancient rode in sympathy with a new *Fiat Pininfarina*.

What about the order for *I Tessuti?*"

"Hhha. I completely forgot."

"*Appunto*—That's the point."

"Tell Sara—she knows the fabric—she can take care of it until I get back."

"Okay," he says "*Va bene*," with a lingering on the long vowels which makes her cringe. "*Allora ciao*—Goodbye then, I'll see you tomorrow. *Ciao, Bella.*"

Skimming the last sweet froth of espresso, her demitasse spoon clinks against the sides of her cup. She sits back luxuriously, taking in the Tuscan Hills, the sunny terrace fragrant with wisteria and rose; their close warm breath, attentive: brazen-red geranium tip toward them from terracotta pots, lemon trees, and orange strain closer.

"*Embè*—"the old woman says, with a faint clink of finality as she sets her cup in its saucer and places them delicately onto the cloth. She gives Elena's head a pat, presses her to stay while she prepares for her nap: arranges the room, fresh sheets. She dusts a stray spec of straw, traces of wool from green-gold threads of her dress and vanishes into the view. Woven into the landscape's course chestnut and turkey-oak, terraced vineyards, twists of cypress, tobacco, and metallic shimmer of olive grove.

The hills gather and cascade before her like the mantle of an angel, textured like velvet brocade with warp or chain and wefts of silk. Brilliant green fabric, spun gold; lamè course grain fields, crème-colored and beige, sunflowers' fine yellow-gold, poppies' scarlet-silk, strands run in rivulets are quickly caught up, wound into distant tangles of rooftops, coppery villages scattered over the hills. Far off Florence's lofty towers, spires and palaces, cathedral, campanile, and cupola tightly gather through the silvery haze of olive groves and gleam in the midday sun like a dream, ancient gold clinging to Paradise.

Elena reaches up her arms, her fingers stretch skyward, nearly touching, her face tilts toward the sun, like a poppy pulls delicate and long in the wind, and yawns, sleepy with wine.

She falls asleep easily in the unfamiliar bed, her hand rested on its cool patina, her head on a pillow of white down, drifting in and out of dreams filtered like sunlight through the netting that falls from its height on the high posters. The sun streams in with the heat, through the slightly parted shutters of the balcony, slants through the slats onto the bare boards of the floor, onto edges of creamy cut-linen sheets, pools of white netting, white-washed walls. A slow breeze pulls on the filmy curtain, the fronds of Easter palm that fan out above the bed, rushing. Her eyes close before the pale blue light of cornflowers' still-shimmering and warm from the fields, a plain polished cross, a Madonna, reclining—mingling with her dreams.

She drifts to a place in the sand—somewhere she's never been. The Tuscan coastline, Maremma moorland: even grey-green sand, cypress, pine, and scrub-scented dunes. Corsican mountains distant ascent, abandoned hills inhabited by fox and wild boar, savage; startling, the Island of Elba rises abruptly from the sea.

Oars dip from a small *moscone* as it glides toward shore. A taught white sail strains at the horizon and darkens before the blazing backlight of the sun. Like the solitary figure of a man as he dives cleanly through the molten surface of the water, infused with the fiery light that melds and flows lava-like from the edge of the setting sun as it dips into the coal-blue sea-calm.

Emerging nearer the beach, his flanks surge through the surf of white foam, he tosses off the salty spray, the water slips and beads over his skin still streaked with oil, red-brown, sun-stained. The white edge of sea washes over his feet, breaks about his ankles as he shields his eyes from the glare of the sky and sand, searches for something on the beach, and catches as if on some treasure, a shiny thing like sea-glass, shimmering. The brilliance of a baby: bare-skinned, sun-browned, with hair the color of spun-gold, sunlight, rests his head on one hand, cherublike, his cheek pressed in the other, his bare bottom tilting toward the sun. His mother lies majestic beside him, Etruscan-style, her left arm bent beneath her, holds up her head with its heavy coil of hair. She barely moves, but to smooth her hand over the baby's skin, to brush away specs of sand, bits of beach as they stick in the creases and folds, light on her baby's flawless flesh, and expanse of her own. Only the almond-whites of her eyes alter as her gaze shifts from the sand, the baby's skin, seek and fix on the figure of the man walking toward them from the sea.

He lowers himself onto the sand, crouches down beside them. He takes a cluster of grapes from a straw hamper, eats one himself, and some he peels and offers in small pieces to the baby, and the woman's mouth opens in turn, her lips part to accept the fruit—hot, dark and sweet.

They pack their things, preparing to leave. He wraps his arms around her and leaning in slightly from behind, his arms twine around her torso, crisscross her breast. They stand together for a long time, very still, looking out over the water at the horizon.

With only the bright sheet left to fold, they each take an end, making a game as they lift it up over the baby, letting it drop to the top of his head, fly up again and fall. His arms reach, fingertips touch beneath the sheet as it fills with wind and lifts toward sunlight like a brightly colored sail. The ship pitches toward the open sea 'till the sailcloth flutters, slackened, and it drifts to where the waters of the Arno ebb and flow, wash up over her sides, lap against the city's walls.

The streets of Florence, deserted at midday (even the swarms of tourists take shelter from the sun, scattering in the humid heat to their hotels, finding sanctuary, if only fleetingly, potent, within palace walls and churches' cloistered secrets, mysterious, cool, candlelit *Madonnas*, locked gates), wakens with a clamor of shop gates and fresh scattered bursts of life.

An old vending woman motions to her, as she circles the Straw Market on her way home from work. "*Signorina*, your sheets—they're ready." Elena edges her way through the crowded market, over to the woman's stall, beneath the loggia of the *Mercato Nuovo*, where modern merchants trade in lace and straw. It exudes its past, she senses instinctively—the selling of silk, beating of gold: its essence of wools and dyestuffs, ancient colors, cloth called indigo, *verzin*, and cardamom, red sandal brought from exotic places; cities like Damascus. And the precious fabrics of the Florentine, so splendid they sparked a Renaissance; a triumph of velvet.

The old woman tucks away the lire notes Elena pays for the set of creamy white sheets with hand-crocheted edges, and settles back in the chair, working now, with a hypnotic, almost imperceptible urge, her fingers show signs of a lifetime cramped about crochet hook and thread. She finishes and sighs with the satisfaction of a spider having spun a perfect white web, cuts off the tailing strand with a pair of fine pointed scissors. "*Per la Sposa*—For the Bride," she says to Elena, handing her the handkerchief along with the package wrapped in thin silvery paper and tied with string. Elena slips a finger over the delicate lace edging, lost in the intricate patterns of the thread.

She stops at a *café*, orders an *Anisette*-laced espresso, and takes it standing up at the bar.

Images of the city pour over the screen, (at the theatre where she meets Alessandro, *A Room With a View* plays every day at five), washing over his skin and hair, his clean white shirt—but so startlingly clear in her dream and real. She leans her head on his shoulder, presses her warm cheek against his cool face. His eyes fixed on the film (within the frescoed and funerary walls of *Santa Croce*, Lucy, George and Mr. Emerson falter between tombs and ascensions).

She loses time (Lucy's tumbled onto a terrace of violets). Feeling suddenly vertiginous, a sinking in the pit of her stomach, she takes in breath, fights the sensation; sweat chills her palms and her forehead—throbs, blood turned to ice-water shoots though her veins, seems to emanate from the persistent waves of nausea, a cold painful surge and pulse in her hands and feet, each part of her left separate frozen. She sucks in; the air, pressing impossibly close, cuts off. Her head whirls and she's falling, startling awake, soaked with sweat.

She plugs up the basin in the small wall-hung sink in the bath and turns on the faucet. The pipes vibrate, threateningly, give a fantastic shudder, one powerful surge and the water drips into a shallow pool. She washes with a sponge and honey-scented soap, drying herself on the small, embroidered hand towel folded neatly over the side.

Pulling open the shuttered doors, she steps out onto the balcony, hovering below the first star's quiver, close, nearly touching. The soft breeze laps against her still damp skin, twilight quickens round her like a cloak of velvet *alucciolato* green-gold with loops of gold silk, like the sparkle of fireflies in a field.

A song lifts up from the terrace like the sound of wind rushing through wheat. Strands of guitar quiver beneath the raw insistent press of fingertips, tough of earth-stained brown hands, strumming. Sun-bleached strands of his hair fall before heavy half-closed lids, slightly parted lips whisper the words, raspy and sweet. Chords fall softly on the silence.

In the kitchen Elena's fingers trace over a *Pattarino* jug. "*Ho deciso*—I decided to take the house. I put a binder..." she says, cocking her head towards the open door: she can see the old woman, her back arched, head craned, her broomstick flailing in the direction of the rabbit hutches, roosting hens. Her son, hearing her fierce cry of "*Il Volpe!*" reach crescendo, leaves his song, and seeing his *falce*, a small sickle, leaning up against the low ledge of the garden wall, hurls it after the fleeting tail of the animal as it darts into the brush.

"What on earth?" Alessandro implodes.

"A fox —" Elena says, "Never mind," as the old woman comes toward the house sweeping a path in the moonlight; she reaches her broom up high to brush cobwebs from the roof beams, and enters the kitchen with a fresh sprinkling of dust.

Risk Taker

by Elizabeth Primamore

"Risk Taker" is a portrait of a man who escapes his
humdrum life as a teacher and a husband through a deck of cards.
But when a snowstorm holds him captive, he's forced to take
the kind of risk this small time gambler could never have imagined.

Chalks pulled the '72 Corolla into the faculty parking lot. Keys in his pocket, he hurried across the lot, waved to the patrol guard, walked up a few stairs, and went through the double brown doors of Harding in Kearny. He shook in his coat a little. The day was overcast and sleet was starting to fall–unseasonal weather for early November. It felt good to be inside.

Harding was a typical public elementary school: a large brick building with a flag out front, a portrait of George Washington in the foyer. Chalks walked along the main corridor past empty classrooms, headed to his office, which was locked. Not unusual but a pain all the same. Robbie the janitor came around the corner and let him in. Chalks liked Robbie, a young Polish immigrant who was always happy to do a little favor. Chalks made sure he gave as good as he got. During the day sometimes Robbie liked to sneak a beer. Chalks once saw him down a can of Budweiser in the Men's Room, but said nothing. Live and let live.

He glanced at the big wall clock. Six-thirty a.m. He had time to practice, something he couldn't do at home because his wife Giovanna hated the sound of playing cards being shuffled. The repetition got on her nerves; it calmed his.

Something in the air made him feel itchy. He rubbed the side of his nose with his index finger, his face scrunching up. When he opened his eyes, they were watery. He was uncomfortable enough to blow his nose and dot his eyes with the same hankie he used to clean the fog from the car windshield. That gave him relief. Shoving the hankie back into his pocket, again he looked at the clock. Ten minutes passed. He was losing time, but first things first.

He took out the Math tests he'd graded the day before and put them aside for later. Then he took out the deck of cards and closed the drawer. He slipped off the elastic band and began shuffling. Jory Blake, the new fifth grade teacher, stuck her head in and said, "Aces high?" She handed Chalks a mug of coffee.

He raised it in a salute. "Thanks."

When Jory started in September, he noticed her passing by the office. At first her presence startled him. Usually the other teachers got there minutes before eight o'clock when classes began, but Jory wanted to make a good first impression, arriving early and making a fresh pot of coffee in the teacher's lounge. Shortly after Jory's arrival, Chalks started looking forward to that cup of coffee.

"Going to Resorts?" Jory said.

"With this weather, I don't know."

"Suppose to clear up for Sunday."

Chalks said nothing. He just sipped at his coffee the way his father used to do. The cards itched his hand, wanting to be shuffled.

"Where did you go before Atlantic City?"

"Vegas. Mississippi."

"Why Mississippi?"

"They got boats there."

"Boats?"

"You know, gambling boats. On the river. Nice Blackjack tables, too."

"That your only game?"

Before he could answer, the sound of voices in the hallway broke into their conversation. Chalks thought it was probably Robbie or the cleaning girl, but he decided to play it safe and tucked away the deck of cards. Jory scooted off down the hall. Both good calls: the principal and his secretary said good morning as they passed by.

The cards would have to wait.

• • • • • • • • • • • • • •

Chalks handed back the Math tests just before the three o'clock bell. When the students had gathered their books and scuttled out the door, he peeked through the window blinds. Sleet was still falling and had crusted his car, wipers frozen on the windshield. He hoped he had an ice scraper in the trunk. The thermometer mounted on the outside wall was just above freezing. Was the sleet sticking? He looked at the black tar. A little. Start up the engine, let it run, and the ice'll melt. As always. He'd lived through so many New Jersey winters.

Something about his car didn't look right. When he was driving on Mill Street this morning, he'd felt a pull to the left. Now he was hoping it wasn't what he suspected. But it was. The front tire was flat. Luckily, this time the car was parked in the school lot and he wasn't driving on the Garden State Parkway to Atlantic City like last time. But he had no spare tire and the car would have to be towed.

Chalks went to the main office to call his wife.

• • • • • • • • • • • • • •

Mrs. Stafford, the school secretary, had red hair like Lucille Ball and thin lips painted pink and when she looked up from her typewriter, her small eyes peeped out of huge glasses.

"Sorry about your car, Mr. Parente. By the way, Sears is having a tire sale. My husband replaced the tires on our Impala and now it's running smoother than ever. Even in bad weather."

"How long has he owned it?" Chalks's hand was on the receiver.

"About five years, I think. But I'm not sure. You'd have to ask my husband. He'll be here in an hour. Can we give you a lift?"

"My wife'll come get me. We have to go to the gas station." Chalks didn't like favors. Favors meant you had to reciprocate.

"How is Mrs. Parente?"

"Fine. Fine."

"And Charlotte?"

"Getting bigger and bigger."

"Dial nine for an outside line," she said, and started tapping away again.

Chalks picked up the receiver. For a second, his own phone number slipped his mind. Then he dialed and waited for Giovanna to answer.

· · · · · · · · · · · · · ·

Giovanna was pleasant at first; she only asked him to wait until Charlotte finished her graham crackers and milk. But then she realized he wanted her to pick him up and follow the tow truck to the gas station and then drive him home because he was too cheap to invest in good tires. He couldn't argue with Giovanna because he knew he was wrong. He liked a bargain, so he bought tires from the junkyard.

As his wife went on and on about his bad habits, Chalks looked out the window. The sleet was turning to snow. Now his wife was sniffling. Soon she'd be crying. Then he thought he heard a gasp, but it was too late—he'd slammed the receiver down.

Mrs. Stafford had on her hat and coat and her pocketbook over her arm. She paused in the doorway as though she were thinking something over, then said: "Don't be too hard on Mrs. Parente. She's frightened for you."

Chalks watched her leave. He felt something he didn't want to feel–the uneasiness of a man who was either angry at life or afraid of it, but couldn't admit either one.

• • • • • • • • • • • • • •

The atmosphere in Harding Elementary had changed. No shouting in the hallway. No banging of locker doors. No bells ringing. Chalks walked through the lonely corridors. He was going to be stuck here longer than he expected. Giovanna would take her time.

He stepped out for a moment into the cold. In the parking lot, tire tracks from the Chevrolet were the only marks on the blanket of white. The Corolla looked like a lopsided igloo. Traffic was light. He hoped to see his wife's car, but there was no sign of the Cadillac. Usually it took twenty minutes from home to work.

He went back inside. He shoved his hands into his coat pockets then took them out. Then he put them back in again and paced. Then he stopped. He was tired. Not of pacing so much but of waiting. Though he actually didn't mind the wait because he knew he was calmer now than he would be at home.

The later it got, the colder it got. A chill ran through him. He went to the nearest classroom and dragged a heavy brown chair into the corridor and placed it near a radiator. When he sat down and touched the cast iron, it was cold. The heat had been turned off for the day. He wrapped his long, thick scarf around his neck and around his ears and under his nose. Then he did what he'd yearning to do all day. Out of his pocket came *Beat the Dealer: the Winning Strategy for Twenty-One*. But there wasn't enough light to read, and he didn't feel like getting up and turning on the lights.

Chalks leaned back and looked at the portrait of George Washington, the American flag, and down the long dark corridor of empty classroom. He closed his eyes to nap. But after a few tries, a few shifts in his seat, he found he couldn't do that, either. The book slipped off his lap and fell to the floor. He didn't bother picking it up.

The cold and the silence gave him something he only wanted at the Blackjack table: time to think. It made him feel uneasy again, uncertain. He pulled out his wallet and looked at the photograph of Charlotte he always carried with him. The impish smile and the dark eyes came from him, not Giovanna. The girl was only ten years old and doing the school work of a child five years older. That was him, too. He snapped the wallet shut and put it away.

"Call the missus?"

There was no mistaking that gruff voice. It was Robbie, standing there with a large ring of keys. "My pleasure to open the office door."

"I'll wait here," Chalks said. "My wife'll be here soon."

Robbie picked the book off the floor and handed it to Chalks. "When you will take this poor fella to this new A.C.? Teach 'im a trick or two?"

"No tricks to card counting, only hours of practice and study." He held the book out to Robbie. "Start by reading this."

Robbie said he would, but Chalks knew he wouldn't. The janitor shuffled away, book in hand.

The next time he appeared, Robbie was closing the top button of his coat. The cleaning girl was with him–Chalks had once caught them kissing in a broom closet. Robbie took the girl's hand and turned to Chalks. "When you leave, the door'll lock." The two stepped out into the falling snow.

Chalks watched Robbie and the girl fooling around in the storm. Tossing snowballs at each other. Laughing. Sliding down the cracked pavement. And as they turned the corner of Mill, they held hands.

Chalks leaned against the wall and folded his arms across his chest. The day was so long, so long and weary. That terrible feeling of unease returned, the feeling he dreaded most, that brewed inside him, to keep his hurt and frustration where they belonged, buried deep below the surface, out of sight, forbidden.

Outside the wind blew against the windows and doors.

It's only snow, he thought. *Only snow.*

What about the car?

He decided to step out and examine the Corolla. Hands jammed into his coat pockets, shoulders hunched, Chalks walked the storm toward his car. Snow was piled on the tops of street lamps and traffic lights. The Corolla was nothing but a big lump in a field of white. Tomorrow there would be talk, snowballs, and a whole lot of digging out. And a whole lot canceled. And happy kids. And if he had his way, he would be at Resorts International where none of this would matter, where not even a blizzard could beat the stacks of chips on the green felt tables.

But there was no dealer to face now. He thought of his wife and figured she wasn't coming for him. Giovanna wanted him to call a cab, but he couldn't see spending the money. Maybe she was right. But it was too late now.

And so, calling it a day, Chalks turned around to go back inside.

The door wouldn't budge. He pressed the handle again. Pushed harder. Nothing. In a sudden burst of energy, he hurled himself against the heavy wood, but only hurt his shoulder. Bent over, he took a few deep breaths, let his hand drop and came up. It was no use. Damn it. That's right. He forgot. The door would lock behind him.

· · · · · · · · · · · · · ·

There was nothing else to do but take a few deep breaths and push himself forward. For the first time in his life really push himself and, like a man resigned to his fate, step into the storm. In the arctic chill, one foot after another, on and on, he went. He made it across the parking lot to the curb and crossed over the main street. Would the gas station still be open? As he trudged along, chin on his chest, he came to a realization. He didn't care.

Trash cans, broken branches and debris blew down the snowy streets. A dog was howling. Face stinging, Chalks pulled his scarf over his mouth. Snow got into his shoes, freezing his toes, but he kept going. He passed the darkened luncheonette, the convenience store and, as he went by Sal the Barber, Chalks thought he heard something but ignored it. The sound got louder. Was it a police siren? As far as he could see, the roads were empty. He threw his head back to let the snow blow into his face. It was piercing but invigorating.

The falling of the snow was seductive, pressing, inviting him to wander in the white expanse of silence. He thought of his wife and child. They were a part of his life. They thought they owned him, that he was their possession. For a second that feeling of unease flared up, then thankfully disappeared. Chalks heard that sound again, the siren. No, not a siren—there was no surge and ebb. He tried to listen more closely but the snow and the wind dampened the sound. The sound, a kind of blare, happened again. It was a car horn honking. And a voice, a woman's voice, rose like a vague shout, lost in the vigor of the storm. His wife?

He turned the corner on Mill, too far away from the school to find out.

It seemed to Chalks, wrapped in the storm's swirl, for the first time in his life he was leaving his mother's home. Foremost and always. He was taking a risk. And whatever the consequences, he knew he'd come out a winner.

This is Sicily

by Tony Reitano

*American Joe Russo discovers he has inherited an apartment
in Sicily from a relative he never knew existed.
But after traveling to Siracusa to sell it, he quickly discovers that
"business as usual" means something quite different in Sicily.*

He changed their names and never told any of his kids?! *Pazzo*!!

Okay, to be fair, I hardly knew him; he died when I was six. I don't remember what he looked like at all. I just had heard he was a mean old man. Mostly from my mother, who said he hated her because my father was divorced and she was his second wife.

So, back to my Grandfather. He was a cranky old man who had a little jewelry shop on William Street in Newburgh, New York. Well, I'm not sure how much jewelry he actually sold. It was more of a watch and clock repair shop. I only have a few vague memories, and they're not exactly warm and fuzzy. My Aunt Carmelina would sometimes take me to his store when she took me shopping for him. It was really dark inside and I don't think I ever really wanted to go there. One time he was being mean to her and I remember screaming at him, "Don't you yell at my Aunt Lena!," who was his oldest daughter and my favorite Aunt. She was a saint, God rest her soul.

But the main thing that sticks out in my mind is I remember he always had a big pot of beans cooking on the stove in the back room. All the time. It was always there, bubbling on the stove. I honestly think he just kept adding beans to the pot. I swear there was probably one original bean still in there somewhere. Gives me the willies just to think about it.

Jure Sanguinis—By Right of Blood. That's the law in Italy. I am entitled to Italian citizenship because my Grandfather, an Italian citizen, did not become a U.S. citizen until *after* my father was born, which means that my father was technically an Italian citizen and therefore *I* am technically an Italian citizen. When I found that out I thought, "Wouldn't that be awesome if I was an Italian citizen? With an Italian passport?" All I had to do was prove the line of descent with birth certificates, death certificates, and a bunch of other certificates...but this name change thing really threw a monkey wrench into the works, after all the work I did, trying to get all the documents. My own records were easy to get. But my parents, that was a different story. I rummaged through my parents' papers but there were no birth records anywhere. I would have to order new certified copies from the State. Then, come to find out you can't get birth or death records in the State of New York unless your name is on them. So how in the world could my name be on my parents' birth certificates?? Tell it to the judge, as they say, which is exactly what I had to do. I had to hire a lawyer, which cost me thousands of dollars. I get Mom's birth certificate—that was all straight forward. But Dad's?

The name on it is *Antonio Vitale.* "This must be a mistake," I think. "This belongs to someone else. They had to have made a mistake. He spent his whole life as Anthony Russo. It's on his school records, his World War II Navy records, even his marriage certificate! This birth certificate from the State of New York, everything else is correct, including the date of birth, the address, the city, and even the hospital. So I write to New Jersey (they're not as strict) to get my grandfather's marriage certificate to double check, and there's his name. Not Joseph Russo. Not even close. *Santo Vitale.* WTF!

My friends tell me, "you should go ask a relative." Who would I ask? There's no one of that generation left. They're all dead now. I'm the only one left. Besides, by now I've moved to Chicago. Well, this is a big roadblock. This breaks the line of descent. The Consulate needs to clearly see the line of descent or they won't award citizenship. I thought New York was strict! They make New York look like Amsterdam. So now I needed to get documents amended, to show that the names were changed but I was still the grandson of my grandfather. Jure Sanguinis. By Right of Blood. More like a Gallon of Blood for what I went through.

So, again, back to my grandfather. I need his certified birth certificate from Sicily. I had to find someone fluent in Italian to help me write to my Grandfather's hometown in Sicily, which, thank God, was listed on the ship manifest of the boat he came over on. This was the only way to get his birth certificate, except they won't respond, no how, no way, to correspondence in English.

Everyone I ask recommends I go to see Cesare, but everyone calls him *Caesar.* He has a shoe repair shop in an old metal Quonset hut on West 13th Street in Little Italy. He's been there forever. He has almost no customers. I don't know how he stays in business. So I offer to pay him to translate my letter to Italian. He refuses to take any money. "Wonderful!" I think. But as the saying goes, there is no free lunch. Oh, no, there is a price to pay. Cesare loves to talk. And talk. And talk. He'll write a sentence for me, and then have a long conversation about it. Then write another sentence... well, you get the idea. Three and a half hours later I walk out of his shop with my one-page letter, go to the post office and mail it to Siracusa, Sicily.

And then I wait. And wait. And wait. After six months I come to realize the wheels of bureaucracy turn very slowly in Italy. I'm getting anxious because my appointment at the Consulate for my application for citizenship is coming up. Finally, I receive a reply, but it's all in Italian, so, you guessed it, I have to go to back to Cesare to listen to another dissertation.

"Hmmm. They send your Nonno's birth certificate. Here."

"Nonno? Oh, grandfather. Right. Excellent! This is the last document I need for my appointment next week. Thanks, Cesare."

I reach for the letter and he stops me.

"Wait. It says your Grandfather's brother died. They want to talk to you. It says here you need to contact them. Do you have uncles, aunts, brothers or sisters?"

"No, I'm the only one left."

"Congratulations. Your Great Uncle left you an inheritance."

"What?"

"And congratulations again." He showed me the letter, "You have to go to Sicily to claim it."

The letter included the name of an attorney, an 'avvocato' that I was supposed to contact. I was assured that he spoke English. I called him and he was kind enough to suggest, "There is no rush. You should wait two or three weeks before coming to Siracusa; the air fares will be cheaper." I agreed and made the arrangements.

• • • • • • • • • • • • •

"She is *sgangherata*," said Signor Bendinelli, standing on the cobblestone street, looking up at the façade. There was a terracotta tile roof, stucco exterior, and there were little balconies with wrought iron railings overlooking the street.

"*Sgangherata?*" I asked.

"Come si dice…dilapidated? Look for yourself."

"You see, there," he pointed as he spoke, "the stucco is coming loose. Those railings are rusted. The roof is old."

I nodded that I understood,

"And the foundation is not good," said the lawyer. He took the keys and opened the door and ushered me in. "Per favore."

As he led the way up the stairs, he said, "You didn't know Signor Vitale?"

I shook my head. "My Grandfather left no clue he even had a brother. My father never said anything when he was alive. I had no idea." I said, looking around. He stopped in front of a door at the top of the stairs and turned the key. As the door swung open, I stepped inside. It struck me that the apartment didn't look like that of an old, single man. There was evidence of some homey touches. "That's odd." I said. "It's pretty clean. How long has the apartment been closed up?"

He hesitated for a moment, like he was unsure of how to answer. "Yes, about that. When I knew you were coming, I took the liberty of bringing in someone in to clean it up."

"I see." I said.

"As you know, I was Signor Vitale's *avvocato*. I'm sorry, his lawyer. When he died, we failed to find his brother, your grandfather, because when your grandfather arrived in America he changed his name, as you know. By law we had to try to find his heirs. It just so happens that, fortunately, you contacted the commune just before the waiting period expired. I'm sorry they made you come all this way across the sea. I could have handled this for you from here. Now, just to be sure, there are no other living descendants, this is correct? No one who would have a claim on the inheritance?"

"No. There is just me."

"Then apartment is now yours to sell. Never fear, I will find you a buyer. You would be surprised," he chuckled, "that foreigners will buy these apartments no matter what the condition."

I had to think. Do I sell it? An apartment in Sicily! Siracusa, no less. I like to travel; I could have a place to come in the winter. I hate the winters in Chicago. Too cold for far too long. But how could I take care of it when I'm not here? I could rent it out, I suppose. Or hire an agent. Or just leave it. After all, I would own it. Put a little money into it and it would be nice.

"I have to think about it. How long do I have?

"You're not thinking of keeping it?" He seemed stunned that I would even consider it.

"I'm not sure. I'm planning on retiring soon, maybe…Why? Can't I keep it?"

"Well, yes, except..."

"Except..."

"You are American. You would have to have an Italian resident card to own property in Italy."

"That's not a problem. I was just approved for dual citizenship."

After a pause, "But there are tax implications. And you don't speak the language. It would be very difficult. I don't recommend it."

"I need a few days to think about it."

"Very well," he replied reluctantly. Then he checked his watch. "I have meeting with another client. We should go."

"Actually, I'd like to stay for a little while."

Signor Bendinelli looked concerned.

"That's not a problem, is it?" I asked.

He shook his head and handed me the keys. "Not at all. Come see me at my office Tuesday *dopo pranzo*—after lunch. We can discuss it then." As he turned to go, we were surprised by an old woman coming up the stairs. She gave Signor Bendinelli a cold look, then she went inside her apartment down the hall as he started down the stairs, mumbling to himself.

The apartment looked to be very spacious, around 1200 square feet, with lots of light, a narrow foyer, living room, dining room, a balcony overlooking the street, and kitchen with a shared terrace.

I made my way down a hallway and turned left into a master bedroom. The room, like the rest of the apartment, was flooded with light. That beautiful, warm Sicilian sunlight. I could hardly believe it, there was even a walk-in closet. The ceilings were high, good for the hot weather. Across the hall were two single bedrooms—one could certainly be made into an office, and the other for guests. There were two bathrooms. With access from the entrance of the house was a terrace overlooking the roofs of the adjacent buildings. Signor Bendinelli was right; I would have no trouble selling this. But now, after seeing it, did I really want to sell? True, I didn't really know what life would be like in Sicily, but I had a lot of vacation time built up at work, and I could stay for a while and see how I felt.

Since the apartment was filled with my Great Uncle's furniture, I moved out of the hotel and relocated. I enjoyed walking the narrow streets off the main boulevard, all the while admiring the sun, the cobblestone streets and the teeming life on the streets. I found myself looking up like a tourist to admire the architecture of even the simplest of buildings. I seemed to have so much more energy. Even if I got tired after walking for hours, I could just sit at a café in a little piazza, have a coffee or an aperitif, and be refreshed to continue on.

My first morning there, on my way back from a walk, I passed that same elderly woman while climbing the stairs. She was leaving the apartment opposite mine, locking her door. She was what you would imagine as your stereotypical Sicilian widow, short, hair in a bun, dressed all in black, clutching a rosary in her hand. I offered a "Good morning" to her. She looked me up and down, and gave a short, brief nod and smile with a, "*Buongiorno*," and was off down the stairs and, I assumed, on her way to church. This became a ritual of sorts. The exchange of "*Buongiorno*" in the morning and then each going our separate ways.

Attorney Bendinelli had a small office, two rooms really, and an assistant who spoke no English. Every so often the assistant would come in and have a short conversation, then give him some papers to sign, and then whisk them away back to his own desk in the front room.

"Why did no one tell me my Great Uncle was dead all this time?"

"We couldn't find you. Understand, we were looking for the descendants of Santo Vitale. That Vitale line in America ended suddenly in 1924, because your grandfather changed his name. It was not uncommon for immigrants to America to change their names. This is why your name is not Vitale. Although it seems an odd choice for a change of name."

"I'll say."

"In any case, I was retained by the commune to try to find any living heir. I searched for records but, it wasn't until you applied for citizenship that the Commune connected your Grandfather with his brother.

"So, you never found me?"

"My dear sir, I have other clients, those who pay me. You were, how would you say…a hobby? I worked on it when I had time."

He lifted a sheet of paper from a file folder and handed it across the cluttered desk.

As I took it, he said, "I don't expect you to pay this all at once."

I took a look at the bill. I didn't speak or read Italian, but the numbers were evident in any language. I almost swallowed my tongue.

"Unfortunately, I spent two years and many hours. And much correspondence."

This was a lot of money. I had to ask, "Did Signor Vitale have any other assets? Maybe a bank account, or…"

"Signor Vitale was quite old. He had a small pension, but that ended when he died. What little he had saved up paid for the burial."

"I see."

"It would be helpful if you could make a payment?"

"All right. Well, right now I only have dollars. I'll need to change them to euros and then…"

"You have dollars?" he interrupted.

"Yes."

"Cash?"

"Yes."

"Dollars would be fine."

"Really?"

"Signor Russo," he said quietly with a shrug and a wave of his hand, "this is Sicily."

I heard from Avvocato Bendinelli often after that first week. He would come to the apartment, and offer to take me to lunch, and ultimately peppering me with advice on how I would be better off selling the apartment.

"Life in Italy is not as it appears. To live here as a foreigner is difficult."

"I've moved to new places before."

"Yes, but this is different. Sicily is a different country. A different culture. The people here are closed to outsiders."

"They seem very friendly to me."

"Oh, on the surface, yes. But, to be honest, you will never be accepted as one of us."

Just then, my elderly neighbor returned up the stairs. As she passed, she gave Signor Bendinelli the same icy stare. She stopped at her door, gave me a scrutinizing look, and then entered her apartment. He gestured in her direction, looked me in the eye, and said, "You see, Signor Russo?" Then with his trademark shrug, "This is Sicily."

I spent the next couple days thinking about what Sr. Bendinelli said. Was I making a mistake? Was I just seeing what I wanted to see? Then on Friday evening at around seven o'clock, there was a knock at my door. I was sure it was Bendinelli with more unwanted advice. Instead, I opened the door to find my neighbor, holding a steaming plate of linguini with clams. She nodded, pushed the plate in my hands, and said, "Buon appetito", then turned and went back to her apartment. I stood, stunned, holding the plate, unsure of what just happened. I was sure of one thing, though, the pasta smelled delicious! I poured myself a glass of wine, sat down and tasted probably the best meal of my trip.

The next day, I knocked on her door, wanting to return the plate and thank her. I waited a few moments. I figured she was old, she didn't move too quickly when I saw her in the mornings. The door opened, she looked at the plate, then looked up at me.

"*Grazie,*" I said.

"*Parla italiano?*" she asked, expectantly.

"Oh, no. Sorry. I don't speak Italian."

"*Ah. Triste.*" She said as she took the plate and closed the door.

Another plate of linguini arrived the next Friday. The longer I stayed, the longer I wanted to stay. I tried to explain to Sig. Bendinelli that this was paradise to me. The weather was hot; I hated the cold. The sun shone brightly all day long; I hated the dark. The food was fresh, delicious, and the streets were filled with life.

I awoke that next Friday morning planning my day around the highly anticipated *Linguini con Vongole.* (Linguini with clams. I looked it up.) However, this Friday evening was different. There came a knock, but when I opened the door, it wasn't my neighbor.

"Buongiorno. Signor Vitale?" said a woman with a heavy Italian accent. She looked so Sicilian. Olive skin, well dressed, but she was not wealthy. Her hair was dark and wavy. But her eyes...they were a brilliant green, piercing, yet open and friendly.

"No," I responded. "Joe Russo. Signor Vitale was my Great Uncle."

"I thought your name was Vitale. What is a Great Uncle? I'm sorry, forgive my English."

"No, your English is very good. Much better than my Italian. Signor Vitale was my grandfather's brother. Can I help you?"

"My name is Saverina. I am sorry to bother you."

"Not at all. Please, won't you come in?" I said, embarrassed at my lapse of manners.

She checked the hall behind her, then came into the apartment.

"You were expecting linguini con vongole, I imagine."

"Yes, how did you know?

"My Mother," she gestured to the hallway, "she makes it for you, no?"

"Oh. Yes!"

"On Friday evenings."

I smiled. "Yes. It is delicious."

"It is something she did for Signor Vitale. They were friends. She wanted me to apologize for her. She is, how you say, under the weather. There will be no linguini this evening."

"Oh, I'm sorry. Is she...?"

Saverina waved her hand, "No, not serious. I have come from Palermo to help. I've made her some soup. She's resting quietly. Sometimes I think she gets sick on purpose, because she's lonely and she knows I will come visit her for a week."

"Sometimes so do I. Get lonely—not sick."

She got the joke and laughed. Her smile was dazzling. "Since there is no linguini," I asked, "would you care to have dinner with me?"

She considered for a moment, then said, "All right. I know a good restaurant. It's a bit of a walk but the weather is nice and the food is good. I'll let my mother know I'm going out and be back in thirty minutes?"

"That would be fine."

It was a beautiful evening, indeed. We arrived at a small, family run restaurant. We walked down a few steps, and Saverina waited for me to arrange a table. The owner said a few sentences in Italian and I had no idea what he was saying. Saverina leapt in and had a quick conversation with the owner, and were shown to a table near the front window. We picked up our menus and I must have looked lost.

"You really need to learn some Italian if you are going to spend any time here," she laughed.

"I know some. I did grow up in an Italian family."

"Yes, in America. You know how to say, what, *buongiorno, arrivederci*, and *lasagne?*

She saw right through me.

"Are you planning on staying?" she asked.

"I'm not sure. I'm thinking about it. I was unhappy at home. Divorced, no children, and sick and tired of my life there."

"Did you expect to work here? It would be difficult."

"I have dual citizenship."

"Well, then you really *do* need to learn some Italian if you plan to work here," she laughed. "And there are the taxes."

"Yes, I've heard."

"Where are you from?" she asked.

"I was born in New York, but now I live in Chicago."

"What is your occupation?"

"I'm an architect. And you?"

"I am in finance."

Just then the waiter arrived with a bottle of wine. He poured, then I ordered, with Saverina's help. I offered a toast with my glass.

"Did you know Signor Vitale? What was he like?"

"I met him a few times. You should ask my mother. She knows everything that goes on in that building."

We had a lovely dinner. Saverina was so Italian. She had an elegant, intriguing air about her.

"It must have been hard for your mother after Signor Vitale died, having that apartment empty for those years. I suppose I should consider myself lucky that Signor Bendinelli took care of it and paid the bills all that time."

Saverina looked at me without saying anything. But she didn't have to. There was a look in her eyes. A hesitation.

"What?"

"You don't know."

"Know what?"

"That apartment was not empty. There was a family living there."

"There was a family...?"

"I'm sorry. I don't think I should have said anything."

"The apartment wasn't empty? But the lawyer said..."

"Signor Bendinelli will say whatever is in Signor Bendinelli's interest."

"Someone was living in the apartment? For how long?"

"According to my mother, from right after Sr. Vitale passed away. Why don't you come up for coffee after dinner? I think you should talk to my mother."

I nodded. "And I can return her plate from last week."

"Oh, and another thing you need to learn. When someone gives you a gift of food, you don't return an empty dish"

I winced at my faux pas.

"Maybe we should stop on the way for some cannoli."

She shook her head in amusement. "So American. Maybe some sfogliatelle." She laughed.

We sat in Signora Parisi's apartment. She seemed very pleased that her plate was returned full of sfogliatelle. She rattled on in Italian as her daughter translated. I heard all about the family who had moved into the apartment shortly after my Great Uncle had died. How it was the handyman that would do repairs for him. How she didn't like them very much, and how she didn't like Sig. Bendinelli, who would come by and knock on the door. One day she was leaving her apartment to go to morning mass, and she saw the father counting out cash to Sig. Bendinelli.

"Mamma says that he definitely didn't like that she saw the transaction. After that, she would see Bendinelli hiding across the street, waiting for her to leave before going into the building. Then suddenly one day Bendinelli was moving the family out, with a big argument. There was a lot of yelling and cursing at him. Turns out the family was Bendinelli's sister, his brother-in-law and their children. Bendinelli told them that they had to leave because Signor Vitale's nephew was coming. Then, a few weeks later, when she overheard Bendinelli talking to you in the hallway, she knew something was not right about it all."

Well, I would like to say that this was a shock, but all that business with Bendinelli, the efforts to get me to sell the apartment, to pay an outrageous bill, Signora Parisi's icy stare at Bendinelli; it suddenly all made sense.

"I know it seems wrong," said Saverina, "but it's to be expected, this kind of thing." She shrugged. "This is Sicily."

When Signora Parisi had finished her story, she told me all about my Great Uncle. She was a delightful lady, and so was Saverina.

Then Signora Parisi put down her cup and said to me, "Sei sposato?"

Saverina looked frustrated. "Mamma!"

"What did she say?" I asked.

Saverina sighed. "She was being rude. She wanted to know if you were married."

I grinned. "No" I said to Signora Parisi.

She smiled. "Mia figlia non è sposata."

"Mamma!!"

"I think I know what that meant." I smiled.

There was an awkward pause. Saverina stood from the sofa. "It's getting late."

I took the hint. Saverina walked me to the door. She asked for my phone, then put in her number. "In case I can help in any way," she said, smiling and not looking up.

Back in my apartment, I looked at legal bill I was given, then pulled out my laptop.

The next morning, I called Saverina, and asked her to have coffee with me. I asked after her mother, and then got sidetracked in talking about her life.

"I never asked. Where do you live?

"I have an office in Palermo. But I've been thinking of moving here to Siracusa to be nearer to mamma. She needs looking after."

"Won't that disrupt your business?"

"Signor Russo..."

"Joe. Please call me Joe," I interrupted.

"Mmmm, I will call you Giuseppe. I'm sorry, you asked me something."

"Won't the move disrupt your business?"

"Definitely, but I can move to another office here or start my own business. Mamma is more important."

I nodded. We spoke for a while, getting to know one another. I liked her a lot. She was beautiful, funny, and wise. And it appeared she liked me as well. We were there for over two hours when suddenly I realized the time.

"We should go. Your mother is going to wonder if some crazy American kidnapped you!"

"No, she's napping. Besides, she wanted me to come. She was nagging me to get out of the apartment. To tell you the truth, I think she likes you."

"Well, I like her too."

"Then you'd better start learning Italian, so you can talk with her. She won't learn English, that is for certain."

"Let's walk."

We got up, I paid the bill, and we strolled leisurely back home. Home. Yes, it was starting to feel that way.

"I think you wanted to ask me something."

"I did?"

"Yes, when you called, you said you had something you wanted to ask me."

"Oh, right. I was wondering if you could help me. Make a few calls for me."

A week later, I heard from Bendinelli. He asked if I would be able to pay the balance of his bill. I said I'd be happy to stop by his office in the morning.

Once there, and the pleasantries were out of the way, he asked, "Well, Signor Russo, have you decided about selling the apartment?"

"Actually, I'll address that after we address a few questions I have on this bill. I see there are administrative costs over two years…"

"Yes, there were many legal filings with the court, and with the clerks. That takes much time and documents."

"Filing fees."

"Which I paid on your behalf."

"And there were taxes paid."

"Yes, I also paid those on your behalf."

"I see. And then there are repairs and updates made on the apartment."

"Things need to be maintained, and repaired, et cetera."

"Et cetera."

"It was vacant for a long time. Things go wrong. And there were improvements, all which will demand a higher price for the apartment. To your benefit."

"I see." I was silent for a long time.

Bendinelli seemed a bit nervous all of a sudden. "I can handle a sale for you at a discounted rate, since you are already a client."

I nodded. "But, there is something missing."

"Well, if there is, we can just forget about it. I will accept the amount on the bill."

"No, I think it should be on there. I don't see the rents."

"Scusi?"

"The rents. The rents that you got for renting the apartment. For two years. It wasn't empty. I had the utility use checked, there was full use of the apartment. And there are witnesses that can attest to the fact that there was a family living there. The postman verified that there was a family named Amaro living there for two years, and their mail is now being forwarded to another address. *Il Consiglio Nazionale Forense*, yes I know who they are, would not look very approvingly at an attorney renting a deceased man's apartment, and taking the money for himself instead of holding it in trust for the rightful heir."

Bendinelli was starting to sweat.

"And I don't believe you ever tried to find me. I think you discovered that my grandfather changed his name and you took advantage of the fact that no one would ever find me. You just didn't count on my application for dual citizenship. So, I will politely decline your offer of a generous discount for acting as an agent for the sale of the apartment as I have decided to keep it. AND, I will be happy to accept your kind offer, which I expect you will agree to, to write off this entire bill, AND to complete the legal work of transferring the apartment to me, at no cost, in return for the rents you have received illicitly, AND my generous agreement to allow you to keep your license to practice law by keeping my mouth shut and NOT reporting you to the authorities."

Bendinelli's jaw had dropped so low he would have made a great flycatcher.

"It has been a pleasure doing business with you. I will be spending a lot of time here in Siracusa and I'm sure our paths will cross from time to time."

I got up and stopped at the door. "Don't look so surprised, Sr. Bendinelli. After all," I shrugged, "this is Sicily."

Italian Gala

by Michael Riccards

*This story is a fictional account of the author's grandfather
meeting with actress, Sophia Loren, and their discussion
of the education of Italian American youth.*

Retirement revolves around boredom and television, and television at least induces sleep since most of it is so mediocre. Early one night, Grandpa was watching channel 9, the movie channel, which was featuring again *It Happened One Night,* with Clark Gable and Claudette Colbert. He had seen it so often he knew most of the dialogue, but suddenly the phone in the kitchen alcove rang loudly, and he got up to answer it. People rarely called him anymore, even solicitors and politicians running for office. He answered, and on the other end was a familiar voice, "Hello, this is Jim Stafford the Third, do you remember me?"

"Of course, you were kind enough to get me the consultant job at Princeton University. A great place, and I enjoyed it immensely."

"Well, people still talk about you and Dr. Einstein. You apparently were the only person who could relate to him on a human level!

In any case, I am calling you to ask another favor. I am a major donor to a variety of causes: the United Jewish Appeal, Boy Scouts, Catholic Charities, Sons of Hibernia, and the Italian American Educational Foundation. The last group is having its gigantic fundraiser at the Waldorf Astoria Hotel in New York City, and I will be out of town making money in Germany so I can continue to be a philanthropist. In any case, I have given the Foundation a major gift for college scholarships which Lehman Company matched, and the hosts want me to be on the dais with the honorary guest this year. I would have sat right near her, but I cannot go. You really are the only Italian I know who doesn't want anything from me, or is trying to get me to invest in their harebrain scheme. Will you go?"

Grandpa was startled; he surely had no scheduling conflict with his boring retirement. But he could not take the place of a millionaire, whom he had barely met over the years. Nevertheless, it was for a good cause, scholarships for Italian American kids to go to college, an experience he never had. So, on a lark, he answered, "I would be honored to go in your place, but I cannot sit on the dais with the guests and the major donors. That would not be honest."

"No, no, you will be representing me, and it is my contribution that got me that close to the main honoree. By the way, the honoree that night will be Sophia Loren, do you know her name?"

"What? Of course, we all know her name. I rarely go to the movies, but even I have seen her in some of her great films. Sitting next to Sophia Loren, that is really a remarkable turn of events."

"The only thing is that this gala is very formal, and you must go in a full tuxedo."

"Yes, yes, of course."

"Good, I know it is quite a trip to New York City and the Waldorf. I will send my chauffer to pick you up and wait to return you home. He will be at 81 Main Street, at 5:30 pm, next Tuesday; is that ok?"

"Perfect. Thank you."

"No, no, thank you; have a good time. Say hello to Sophia from me!"

Grandpa looked at the telephone, which he gently held onto, *What was happening in his life? He was a retired old man, a working man, now he was eating with the rich in the most extravagant city in the world, more than Rome, more than Naples. It was New York City, the city of the very wealthy and the very poor, and I am going to the Waldorf Astoria for dinner.* The only person he ever heard of at that great hotel was the famed general, Douglas MacArthur, who lived there for the rest of his post-war life. *And his dinner companion, Sophia Loren, this must be some Italian joke, something Punchinello would dream up. But Mr. Stafford was not a man of practical jokes.*

Then he began to worry—he had no tuxedo. Even for his children's weddings, he had worn his one good suit, but not a tuxedo. How would he get one in a week? Then he remembered, of course, Angelo Albino's son owned the Rose City Formal Shop, and people rented tuxedos all the time. Angelo had come over on the boat with his father, who had actually worked for Grandpa in the early days. But he was by trade a tailor, not a gardener, and so he opened up a small shop right by the old YMCA. Business was good, and he gave it to his son, who was proud of the tradition.

So, Grandpa went the very next morning up the hill to the Rose City Formal Shop, and was greeted with genuine affection by the son. Grandpa told him the incredible story, and the young tailor believed it without hesitation. He pulled out his best tuxedos and took one in to fit the old man perfectly, and then gave him a bowler hat to top it off. Grandpa looked at himself, *"I look like a Milanese banker."* And indeed he did. The tailor was patient and caring with his stitches, making sure that they were invisible but strongly woven.

He stepped back and proudly proclaimed, "Ah, papà would be proud of my work. Go and meet Sophia with confidence, my friend. Our family goes with you."

Grandpa took out his wallet to pay, but the tailor insisted, "It is a present from the family that you have done so much for over the years. I do not charge old friends. Just make sure you bring it back the next day."

And on Tuesday, a fully dressed Grandpa with his bowler hat stood in front of 81 Main Street waiting for his limo. It was only five o'clock, but he did not want to be late. People looked at him from across the road as they entered and exited the chicken market. Was this some advertising for a new store, or what? Right on time, the limo came, the chauffer ran out and opened the door, and welcomed Grandpa in. They moved through the ugly industrial areas of Northern New Jersey, though the tunnel, and then past the stately Rockefeller Center and onto Park Avenue, which was beautiful decorated this time of year. There in front was the Waldorf Astoria in gold trim. Grandpa got out, and the driver said he would wait until the whole gala was done.

Somewhat reserved, Grandpa walked in and was immediately greeted by a host wearing an Italian American Foundation button. He looked like one of those ambitious lawyers trying to make it on Wall Street. "Hello, how are you? Good to see you again, please go over to the left banquet hall."

Obediently, Grandpa went left and entered the lavish banquet hall with the gigantic logo of the Foundation behind the dais. As he walked in, they asked him the name he was sitting under, and he said "Stafford."

"Oh, Mr. Stafford, how good to finally meet you. You know you are sitting on the dais, on the left side of the guest of honor tonight. Lucky you!"

A hostess led Grandpa to the dais, and there were the usual wealthy Italian American types with fancy suits cut to make them look thinner and who lived in the world on a shoeshine and a smile. He was quiet and deferential, but they took that as the standards by which the very rich carried themselves. Thus this humble man fit in to the world of the falsely humble. They brought him the very best cocktail, which he only sipped, and a full plate of hor d'oeuvres, meant just for him. His seat was heavily padded while the audience had regular seats in tightly packed tables. There was more silver on the table than in the US Mint, and it would take a college course to figure out which fork to use when. They insisted on talking to Grandpa about the future of the wheat markets in Australia, and the oil deposits of Saudi Arabia. He listened intently, as if he knew what they were asking about, and then they assumed that he had some secrets that they should know if only he would trust them with them.

The chairman of the Foundation was Marco Galena, who greeted Grandpa with a big hug, and told him how excited he was at this year's turnout. They were honoring Sophia Loren, of course, and also the Yankee shortstop Phil Rizzuto, and Joseph Albanese, an old associate of the legendary mayor, Fiorella La Guardia.

"It will be a royal night," he pledged.

Then it happened, from the side door in walked Sophia Loren in a sparkling black dress, with her head erect, on high heels that made her look even taller than her 5'9". She had a long stately nose, rich red lips, and her black dress was cut seductively low so her ample bosom peaked out on top. She was more beautiful in person than in the movies.

She slowly made her way to the dais, and signed autographs and had her picture taken with every man who could make it to the reception line. When she reached her seat, only Grandpa had the good manners to hold her chair for her, Old World manners that she recognized and appreciated immediately.

She gave him a fixating smile, and wondered, *My God, how much money did he give for this honor? He looks like a Milanese banker.* She never cared for those types of people and let her husband, Carlo Ponti, deal with them. But when she started talking with him, she heard the familiar sounds of a Neapolitan dialect. And she lapsed into Italian and began a conversation with him, ignoring most of the fawning men running up to her and taking pictures.

"I think from your accent, you must be from Naples. Did you know that during that awful war I and my family lived in Pozzuoli, near Naples, and once the Allies bombed the munitions plant there, and I was struck by shrapnel and wounded in the chin." She then turned her beautiful face toward Grandpa and showed him her tiny scar. Grandpa was totally fixated by her beauty and tried not to look below her neck. "Are you from Naples, or an outlying province?"

"I am from Avellino."

She sipped a glass of red wine and quietly pronounced, "This wine is terrible."

"Yes," said Grandpa, "it is from the bottom of the barrel."

Then she responded, "'You know you have a very fine white wine from Avellino, Villa Raiano Wines?"

Grandpa told her he knew the wine. In fact as a boy, he had worked in the vineyards there and helped in the pressing of the grapes.

She smiled at him with her wide lips, and then went on "We moved to Naples, but after the war our family returned to Pozzuoli and opened up a pub in our living room, selling homemade cherry liquor. I waited on tables and washed dishes, and the pub was popular with American GIs. Then when I was 14, I entered Miss Italia 1950 beauty pageant, and was not selected.

"Good God, if she was not selected, what was the winner like!, the old man wondered to himself.

"I still love Rome more. Did you see me in *Yesterday, Today, and Tomorrow* with Marcello Mastroianni?"

Grandpa lied and nodded yes.

"Up in the Piazza Navona on the left as you walk in is a second story apartment, and there I played Mara. I came to love the Piazza and almost wanted to buy that apartment."

"I saw the Piazza when I was young," he interrupted. "It is where Julius Caesar was murdered, not the Forum."

"Yes, yes, you are right. It was like Lincoln, Caesar was leaving the theatre when they killed him. 'Et tu Brute.' I always wanted to play Calpurnia in Shakespeare's play."

On and on they continued, and then the chairman abruptly called order, and began to give out the awards to the bright Italian American students chosen last year. As they were introduced, they stood up, and Grandpa could not help but notice that more than half of them were girls. It was then that he felt somewhat ashamed, for he had always forbidden his own daughters to go to college. Women should get married young. He was a man of his times in so many ways. But this was a different world in front of him... and beside him.

The chairman then introduced the guest of honor, and Sophia Loren rose up and in the lights the sequins on her black dress glowed as she tilted her head and began, "I want to thank the Foundation for this great honor, for I was a child of the terrible war and never had a chance to have much learning. Now these boys and girls are going to college, thanks to the generosity of people like my good friend Raffaele, sitting next to me."

The old man almost crawled under the table.

She praised the leadership of the Foundation, and their support for the productions of her husband, Carlo Ponti. She talked about how she interrupted her career to raise her sons Carlo and Edoardo, and then came back into the movie business. Then she stopped and remarked, "Then in the middle of my career, when I left to raise my sons, Carlo and Edoardo, my critics said I was just another 'Italian mamma" and would never come back to the film industry. I guess they were wrong. Whatever you see here is due to spaghetti."

The audience hooted and cheered and rose almost as one in a standing ovation. She was an accomplished actress, and knew when it was time to exit. She then sat down. It was a very short speech, like the Gettysburg Address. But the guests came that night not to hear her remarks, but to say they had seen her, and there she stood luminous in the shaky, bright lights.

The chairman continued on with other awards and recognitions. But who really cared? Sophia turned to Grandpa and said, "Here is my address and phone number in Rome, Villa Ponti, when you come to do business there, call me and Carlo, and we will take you to the Piazza Navona. Right there at the entrance is the best gelato store in the city. He just loves good gelato. She wrote on the program the information, and gave it to him with a smile. Then she was overwhelmed with fans and sycophants. Grandpa left as a group of sponsors were coming up to ask him to fund the next Christopher Columbus Day parade in October. He caught his limo, and they retraced the way back to Jersey.

The next day he brought the tuxedo back, for the romance was over. He simply left it with an assistant and walked home. As he was getting very old, he knew he could never take a long trip back to Rome. And surprisingly he told no one of his experience, for who would believe it, even in his own family? One night, he decided to try the new ice cream store near his apartment house, Luchene, which was patterned on the Café Greco near the Spanish steps, where the great poet Goethe used to eat. It had beautiful mahogany molding and endless mirrors. Grandpa liked the mirrors, for he would look in one and then that reflection of his looking would appear in another mirror which in turn was captured in another mirror, and which became a tiny reflection of the mirrors and of him alone. He once thought crazily that this is what God must be like.

One afternoon, he went in and ordered gelato, limone of course, and sat down to eat it. He began to doze off somewhat, and then he saw eating with him Sophia and her husband who also ordered limone. Behind them, he could vividly see the "Fontana dei Quattro Fiumi," Bernini's fountain of the waters of the four rivers, with children playing and splashing and lovers holding hands.

"

The Devil's Pit

by Aniello (Neil) Russo

*Teenage cousins Franco and Sylvana bravely assist their
somewhat eccentric Uncle Marcello carry out a plan to secretly help
a Jewish couple escape to Switzerland, away from German occupiers.
And the bottomless Devil's Pit plays an important role.*

The sun was just coming up in the small town of Benvuto in the
region of Lombardia. Franco Vertobi and his cousin Sylvana Serafini
were herding the four sheep that belonged to Franco's uncle Giovanni. Franco's Uncle Gio was inclined to drink a bit too much wine, and
needed the extra sleep. Franco was an early riser and he usually brought
the sheep to the foothill of Mount Tatro, a relatively small mountain
that stands before Mount Versi, a great mountain with snowcaps. The
springtime grass was a wonderful treat for the sheep who had become
somewhat tired of hay.

Both Franco and Sylvana were quite uneasy fearing that they
might bump into the patrol of SS soldiers and their police dog. They
knew the Germans would be cranky because of the early hour. They
were relieved to see the patrol group was at the far end of town. Franco

was worried that the soldiers would make any excuse to frighten them, and Sylvana was especially concerned because she was an American who had to remain there when the Germans occupied Versi. She had been visiting with her father, who had to leave abruptly because of a business emergency. Sylvana feared that the Germans would imprison her or kill her. Franco also knew if Silvana was discovered to be an American, his fourteen years of life would be over.

The Devil's Pit was to the left of the path, and they stopped to each toss and stone into the pit—hoping to hear them hit bottom. They heard nothing.

Mount Tatro was of unusual geological construction in that it had many openings and shafts. The Devil's Pit was the deepest, and it had a passageway leading to Mount Versi, causing run-off from that mountain to flow into the pit and follow a seam to Porto Getano that led into Lake Lugano.

The townspeople of Benvuto had constructed a strong, high wall before the pit to prevent any flooding to come down on the town. Over the years, there had been two Grandi Inondazioni—a tremendous fountain of water shot skyward, and caused tremendous damage to Benvuto and Porto Getano. The flood would run down the hill to Porto Getano.

Sylvana did have one advantage since she was blond and had a light complexion. One of the Germans even gave her candy and said that she reminded him of his little daughter Erika. Sylvana always made an effort to smile and offer many thanks. The most difficult problem was striving to control her rapid heartbeat, and not show fear.

After about an hour, Uncle Gio arrived, and Franco suggested that they should walk up the mountain path that led to Uncle Marcello's cabin. He had built it himself, especially high on the mountain because he didn't want neighbors; he wanted solitude. On occasion he would go down to the town to buy some wine and groceries. He usually was not communicative. Some of the townspeople thought he was a bit muddled because he wore a buckskin jacket and a hat made out of wolf hair. Uncle Marcello greatly admired Errol Flynn, and the movie Robin Hood.

He taught himself to use a bow and arrow, and hunted rabbits, squirrels, deer, and the occasional wolf. He especially loved to engage the wolf because he considered it a mighty challenge. The Germans allowed him to keep his bow and arrows. They felt he was harmless...and Colonel Mueller greatly enjoyed the venison and rabbit meat Marcello gave him. What the Colonel didn't realize was that some of the "venison" was wolf meat. He also didn't know that Marcello had Angela and Vittorio Langano hidden in a cave on the other side of the mountain, a cave hidden by a wild bush and only known to Marcello. The Langanos were Jewish and he got them out of town the day before the Germans arrived and it was his intention to get them to safety in nearby Switzerland. The town north of Benvuto is Porto Getano on Lake Lugano, and Porto Getano bordered Switzerland. What the Germans and townspeople didn't also know was that there exists a passageway on the wall of the Devil's Pit, a passageway hidden by heavy, spiked vine. Marcello's father had told him about the hidden passageway which came out in a rocky area in Switzerland that was hidden in a gulley.

"Sylvana, once I have contacted your father, I will make arrangements to get you to Switzerland, but for now, I need your help. You and Franco must create a diversion so that I can get the Langanos into the Devil's Pit, and the passageway."

"So, Mayor Puzzoni, this is the Devil's Pit. You say that it is bottomless. I can understand the need for the fencing, but I am somewhat confused about the tall wall in front of the pit."

"The wall, Colonel, is to prevent a flood in the town. You see... when we have heavy rains, the water pours down the mountain and the wall forces the water into the pit. It is especially needed when the snowcap on Mount Versi melts; the melt finds its way through Mount Tatro and rushes down to the town. Of course, that only has happened two times. The townspeople are always fearful that the Grande Inondazione could happen again. Old Tomaso, ninety-eight-years-old, experienced the last one in 1928, and he has said that it occurred when the weather was unseasonably warm and the snowcap began to melt, followed by heavy rains."

The melt works its way into the porous rock of Mount Ta-tro, rushes into the Devil's Pit, and shoots up into the air like a giant fountain.

Is there anyone around who can support this Tomaso's story? I think not. Well, the wall must come down. It presents a possible protection for enemies of the Reich!"

"But, Colonel Mueller, excuse me... but the possible Inondazione!"

"I'm not interested in old wives' tales—the wall comes down!"

"As you wish, Colonel. I'll have some of the men to tear it down and put up more fencing – if that is agreeable. Fine. It will be done tomorrow. I hope the Colonel is satisfied with my small hotel for a headquarters. If I can be of any further service, I shall do my best to serve you. I do worry though, as the weather has been unseasonably warm."

"I must admit that it is refreshing to have someone who wishes to serve the Reich. Puzzioni, let us take stock of the amount of wine that is available in town. Making excellent wine is one of the best things Italians do—and I appreciate good wine!"

"And you shall have it, my dear Colonel! And your use of my hotel as your headquarters is an honor."

Mayor Puzzioni was the richest man in town. Not only did he own the hotel, but he also owned the bank. His greatest love in life was money. Collaboration with the Germans would be no problem for Puzzioni. He also owned several acres of land next to the hotel on which he grew hay.

In fact, Uncle Gio helped Zano Ameche with the harvesting of the hay. Puzzioni gave him some bales for pay, and Uncle Gio bought enough more hay to carry the sheep through the winter. He had been a cheesemaker in his youth, and delighted in making cheese from the sheep milk. The sale of cheese and lambs—he borrowed Zano's ram to impregnate the ewes for a bundle of cheese—allowed Uncle Gio to live rather comfortably.

Shortly after Colonel Mueller had returned to the hotel, Pietro Galenti, alias Stogie Pete, arrived in his truck with supplies he had bought in Switzerland, food stuffs for the Germans. He parked his truck in front of the hotel and lighted up a stogie. As a matter of fact, he just about always had a stogie in his mouth, and was prominent for always smelling of tobacco. He knew it upset the German and delighted in the fact that they couldn't be happier than to see him leave. Some of the clerical staff made any excuse to avoid him whenever he arrived.

Major Hiller had the cook and his staff unload the truck and then went over the paperwork with Stogie Pete. Pete loved it when the major winced each time, he had to pay Stogie, and Stogie knew that once he left, the major always rushed to open his window...seeking fresh air!

Stogie and Marcello were good friends, and he often climbed the trail to Marcello's house and brought a bottle of wine and some provolone cheese with a large round loaf of wonderful bread, bread that the southern Italians loved. Stogie was originally from Naples, and only landed in Lombardia because he fell in love with Vera when she visited friends in Naples. She insisted that they had to live in Lombardia near her parents, and he would have gone to the moon for her.

Pete—he didn't smoke at that time; Vera didn't like it. He didn't want to leave his beloved Naples, but he didn't want to lose Vera. He solved the problem by spending a month each year in Naples. Of course, that was before the German occupation. He and Marcello always had a great time during the weekly visit. The wine went down smoothly, like melting snow, the bread and provolone did their job of keeping the palettes dry, and Marcello always roasted some deer meat. Both considered the visit a gift from heaven. Stogie always slept over, not wishing to drive at night.

Before he left the following morning, Marcello told him to be ready. If the plan worked, the Longanos would be waiting next to the abandoned farmhouse. Stogie was to drive them to Angela's brother's house. He had contacted him earlier. Stogie always went to Switzerland on Thursday to pick up the supplies for the Germans and the grocery shop run by Vera's brother. Marcello planned to move on a Wednesday night, but it had to be an overcast night, a night when the moon would be in retreat, a black night. He anxiously listened each day for the weather report. Several times it looked promising, but then the weather cleared and the moon appeared to be smiling constantly, confident that it was being appreciated by mankind.

Two weeks later, the weather seemed promising. Monday and Tuesday had been overcast and the weather report expected clearing on Friday. It was time!

Franco and Sylvana followed their same routine that Wednesday morning. They brought the sheep to the mountain pasture, visited Uncle Marcello, went to Aunt Ida's for school instruction—schools were closed after the Germans killed two instructors who made protests—and took their nap during Mezzogiorno. The remainder of the afternoon was spent reading. After the evening meal, they relaxed and quietly went over the instructions that Uncle Marcello gave them.

"I've got the German cigarette package here and the German matches. I picked them up in front of the hotel. We have to wait until about eight o'clock—that's when the motorcycle currier usually arrives. We'll wait behind the bushes across the street. We have to allow about 10 minutes to pass, and then make certain there is no one around. I hope Old Fabrizio doesn't show up taking his nightly walk. You light the grass next to the Colonel's staff car, I'll light the far side, and drop the empty cigarette package and book of matches on the sidewalk—far enough away so that they don't get burned, and then we'll keep low and head back home. You're not nervous, are you? Okay, I know you can handle it."

Franco and Sylvana made their way stealthily toward the hotel. They were relieved to see the two soldiers and police dog at the top of the hill that led to Porto Getano by the light from Nicodemo's restaurant.

About fifteen minutes later, they heard the distinctive sound of the currier's motorcycle. They were both nervous, but determined to succeed.

"Okay, it's time. We're in luck—there is no sign of Fabrizio or anyone. Keep low. Let's go," whispered Franco.

Once in position, Franco waved his arm—the signal to set the field on fire. The grass was just beginning to turn brown and made fine kindling. In fact, the blaze arose so quickly that Franco and Sylvana had to run away with great speed. They headed back to the bushes and hid, no time to get back home.

It was actually Old Fabrizio who sounded the alarm. He just was closing his front door when he saw the flames. He ran down the street, tapping his cane, quite rapidly for an elderly gentleman with a severe case of arthritis. The patrol was also running toward the fire with the police dog barking loudly.

Colonel Mueller rushed out half-dressed as the lady of the evening quickly dressed and left. The ten soldiers and currier ran out and waited for orders. Mueller yelled that he wanted them to move his command car. It was a classic Mercedes that General Rommel had once used. Corporal Heinz was the only one to remain somewhat composed and called the fire station at Porto Getano. The call was unnecessary because the firemen at Porto Getano had already seen the flames and moved quickly. They soon had the fire extinguished, and left after speaking with Colonel Mueller.

Mayor Puzzioni and the rest of the townspeople all seemed to be there. Puzzioni kept yelling, even after the fire was out. "Save my hotel, save my hotel!" Colonel Mueller was livid. His face was as red as the fire at its height. The command car was history!

"Major Hiller! Do you have any information about who started the fire?'

"Nothing conclusive, but Corporal Hein has found a book of matches and an empty cigarette package. Private Scneider said he was looking out the window just before the fire and thought he saw the currier smoking. Scneider actually owed Currier Pranz some money from card games and saw his chance to eliminate the debt.

"Arrest him, Hiller! Arrest him! I want him in my office in five minutes!"

"What do you have to say, Pranz? Speak up!"

"Colonel, I did not light the fire! I don't understand the accusation. Who would accuse me?"

"Lock him up! Tomorrow he goes to headquarters in Milan! Get him out of my sight!"

Pranz looked to Sergeant Nitz for some solace as the sergeant locked the door to the jail cell that had been constructed in the hotel basement. "Sergeant Nitz, I don't even smoke. I don't understand..."

"Look - the best advice I can give you is to keep quiet. Do you want to face a firing squad? If you keep quiet, they'll probably send you to Montecassino—a large battle is going on there. I'll tell you one good thing: the food is terrific down there! And one more thing—duck! You know how to duck?

"Duck? What do you mean?"

"Those Americans are throwing a lot of lead at our boys! If you want to enjoy some of that unbelievable food—duck! Of course, you'll probably be locked up for a while. And forget about the no smoking—nobody will believe you. Remember—duck!"

Marcello got the Langanos to Switzerland through the passageway. Stogie Pete brought them to the brother, and was invited to supper. They all enjoyed a great meal with enough garlic included that Stogie's fragrance was undetectable.

Colonel Mueller packed his bags for his new assignment in Russia, and left town just before the Inondazione. So much water shot out of the Devil's Pit that Mayor Puzzioni's hotel was swept away with him as a passenger.

Marcello basted the roast venison and Stogie and the two young "commandoes" sat at the table awaiting a meal only Uncle Marcello could put together, with sweets to follow. But first they had to make a toast—the youngsters had a small bit of water added to their wine—to a job well done.

The townspeople and people of Porto Getano were not happy about the flooding, but the Germans had pulled out—never to return.

Nonna's House

by Paul Salsini

A Cleveland family discovers that
timing is everything when they decide to move to Italy.

IF DANNY HADN'T noticed the large white envelope stuck in the pile of junk catalogs and pleas from charities, his mother wouldn't have opened it and their lives wouldn't have been changed forever.

"Mom! Is this for me?"

"I don't think so. Let me look." Elizabeth Donato cracked another egg in the bowl and wiped her hands on her apron.

"It's for me, right?"

"No, afraid not. Odd, though. It's from Italy. Look at the great stamps, Danny. Maybe your father can help you start a stamp collection."

"Really?"

"Who could be writing from Italy? 'Simonetta e Bandettini. *Avvocati di diritto*. Lucca.' A law firm in Lucca?"

It took ten minutes to find the letter opener that someone had artfully concealed in the drawer with plain envelopes and stamps. She slit the envelope open.

"What? What? Oh my God! No!?"

"Mom, what is it? Mom, what happened? Why are your hands shaking?"

Four of the six pages fell to the floor but Elizabeth continued reading from those in her trembling hands.

"Why are you crying, Mom? Did somebody die?"

"This can't be true."

"Who died, Mom? Who died?"

"Danny, where are your father and your sister?"

"They're raking leaves in back. Why are you crying? Mom, please!"

"Go get them, Danny."

Elizabeth sank into a kitchen chair, almost knocking over the bowl on the table. Sniffling, Danny ran out the back door, returning in a minute with his father and Sarah.

"What's up, hon?" Robert said. "Why is Danny crying? He said somebody died. Who died?"

Sarah started crying, too. "Who died, Mom? What's going on?"

Elizabeth handed the pages to her husband.

"Really? Oh my God!"

• • • • • • • • • • • • • •

Elizabeth and Robert had gone to Italy for the first time on their honeymoon, landing in Rome, then driving north to Florence, Venice, Milan, and then down to northern Tuscany. Robert wanted to discover the village of San Martino where his father was born and to meet his grandmother.

The visit went beyond their wildest expectations. Ever since her son and his wife were killed in an automobile accident in America, Nonna had never thought she would see her only grandchild.

Roberto! Roberto! Santa Maria! Vieri qui! Dammi un bacio! Dammi un abbraccio!

Having taken an Italian course at a Cleveland technical college before the trip, Robert knew that he should give her a kiss and a hug, which he did, except that it went on and on, and then the whole thing was repeated with Elizabeth.

"Elizabetta! Elizabetta!"

Nonna practically pushed them into chairs at the table and proceeded to bring out plates and bowls and platters. Ravioli, chicken in a red sauce, an omelet, a vegetable torte, fresh lettuce, tomatoes, celery, crusty bread, cheeses.

"Mangiate! Mangiate!"

Throughout the meal Nonna told stories about how she was born in this very house and that during the war she ran food and supplies to members of the Resistance who were fighting in the hills. One time, she said, she was almost taken prisoner by the Nazis when she caught her scarf on a tree.

"Bastardi!" she exclaimed.

But Nonna could barely get through the story about her husband being killed by the Nazis in an ambush just before the armistice.

"Bastardi!" she exclaimed even louder.

She told stories about Robert's father, how she had to raise him alone and how he was a *mascalzone*—a rascal—and was always getting in trouble with the teachers. She was so upset when he decided to go with some friends to America. Only nineteen years old—*un giovane!* And how he worked in a factory in Cleveland and married a girl whose family had left the San Martino area before him. Nonna never saw him again.

In faltering Italian, Robert told her about the accident that killed his parents when he was twenty-three years old and about to get married. Elizabetta saved his life, he said.

When they said their *"Arrivederci!"* three hours later, after visiting his grandfather's grave in the church cemetery, after going through photo albums and scrapbooks, and after eating too many cookies, there was an abundance of kisses and hugs and promises to return.

"Presto!"

The second visit was six years ago, shortly after Sarah was born.

"Che bel bambino! Bel bambino!" Nonna cried. She gave the baby a porcelain doll that she had been saving for the daughter she never had.

Sarah was two and Danny was just born when they visited four years ago. They stayed two weeks this time because Robert wanted to do some repairs to his grandmother's house. Tiles were cracked on the roof, the electricity was haphazard and the outside balcony needed bolstering.

The visits became annual. They would stay for two weeks, Robert would repair things, Elizabeth would take cooking lessons from Nonna, and the family found good friends in the neighbors next door, the Lucchesis, Nico and Francesca and their children, Marco and Livia. The couple taught the Americans how to play *scopa* and *briscola* and what to buy at the little *mercato* in the center of the village.

Nonna clearly wasn't feeling well on their visit last year. Instead of the extravagant meals she had always prepared, she offered a frozen pizza.

"Sono malata," she said.

Robert didn't want to talk about it, but Nonna said she knew she wouldn't have long to live and didn't know what would happen to her house.

"Someone would surely buy it now that it was in better shape," Robert said.

Nonna said she didn't want strangers living in her house. And that ended the conversation. When they left, Robert and Elizabeth knew they would never see Nonna again.

Last August, Francesca Lucchesi called in tears to say that Nonna's body was found on her kitchen floor. She'd had a heart attack trying to bake bread. The family couldn't attend the funeral, but went to Mass the next day at their local church. Elizabeth made Nonna's ravioli and they shed many tears.

"Well," Robert had said, "maybe we'll go back to Italy someday, but there's not much reason now, is there?"

• • • • • • • • • • • • • •

WITH THE KIDS shooed out to the backyard to play with Rosie, their new kitten, Robert and Elizabeth sat at the kitchen table, the pages of the letter spread before them.

"I can't believe she did this," he said.

"She said she didn't want strangers living in her house, but I never thought…"

"You'd think she would have asked us."

"You know Nonna. She wasn't the kind to ask. She just did it."

Robert put down his coffee cup and stretched.

"Poor old lady. I can just imagine her worrying and worrying about what would happen to the place. And then she died like that. Well, I'll write to the lawyers tomorrow to see if they can find a real estate agent for us. I don't think it will be too hard to sell."

Robert was exhausted from the leaf-raking and he and Elizabeth went to bed early. Within minutes, both were fast asleep.

It could have been the shaft of moonlight that struck the bed after clouds had parted. It could have been a bare tree branch switching against the window. Whatever it was, Robert suddenly woke and stared at the dark ceiling.

He turned over. And again. And stared at the ceiling again. Then he poked his wife.

"Hon?"

"I'm awake. Couldn't sleep."

"You're not thinking what I'm thinking."

"Um. Maybe."

"We can't, right?"

"No, we can't."

"Dumb idea."

"Really dumb."

"Go back to sleep."

"Night."

At 2 a.m., they were both lying on their backs, staring at the ceiling.

"The kids would have to make new friends."

"Danny might like it but Sarah would scream bloody murder if she had to leave her friends here."

"You'd miss your students, too," Robert said.

"Yes."

"Of course, I can do my online stuff anywhere."

They were silent for another fifteen minutes.

"We've always loved San Martino," Robert said.

"The people are so friendly."

"Not much to do, though."

Another long silence.

"I love the new kitchen cupboards," Elizabeth said. "And the second bathroom was really needed."

"Nice big windows."

"The stove is old."

"It can be replaced," Robert said.

They thought some more.

"There's been so many murders in Cleveland lately."

"Hardly any over there. We'd all be much safer."

"Let's sleep on it," Elizabeth said. "We can think clearer in the morning, OK?"

"OK."

Since neither had slept much, both came into the kitchen rather bleary-eyed.

"Mom," Danny said as soon as he saw his mother. "What did that letter say? Who died?"

Elizabeth and Robert exchanged glances and sat down.

"Now," Robert said, "you know how you loved to go to see Nonna in Italy?"

"Yes."

"Well, as you know, she died about eight months ago..."

"And we couldn't go to the funeral because Mom was teaching and Dad had a deadline," Sarah said.

"Right," Elizabeth said. "Well, Nonna's only relative is your father."

"Because," Danny said, "Daddy's parents were killed in that car accident before we were even born."

"So," Robert said, "she didn't have anyone to leave the house to, so, guess what? She left it to us!"

"Really?" Sarah said.

"Wow!" Danny said.

"So," Elizabeth said, "at first we just thought we'd sell it. But we've been thinking all night and we think, maybe, just maybe, we could move there! What do you think?"

"To San Martino?" Sarah asked

"Yes."

"And leave here?" Danny said.

"Yes."

There was a long silence as the children stared at the table, at each other, and at their parents.

"When?" Danny asked.

"Well," Robert said, "we'd have to wait until after the semester, so it would be over the Christmas break."

"Can we take Rosie?" Sarah asked.

"Of course!"

In the next week, Elizabeth gave notice at her school and Robert told his clients that he would complete their projects but would wait until late January to take on others.

He called the law firm in Lucca and Signor Simonetta told him that since Nonna had left a formal will *(Testamento)*, the house could be turned over to the Donato family immediately.

Their house needed work before it could be sold—plastering, painting, wall papering, electrical stuff—but it was a seller's market in Cleveland and they received three offers. It wasn't hard to pick one.

Their friends were truly sad to see them leave. Although Robert was doing well as a graphics designer and Elizabeth taught in elementary school, they were better known for their performances on the cello (Robert) and violin (Elizabeth). The "Donato Duo" often gave free performances in schools and coffee houses and had even been featured in a story in the Cleveland Plain Dealer.

They wondered about taking the instruments, but Robert said, "What the hell, we'll regret it if we didn't take them."

"What the hell," Elizabeth added.

At a farewell party in the church hall just before Christmas, they gave their last concert, consisting entirely of Christmas carols and ending with "Ave Maria." Everyone came up afterward for hugs and kisses, and Johnny Greco, Robert's best friend, raised a glass of beer.

"To our dear friends, the Donatos. We're sorry to see you go. We're gonna miss your concerts, but mostly we'll miss you. Robert, Elizabeth, Sarah, Danny, you are Family Numero Uno! But, hey, what could be better than going to Italy in 2020?"

• • • • • • • • • • • • • • • •

THE FLIGHT seemed to last forever, but eventually the plane landed in Pisa and they managed to cram two kids, a cat, five suitcases, a cello and a violin into the rental car.

"Look at those trees," Elizabeth said as they approached San Martino and saw the ancient cypresses standing like tall guardians over the road.

"They never change," Robert said. "Just like everything else here."

"Except," his wife said, "now they're going to have a new young American family as permanent residents."

"They're so lucky."

Unlike the picturesque hilltop villages seen on countless calendars and in movies, the nondescript San Martino mainly consisted of houses built after the village was bombed by the Nazis during World II. There were a few, like Nonna's, that had somehow survived for a couple of centuries.

A massive church, much too large for the village, stood in the middle alongside a creek that was mostly a trickle. The business "district" consisted of the *mercato* and a *bar* for coffee and sweets. A canning plant at the edge of town provided some employment.

"I love this place," Robert said.

"You know," Elizabeth said, "it feels like home already. It's so quiet, so safe."

They felt even more at home when they pulled up to what would always be called "Nonna's House" and saw the big sign on the lawn: *"Benvenuti Americani!"*

"Oh, wow," Robert and Elizabeth said together.

They had barely opened the car doors when they were engulfed by the hugs and kisses of their new neighbors, the Lucchesi.

"We've been watching from the window all morning," Francesca said.

With their neighbors' help, Robert and Elizabeth unpacked a few things and then enjoyed the bottle of Rosso di Montalcino that Nico had brought.

"Welcome to Italy," Nico said. "May you always find love, happiness and good health here."

Francesca gave Robert a sealed envelope: *Cari Roberto ed Elizabetta.*

"Nonna gave me this to give to you after your last visit," she said.

"Look," Robert told Elizabeth, "she says, *"Dio vi benedica nella vostra nuova casa."* God bless us in our new home. She knew then she was going to give it to us."

"God bless her," Elizabeth said.

Unpacking took much of four days, with some things lost forever and only minor damage to the cello and violin. Robert thought he could restring and tighten.

Robert set up an office in an alcove on the second floor and Elizabeth enrolled Sarah in the bright new school in the neighboring village of San Matteo. Rosie found a nesting place on a window sill where she could observe the variety of birds in the back yard.

The children spent much of their time with Marco and Livia and a bunch of other kids at a well-equipped playground that had swings, slides, trapezes and even a playhouse.

Tears were shed whenever they found something of Nonna's—a piece of jewelry, her hand-written recipes on index cards, photos of her and her young husband.

One afternoon they visited her grave. Amabilia Bianchi, 1934-2019. Her marble tomb was next to her husband's, Roberto Donato, 1922-1943.

"Look, Dad," Danny said, "you were named after your grandfather."

"I know. My parents thought he was a hero, killed by the Nazis like that. And notice that your grandparents had different last names. That's a custom in Italy, the wife keeping her maiden name."

"I'm going to keep my name when I get married," Sarah said.

Friday night was reserved for playing *scopa* with their neighbors and they alternated houses. Toward the end of the evening in the middle of February, Francesca wondered if the newcomers had been watching the news.

"Afraid not," Elizabeth said. "We've got so many projects going."

"Well, there's something strange going on. They're talking about a new disease that's baffling doctors. It was found in a man in Codogno."

"That's in the province of Lodi, which is in Lombardy," Nico said.

"This man," Francesca said, "was 38 years old and he was having respiratory problems. The doctor said he just had the flu and prescribed some medicine. But the man got worse, and he went to the hospital in Codogno."

Nico continued the story. "The doctors found it interesting that that the guy recently met an Italian friend who had been in China. Now, this disease was first reported in China, so the doctors tested the man and his wife and they tested positive for it."

"What's scary," Francesca said, "is that this man had a lot of friends and may well have infected others. He's now in a clinic in Pavia."

That's about 35 kilometers south of Milan," said Nico, who was obsessed with maps.

"Anyway," Francesca said, "They think the disease has been spreading in other areas."

"It has a very odd name," Nico said. "When I first heard it, I thought it was a name for a new planet. It's called Covid-19. But we don't have to worry. We're nowhere near Codogno."

• • • • • • • • • • • • • •

A FEW DAYS LATER, Robert suggested watching the news to see if there was anything new about the disease.

"We should get used to finding out what's happening in Italy," he said. "Probably nothing as exciting as an Indians game."

All four lined up on the couch.

"There are now," the announcer was saying, "79 confirmed cases of the coronavirus. Of the new ones, 54 were found in Lombardy, 17 in Veneto, eight in Pavia, two in Emilia-Romagna, two in Lazio and one in Piedmont."

"Oh my," Elizabeth said.

"It's spreading all over," Robert said.

While Sarah clutched Rosie, Danny grabbed his mother's hand.

"What's happening, Mama? What's going on?"

"It's OK, Danny. There's a bad sickness going around up north, but it's far from here. We'll be fine."

The next night the announcer reported that there were 984 confirmed cases and that two government officials in Emilia-Romagna had tested positive.

"Even government officials," Robert said.

The news was even grimmer the following night.

"We can now report," the announcer was saying, "that the first deaths have occurred because of Covid-19."

"Deaths?" Elizabeth whispered. "There have been deaths?"

"The first was a 77-year-old woman from Casalpusterlengo, who visited the same emergency room as that 38-year-old man from Codogno that we've mentioned. She died in Lombardy. There was also a 78-year-old man who died in Veneto, so we see the coronavirus in both the northwest and northeast parts of Italy."

"Oh, my God," Elizabeth said.

"But people are dying?" Danny said.

"It's fine, Danny, it's fine."

"You think so?" He climbed on his mother's lap.

"Yes, Danny, it's fine. Let's listen to the man on the TV."

The man on the TV was continuing.

"There have been many cases reported in other countries, and now in the United States."

Robert pulled out his phone.

"I'm going to text Johnny."

His thumbs seemed numb so it took a couple of tries.

"Hey! Bad virus around here. There?"

"Hey! No prbls here. Pres says under control. Only 15 ppl with it. Only one sick, others fine."

"Really?"

"Yeah. Pres said going to be miracle. Going to disappear."

"U believe in miracles?"

"Why not?"

Robert had long ago learned not to talk to Johnny about the president of the United States.

"Take care, Bud."

When Robert put the phone away he noticed that Sarah was staring straight ahead, not even looking at the TV.

"You OK, honey?"

When she didn't respond, Robert put his arm around her.

"Don't worry, hon. It's not something near us. Hey, how's Rosie doing? I think she's grown, don't you? Hon? Don't you? Such a good kitty."

He patted the cat. Danny, meanwhile, snuggled closer to his mother. Elizabeth stroked his back.

"Well," Robert announced, "it sounds bad, but I'm sure it's not going to spread very far. Not here, anyway."

· · · · · · · · · · · · · ·

BY MARCH 1, the death toll in Italy had climbed to 40 and with Danny tight against Elizabeth and Sarah staring straight ahead, the Donato family sat transfixed in front of the television as the announcer listed the victims.

A 68-year-old woman in Crema. An 84-year-old man in Bergamo. An 88-year-old man in Codogno. An 80-year-old man in Milan. A

62-year-old man in Como. An 84-year-old man in Nembro. A 91-year old man in San Fiorano. An 83-year-old woman from Codogno.

"You see," Robert said, "these are all old people. And they're all far away. No need to worry."

The announcer continued. "Also, a 26-year-old Norwegian man who has been living in Florence has tested positive."

"OK," Elizabeth said as she adjusted Danny, "this guy is 26, younger than we are, and he's in Florence, which isn't far away."

"We've also," the announcer said, "had reports of young people who have tested positive, A 4-year-old girl from Castiglione d'Adda, a 15-year-old in Bergamo, two 10-year-olds from Cremona and Lodi, a 17-year-old from Valtellina who attended a school in Codogno, and a school friend from Sondrio.

"Mama," Danny whimpered, "we're all gonna die!" Tears ran down his pink cheeks.

Elizabeth grabbed the remote and turned the TV off.

"Time for bed, kids."

Sarah and Danny were at her heels as she ran up the stairs.

When she had put the kids to bed and returned to the living room she saw that Robert had turned the TV back on. She turned it off again.

"OK," he said. "why is Danny obsessed with death?"

"He's always been that way. Remember when we found out about your grandmother's death? He came into our bedroom every night with his teddy bear wanting to sleep with us. And when we got the letter about the house the first thing he said was 'who died.'"

"Well, you were crying. But what's up with Sarah? I don't think she's said three words in the last week."

"She retreating. She does that. This is a bad time, Robert, and it's going to get worse."

Elizabeth told Robert that she didn't want to watch the news anymore, but Robert said they had to be aware of what was going on.

The news was always bad.

"This is like watching a horror movie," Elizabeth said.

"Except that we don't know how it's going to end."

"Badly, I'm afraid."

Since it couldn't control the virus, Italy began to take steps to protect its citizens. A lockdown at the end of February covered ten municipalities in the province of Lodi and one in the province of Padua. About 50,000 people were affected, including 16,000 in the most affected town of Codogno.

On March 4, the government closed all schools in the country. Elizabeth had mixed feelings about that. Sarah was having trouble adjusting to the school in San Matteo, and now she'd be taking classes online. That would be difficult.

On March 8 Prime Minister Giuseppe Conte announced the expansion of the quarantine zone to cover much of northern Italy, affecting over sixteen million people. The last two days of the Venice Carnival were called off, major league soccer matches were canceled, and the famous La Scala theater in Milan was closed.

At the time of the decree, over 5,800 cases of coronavirus had been confirmed in Italy, with 233 dead.

Listening to all this, Sarah hugged Rosie and stared straight ahead. Danny began sobbing.

"Mama," he cried, "What does that mean? Is everybody going to die?"

"No, no," Robert said. "It just means that people should stay inside so they are safe and so that the disease doesn't affect them."

He took Elizabeth aside. "I think we're going to be quarantined soon. We'd better stock up."

"Agreed."

There was no point going to the little *mercato* in San Martino so they drove to the supermarket in San Matteo. Dozens of other people had the same idea and although they filled two shopping carts, mostly with frozen foods, they also found empty shelves.

"Look, there are only six packages of toilet paper left," Elizabeth said.

"Take three."

At home, two of Robert's four clients in the United States said they were canceling orders because they couldn't afford his design work for now. They reported that there were 1,300 cases now in the U.S. Robert texted Johnny Greco.

"Hey. How u?"

"No prblm. Pres said will go away."

"Really?"

"He says summer coming and heat will drive away."

"Heat will kill virus? U believe?"

"Course."

"Take care, Bud."

Robert put the phone away.

· · · · · · · · · · · · · ·

THE NEWS THEY HAD EXPECTED came on March 10. With more than 1,000 deaths, Italy ordered the lockdown of the entire country.

"Tell the kids what that means, Robert."

"Well, the rule is *'Restate a casa'*—stay at home. We have to stay indoors except that we can go to a grocery store or a pharmacy once a week. Many stores will be closed. We have to wear masks outside. We need to carry ID cards. Oh, and there won't be any Masses in churches."

"I can't play with Marco?" Danny said.

"Afraid not," Robert said.

"We can't go to the playground?" Sarah said in her first words of the day.

"No," Elizabeth said. "You and Danny can play on the balcony."

"We can't go to the *mercato* and buy candy?" Danny said.

"Not for a while."

"We're in prison!" Sarah shouted.

Elizabeth, who was not known for being religious, began fingering a rosary they'd found in Nonna's jewelry box.

"You know what I've been thinking, hon?" she said. "I've been thinking how terrible all of this would have been for Nonna. She was always out and about, talking to all the neighbors. I'm glad she isn't here for this."

"One of the few things we can be grateful for, I guess," Robert said.

The next day, pointing to 11,000 cases in more than 110 countries, the World Health Organization declared Covid-19 a pandemic.

Unfortunately, a talking head on TV then said that Italy was being menaced by a *mostro silenzioso*—a silent monster.

"A monster!" cried Danny, who had been terrified of the creatures for all of his four years. "A monster is going to get us? Mama!"

"No, no."

"But he said a monster, Mama!"

"It's OK, it's OK, honey. Robert! Turn off the damn TV!"

• • • • • • • • • • • • • •

THE FAMILY ENTERED a time of tears and tensions. Danny was permanently attached to Elizabeth's pants leg. Sarah tried to put her doll's clothes on Rosie, who didn't cooperate and fled under the bed. With the TV virtually banned, Robert spent hours online with *La Repubblica*, *Corriere della sera*, *la Stampa* and CNN.

Soon, the days seemed endless and nerves were frazzled.

"I thought you were going to empty the dryer."

"I thought it was your turn. I did it yesterday."

"No, I did it yesterday. It's your turn."

"OK, OK, OK."

Dinners, which had always been a time for sharing the news of the day, became a time of silence or arguments.

"Mom, this hamburger isn't cooked," Sarah said.

"Should I reheat it?" Robert asked.

"Why the hell don't you cook it yourself?" Elizabeth shouted. "In fact, why don't you cook all the meals?"

"OK, OK, I will."

Robert's pasta the next night was denounced by the children as hard, cold and inedible. Elizabeth had skipped dinner.

Elizabeth and Francesca took to daily phone calls, waving at each other from their kitchen windows, their children at their sides.

They talked about when they were allowed outside.

"It's so strange," Francesca said after a shopping trip to San Matteo. "I saw two people being ticketed just because they were talking to each other in the piazza."

"I've noticed," Elizabeth said, "That people try to avoid eye contact. You think the next person you meet might get you infected."

"This is so hard," Francesca said. "Italians are so gregarious. We hug, we kiss—on both cheeks! Now we can't even go outside."

They worried about their neighbors, all of them elderly.

"Poor Signora Franchi," Francesca said. "She was always going out and she had some other old ladies in every week to play cards. Now she has to stay in all the time. She must be going crazy."

"Those two men who live in the next house," Elizabeth said, "I wonder how they're doing. They always seemed so nice."

"The came here because they were harassed in Pisa. And now this."

"What are they doing for food?"

"I see the kid from the *mercato* put something on their doorstep every day at 5:30. Not that I'm watching or anything."

"What about Signor Chen?" Elizabeth asked. "Doesn't he go to Codogno to buy things from China?"

"Yes. I know he shouldn't, but Nico says that's his job."

They talked about their lives.

"I cook, I clean, I take care of the kids," Elizabeth said. "I'm so stressed."

"I'm not used to having Nico home all the time," Francesca said. "I wish he'd help with the kids more."

"Tell me about it," Elizabeth said.

On her own laptop, Elizabeth tried to find out how to talk to children about the pandemic.

"Nobody knows!" she told Robert later. "Be honest, they say. Correct misconceptions. Support your child. Follow a routine. Good grief! Have any of these people ever had children?"

"It's sort of good advice," Robert said.

"How would you know? You're up there on your computer all day."

"Elizabeth, I'm not..."

"You don't have to deal with Danny and Sarah. I don't know what to do with them. They're freaking out."

"But I am helping..."

"I'm so tired. I can't sleep at night so then I'm tired in the morning."

"I know, hon."

"Well, I WISH TO HELL YOU'D HELP OUT MORE!"

When she burst into tears Robert tried to take her hand but she brushed him away and ran upstairs, followed, of course, by Danny and Sarah.

• • • • • • • • • • • • • •

ROBERT AND ELIZABETH made up that night—sort of. Elizabeth said she was sorry she had bitten Robert's head off, and Robert said they were under such strains now and he would help more with the children.

"Are you sorry we moved here?" he asked as they were lying in bed after returning Danny to his own bed.

"I don't know. We can't go back."

"I sure don't want to go back to Cleveland. Johnny said there were two more murders overnight."

"We've been in lockdown for three weeks," Elizabeth said. "When will it end?"

Robert suggested that they have a family meeting—one the kids called a family council — to discuss what was going on.

"We know," Elizabeth said as they gathered at the kitchen table, "that this has been a hard time for all of us, but we have to live together so let's make the best of it."

"How about," Robert said, "if we had a routine. Then we could manage things better."

They made out a schedule. Breakfast followed by online class time for Sarah while Robert and Danny made birdhouses. Then a treat and then more class time for Sarah and a board game for Danny. Lunch would be followed by a cleanup time.

"And everybody is going to clean," Elizabeth said, not looking at anyone in particular.

Then they all would work on a 2,000-piece Hogwarts jigsaw puzzle they'd barely started on the dining room table. Then the kids could read or play with Rosie on the balcony and then all four would help make dinner. At night, the kids could play a videogame and then Robert and Elizabeth would bring out the cello and violin and play. Maybe Sarah and Danny could learn some simple songs.

"And once a week," Elizabeth said as she posted the schedule on the refrigerator, "you can have a Zoom session with Marco and Livia."

"Remember how we used to go camping and we stayed in a tent?" Robert asked. "Well, let's pretend that this is a tent and it's raining so we can't go out for a while, OK?"

"OK." Sarah and Danny replied, not very enthusiastically.

Elizabeth sighed.

The system worked well, but sometimes it fell apart. Sarah accused Danny of hogging the console for the videogame. Danny threatened to push Rosie off the balcony and Sarah screamed. No one paid attention to the jigsaw puzzle for days because the kids said it was "too hard."

The news that Robert saw online continued to be bad. On March 23, Italy led the world with a death toll of 5,476.

"I don't want to set a record," Elizabeth cried. "I just want this to be over."

"It's OK, Mama," Danny said. "It's OK."

Robert and Elizabeth were alarmed when they received a call from their neighbor.

"Francesca, why are you whispering?" Elizabeth asked.

"Listen, don't tell the kids but you know Signor Chen has been going to Codogno and three days ago he wasn't feeling well and he went to a doctor who put him in the hospital. He's there now."

"Is he OK?"

"I don't know. Don't tell the kids, OK?"

Elizabeth took Robert aside to tell him.

"Well," he said, "I guess it was just a matter of time before San Martino had a case. Now we really have to stay inside."

Danny was suddenly tugging at Elizabeth's apron. "Mama! What's going on? Did somebody die?"

"No, honey, no one died. Let's work on the puzzle, OK?"

While they did that, Robert opened his phone to text Johnny.

"Hey. How u?"

"OK."

"Just OK?"

"Getting bad here. 14,000 ppl positive in Ohio. 610 dead."

"What pres say?"

"Said drink disinfectant."

"What? U kidding?"

"What he said."

"No!"

"Yes."

"How u feel?"

"Sad."

"Take care, Bud."

Four weeks into the lockdown, Robert and Elizabeth wondered how to celebrate Easter, traditionally a bigger feast than Christmas in Italy with festivals and processions and fireworks.

"In Florence," Robert told the children, "they have a big cart that explodes with fireworks and people come from all over to watch. Maybe we can go next year."

"We're never going to go anywhere," Sarah said. "We're stuck here forever."

Ignoring her, Elizabeth said that she found a cake shaped like a lamb and two chocolate eggs in the supermarket and they'd have them on Easter.

"And after that we can watch the pope give his Easter message, and there's a concert by Andrea Bocelli from the Duomo in Milan and..."

"Big deal," Sarah said.

• • • • • • • • • • • • • • • •

AT THE END OF APRIL, there were a few reasons to be a little optimistic. Francesca reported that Signor Chen had returned from the hospital and had to stay in quarantine but was feeling better. Robert read online that the Norwegian student who had tested positive in Florence had recovered. And CNN said that Italy had posted its lowest number of new coronavirus cases in seven weeks and that Prime Minister Conte would make an announcement that night.

"OK," Robert said, "I think we can watch television for this."

They lined up on the couch again, Danny still sitting close to his mother and Sarah hugging Rosie and staring ahead.

Conte appeared on the screen, a tall man with black hair.

"After 56 days," he said, "I am pleased to announce that Italy will cautiously—very cautiously — begin easing restrictions on May 4."

"Oh, thank God," Elizabeth said. "Thank God!"

"Can we go out again?" Sarah asked.

"Can we go to the playground?" Danny asked.

"Can we go to the the the *mercato* and buy candy?"

"Yes, yes, yes."

Television stations seemed relieved not to be reporting new cases and death tolls. Instead, they showed clips of the country slowly coming back to life: A couple buying ice cream, kids playing soccer, people singing on their balconies. Once again Italians came out of their homes and even though they wore masks and stayed at safe distances, resumed the traditional evening walk of the *passeggiata*.

In a phone call soon after the lockdown had ended, Francesca asked Elizabeth why she and Robert had stopped their balcony concerts.

"Oh, I don't know. I guess we just didn't feel like it. I think we can start again now."

The next night, with Sarah and Danny turning the pages, their concert was a celebration: "Greensleeves," Beethoven's "Moonlight Sonata," a waltz from "Sleeping Beauty," Bach's "Minuet" and finally, "Amazing Grace."

All the neighbors listened from their own balconies, even Signor Chen in his bathrobe, and their thunderous applause could probably be heard in San Matteo.

Robert reached over and put his arm around his wife. "We're going to be OK, right?"

"We are."

The Presence of the Dead

by Mark Spano

*The Presence of the Dead by Mark Spano is part of
a larger work entitled Kidding the Moon.
This is a story of the fragility of life and the intractability of death.*

> YOU DON'T BELIEVE
> THESE DELICATE STEMS OF YOURS HAVE BEEN,
> BY YOURSELF OR THE FATAL SCHEME
> OF THINGS, FASHIONED FOR IMMORTALITY
> — *Leopardi* (from Broom of the Flower of the Desert)

If I have a religion of any kind, it might be described as Proustian. "A mystical atheist," is how Edmund White describes Proust's religion, "someone imbued with spirituality who nonetheless did not believe in a personal god, much less a savior." I am the first to admit that explaining my own faith from such a derived set of not so religious values as Proust's seems to announce many more vagaries than incites. I am able though to say that my evolved religion is creedless and does not concern itself with an afterlife which is not to say that one does not exist. It seems to me there is just too much work to do on this side of a final breath to concern oneself with the undone housekeeping on the other side. Then, there is the matter of the dead. Where have they gone?

Just how gone is dead and gone? Initially, it is the very shock of *goneness* that makes the dead so present. Grief is in the body, and the body never forgets.

At this point, cataloging a few of my losses to death seems necessary to further tell my story. Through the 1980s, Nicholas and I lived in the leafy northern Virginia suburbs of Washington, DC. It was the closest-to-town sight we could find and afford with enough property suitable to Nicholas's conception of what a garden ought to be.

Our neighbors behind us were Ken and Anne-Marie. They were an unlikely couple, he from San Antonio and she from a suburb of Paris. They had two small children that Nicholas and I adored. Sophie and Little Ken were articulate and imaginative children. They had an absolute genius for knowing exactly the minute when Nicholas and I had finished Saturday morning house cleaning and were off for Chinese lunch. Sophie and Little Ken appeared as if on cue. Their parents always permitted them to tag along, and Nicholas and I were overjoyed and genuinely blessed to have such gentle and reasonable neighbors.

On a Monday in December, I returned from work and looked across my yard to see the cars of both Ken and Anne-Marie in their drive. I worked then for a company that started quite early in the morning, which had me most days finishing work ahead of the normal commute. Arriving home just before four, I could not imagine why Ken and Anne-Marie were home so early. Nicholas and I had had supper with them on the prior Saturday. There was no talk of a day off. Something seemed amiss.

I went to knock and found Anne-Marie in her living room with a look of shellshock. It was a look that would stay with her for months to come. At dinner the two days before, Ken had been nursing a sore foot, "An old sports injury," he said, "sometimes it aches like nothing I've experienced."

It was no sports injury but a very invasive cancer that had spread through the seemingly robust thirty-eight year old Ken. It took only about five months for the disease to do its awful work on my young neighbor. Ken was dead by late May.

Through his illness, Nicholas and I looked after Sophie and Little Ken, prepared meals, went to school pageants, and generally stood in for Ken and Anne-Marie who tried mightily to maintain some patterns of normalcy in the lives of their children.

After Ken's death, we continued on with Anne-Marie and the children. The father was gone, the mother in a state of great disbelief. The children had come to depend on Nicholas and me. Our relationship, in those months grew far beyond Chinese lunch. We had become a family.

Through the years I have shepherded Ken and Anne-Marie's children to the tops of the Washington Monument, the Empire State Building and the Eiffel Tower. I have swam with them at the beach, fed them Thanksgiving turkey, and celebrated their graduations. Through those times, a faint and not so faint presence of their father always lingered with us.

. . . .

I once believed Nicholas was less conflicted about his family than I. His family and his mother, in particular, wanted to see him, hear from him, visit him, go on vacation with him, etc. I was included in his family almost immediately—no questions asked. My parents never had this kind of enthusiasm over their children. Most Italians took great pains to emphasize family but, at some point, my parents tired of the notion of family.

I had a much greater desire for a cohesive family than my parents and siblings. I believe my parents upheld some necessary picture of the importance of family, but by middle-age, they let pretense fall. They were too exhausted by the antics of their own siblings to even feign a desire they wanted much from their children than to grow up and move away.

After the first couple of years with Nicholas, I had a family and cohesiveness beyond my wildest yearnings. This went a long way in alleviating much of what I believed was missed in my own family. It did not, though, assuage the pain of my father's refusal to see me for the person I am.

Into my forties, after the deaths of both Ken and Nicholas, my father had some hope that I might marry Anne-Marie. Anne-Marie and I laughed heartily at my father's pure persistence in his attempts to will me heterosexual. There is too a grief that after so many years, he continued to refuse to see who I am.

Nicholas's family being New York Italians to the marrow of the prosciutto bones his mother got from the butcher for pasta con fagioli, lived their lives around the dining room table. They congregated for big meals. Life was food, food, and more food.

• • • • • • • • • • • • • • •

Cal was a senior programmer with the Navy when I worked on a government contract in DC. He was blonde, barrel-chested, and buff from an unrelenting devotion to weightlifting. Cal was a few years older than I.

He was a recluse spending his time away from work, working out, reading, and having numerous and anonymous sexual encounters. His mathematical gifts were far beyond the skills required for his job with the Navy. He was a very quiet man; sometimes, downright sullen.

When I worked for the Navy, there were as many gay men and lesbians as anywhere else I had worked, both civilian and in uniform. This was years before, "Don't ask. Don't tell." It never seemed to be any greater an issue than it was anywhere else, but neither did anyone talk much about it.

Cal had been married once, but his marriage did not last long. He was still on quite good terms with his ex-wife and his successor as her husband.

Cal and I went to lunch frequently and talked about books. He loved the Latin American writers as did I. We also read much of the

New Physics. Cal would frequently take home with him a book I had trouble understanding. After he had read it, we would have lunch so he could explain to me over pasta at our favorite Italian place those parts of the book I did not understand.

Cal also enjoyed recounting for me his many sexual adventures. Cal was physically a remarkably imposing man. He liked to play rough, and he wanted only anonymous, frequent, and the edgiest of confrontations. Before I believed that my life would be touched by the strange disease that seemed to be killing gay men in New York and San Francisco, Cal, who always seemed to be in sparkling good health, was dead of pneumocystis pneumonia.

• • • • • • • • • • • • • • •

Al was a retired Navy Commander and worked on the Navy contract with me. He gave me frequent advice for navigating the bureaucratic waters of Navy work and taught me patience with a system that was not hasty in its decision making. Al was a grandfather and rode a Harley to our office in the Washington Navy Yard. He was still married and living with his wife, and he also had a boyfriend who lived on Capitol Hill.

When Nicholas worked for the Library of Congress, on nicer days, I would walk from the Navy Yard to have lunch with him. On many of those days, he and I would run into Al and Herb, his boyfriend sitting on a bench at the Capitol South Metro Plaza eating carry-out and admiring their meticulously polished Harleys parked at the curb.

Al was very fond of Nicholas and paid us both a good deal of much-appreciated attention.

Herb got sick before Al, but Al died before him from a brain stem ailment having never exhibited any of the usual symptoms associated with AIDS.

At Al's funeral, the family all sat together at the front of chapel as one would expect. Herb sat in the back weeping quietly being attended to by a well-dressed young man I did not know. I am certain that Nicholas and I (and very likely the well-dressed young man) were the only mourners who knew the identity of the thin, pale gentleman in tears being helped along by a well-dressed companion.

The Viewing

by Leo Vadalà

Wakes are usually sad, mournful affairs—but not always.
In 'The Viewing,' the author imagines the Italian-style viewing of a kid
as seen and felt by a young participant as his very first experience of the kind,
and how he manages to transform what would usually be a somber,
grief-stricken event into a spooky but hilarious happening.

I hate viewings—I am embarrassed to admit it but the sight of corpses gives me the galloping heebie-jeebies. I try to avoid them like the plague and I go to a viewing only when it's absolutely necessary, you know, close family members and dear friends.

It's a phobia that started years ago, when I was just a young kid of about twelve or thirteen.

I was still living in Italy at that time and it must have been either summer or on a weekend, I'm pretty sure, because I remember I was off from school. It was around noon, and I was out in the streets with my friends, playing soccer. From a distance I heard my mom holler for me to come home for our noon meal. Mom had this foghorn type voice, she just opened the window on the fourth floor of our apartment and bellowed out my name: **LILLO!**—that was my nickname.

Whenever mom called, you could hear her from two blocks away. All my friends used to make fun of that. As soon as they heard her holler they would start mimicking her voice, all of them shouting, chorus like —**LILLO! LILLO!**

I ran home because I was hungry, plus in those days you just didn't screw around with your parents, and when they called, you ran. More than once I was sent to bed without supper for being late or disobedient. Today it would be called child abuse, but in those days parents were still held accountable for disciplining their children.

When I got home I washed up a bit then sat down for lunch—in Italy, lunch is the big meal of the day. It was during the course of the meal that my mom told me: "I heard your friend Aurelio died. Maybe this evening you should go visit the Fabbris."

I was stunned. "**What? Aurelio died?...**"

"Yes..." —My mother said— "He had polio, and he passed away this morning."

I was so stunned I started crying. Aurelio was this friend of mine, a young kid just about my age, and all us kids had been wondering why we hadn't seen him over the past several days.

Did I say friend? Scratch that. If truth be told, I hated his guts. In fact, we weren't even on speaking terms when he croaked. As kids go, he was a true blue prick, so snotty you wouldn't believe it, everything he did was always right and whatever you did was always wrong. You know the type, always looking for arguments, always picking fights, and always backing out at the last moment.

The only thing Aurelio had going for him was that he was a hell of a good soccer player. I mean, he was good, real good. He not only was fast, but he could do tricks with a ball that I had seen done only by professional players. In fact, only a couple of months before he died, he had even had a tryout with the juvenile team of the Genoa Soccer Club, the city's professional team, the team all us kids idolized and dreamed of playing for. After the tryout he'd become even more hateful, if that was possible, acting like his shit didn't stink.

The main reason we kept him in our group was that everybody wanted him on their team when we chose sides.

After lunch I went outside again to see my friends and tell them about Aurelio. Some of them already knew and they were all subdued. We didn't even get a game going, that's how big of a shock it was for all of us.

You know how it is, kids can hate each other's guts passionately just as much as adults, even more perhaps, but when one of their own dies they only remember the good times they had together and the good qualities he had.

We went on and on: "Remember that goal he scored against Carlo? Man, three guys were guarding him and he still scored... And that one he scored on a scissor kick against the San Tommaso team?"

They forget quickly what a mean, petty louse the guy really was, unlike adults who may act noble and forgiving but, deep down, they'll say *served the bastard right.*

Mom suggested I should go visit the family later in the day to see him laid out. I had never seen a dead person before, and I wasn't too crazy about it, but I put on my best shirt and short pants, even shined my shoes, and went anyway.

I don't know how they do it now, but back then in Italy there was no such thing as a funeral home for viewings. They did have funeral homes, but they only provided caskets and a hearse, usually a horse drawn carriage. Dead people were usually laid out at home in their beds or on some table, with flowers and candles and people praying and weeping all around them.

The Fabbris lived on the sixth floor of an apartment house about a block away from where I lived. The apartment main entrance was half closed as a sign of mourning and a black ribbon hanged from the closed half of the door.

I climbed up to the sixth floor—elevators? Are you kidding?—knocked on the door and was admitted inside. The place reeked of flowers and candle smoke, and just as soon as I stepped in I already started to feel a bit sick, dizzy like.

Aurelio's mom was in the kitchen crying uncontrollably. Three or four ladies were fussing around her trying to console the poor lady, and his dad, plus about a dozen people, all friends and relatives I guess, were gathered around the bed, all of them also crying their hearts out.

It was a sad scene, really, but I felt estranged like. It was a solemn occasion, one I'd never witnessed before, and I wasn't sure of what to do, or how to behave. It was my first corpse, and I was gripped by this fierce sense of both fear and curiosity. Best I can describe it is that I wanted to both have this experience and also get my ass out of there as quickly as possible.

Crying, like laughing, can be contagious. If everyone laughs or cries, chances are you'll do the same thing. This time, however, even though there wasn't a dry eye in the house, I couldn't cry. I had cried at home when my mom had first told me because of the shock, I guess. But here, in the presence of the living corpse and everyone else crying, my eyes couldn't produce a tear if my life depended on it.

I was apprehensive, even scared, but scared as I was, I was determined to see what the dead Aurelio looked like. It was my first corpse and, for once, curiosity was stronger than fear. Another strong motivating factor was that I hadn't seen any of my friends among the crowd, and I wanted to score points with them afterwards, when I gave them all the gory details.

Twisting and turning, I elbowed my way through the crowd until I found myself at the foot of the bed, and finally there he was, laid out and fully dressed in his First Communion suit with his hands resting on his stomach, holding a Rosary.

I focused my eyes on his face. And that's where the trauma began.

I immediately noticed that one of his eyes, his right eye, was just a tiny bit open, just an itsy-bitsy tiny slit, but enough to see a slice of the pupil. You'd think someone would have had enough sense to just manually lower the eyelid a bit, and let him rest in peace, but noooooo....... Either they didn't care, or didn't notice, or maybe they just left it like that so that I could be practically scarred for life.

Whatever—I became so fascinated by that goddamned itsy-bitsy closed eye that I began to concentrate on that to the exclusion of everything else. And the wildest, most fantastic thoughts started flooding inside my head.

I sometime ask myself how our mind functions—when it does function, that is. I mean, I wonder what triggers certain chains of thought, what sustains them, what feeds them, why a random occurrence or even a visual experience can start a prolonged daydream or a recurring nightmare. Like, for instance, we see a leaf gently falling to the ground, and in fragmented yet logical steps our imagination takes us to some vision or conclusion that has no relation whatsoever to that foolish leaf drifting in the wind.

That barely closed eye was my falling leaf and, in the bat of an eye—an appropriate expression if there ever was one!—it felt like the whole goddamned tree trunk was crashing on my head.

How did that occur? Damned if I know! Crazily, I began to imagine that he was looking at us, spying on us, like he was just pretending to be dead, like he was really alive and well but checking out to see how we treated him thinking that he was dead. And as I imagined, I began to actually believe that he was keeping score of who had showed up and who had stayed at home, what people were wearing, how they were behaving.

I tell you, the wildest things. Were the mourners respectful enough? Were they somber enough? Were they truly heartbroken?

At one point, I actually felt that, had he wanted to, he could have fully opened that eye, or both of them, and yelled out: **"AH! AH! YOU! WHY AREN'T YOU CRYING!!!"**

It was some sort of self hypnosis, of course, but I was so totally spaced out that I remember silently repeating to myself over and over: "Now... now... now... he'll open it now... now... now..."

I was even holding my breath, anticipating it so strongly that, had he opened it, I would not have considered it a miracle—it would had been something preordained.

My concentration was so complete, I had become so totally absorbed with that eye that I had tuned out all that was going on around me, crowd movement, crowd noise, everything and totally. Even potential dangers.

You heard that right, potential dangers! To wit, it didn't dawn on me, I just wasn't registering that, one by one, all the people in the room were filing out to get coffee or something. I simply wasn't aware that now it was just he and I in that room.

And the stage for a powerful drama was all set.

Still unaware of my predicament, I began thinking about our rather stormy relationship when he was alive, how we used to fight all the times about the silliest things, the way he hogged the ball when we played, never wanting to pass, the way he would criticize just about everything I or anybody else did, the way we played, what we were wearing, that kind of stuff.

Goddamned kids that we were, we'd come out swinging at the drop of a hat. Actually, neither one of us was much of a fighter but we faked it beautifully, you know, classic boxing stance, circling and circling, lightning jabs that never came close, menacing glares, and all the while silently praying for some nice old lady to come by, give us a good scolding, and separate us.

All the fights we had, I don't remember landing one single punch or getting hit by one for that matter. A couple of shoves, some wrestling, and that's about it.

Afterwards, I would swagger over to the guys who usually surrounded us egging us on, and I would tell them how lucky he was that lady had come along just when I was getting the upper hand, because he would otherwise be begging me for mercy. I'm sure, of course, he probably said the same thing to his friends. If he had any, that is.

Every time we had a fight we would stay mad at each other for a few days or even weeks, not speaking to each other, but we would then silently drift back together, usually when we wound up playing for the same soccer team. As well as I can remember, neither of us ever apologized to the other. We simply forgot our differences and resumed talking to each other, only to fight again later for the silliest reasons.

This, by the way, wasn't just a personal thing between him and me but also between him and just about everybody else in our group. I'm telling you, he was a hateful prick.

We had had our last fight just a few weeks before he died, and we hadn't had a chance to make up because, like I said, he took sick and dropped out of circulation.

As I stood there looking at his eye, I was thinking about that last fight we had. Being just a kid and still quite religious, I began to feel pangs of remorse for whatever had happened between us. The right thing to do, I felt, was to assume all responsibility for our last argument as well as all the previous ones, and I'm talking dozens of them, although just a few of them ended up in a scuffle.

I told myself I was a rotten bastard, or words to that effect, because the word 'bastard' was still a no-no in those days, and definitely not part of our everyday vocabulary.

Yes!... It had all been my fault, and I definitely would have to go to confession and beg God to forgive me for all my sins!

And then came the next, 'fragmented' and 'logical' step in my chain of thought. One tragic, insane thought entered my mind—would it be possible that he took sick and died because he had been so upset about our latest fight?

Holy Mary, Mother of God, pray for us sinners! That's all I needed to totally crack me up. He had died of polio, of course, but what the fuck did I know about polio?

That goddamned thought took root, germinated, and quickly blossomed into a firm certainty. Yes! I was directly responsible for his death. No question about it, nobody knew it, but I was a bloody murderer.

I swear I felt my teeth sweating and shivering at the same time, I knew the 'carabinieri' would be bursting in the room any minute, I saw myself arrested, manacled, tried, convicted, and sentenced to spend the rest of my life chained in some dark and musty dungeon like the Count of Montecristo.

Worse yet, I saw, or imagined to see a million eyes staring at me accusingly, and a million fingers pointing at me, and I heard a million voices chanting tauntingly: "**YOU killed him!... YOU killed him!... YOU killed him!... NOW you must die!... YES! NOW you must die.**"

Man, it was Panicsville! My insides had become a mass of jelly, I felt my lunch, my breakfast, all my past week's meals coming up, my mouth was dry and full of saliva at the same time. Gastric juices in my stomach were churning up enough gas to fill the Goodyear blimp. Air was coming up my windpipe, and I felt this overwhelming urge to belch and to fart so loud that it would have awakened him but—stupid asshole kid that I was!—I held it back because it was impolite to belch or, even worse, to fart, especially in front of a corpse.

I began swallowing hard. Somehow I managed to stop that nauseous feeling, but I broke out in this cold sweat and I felt like I was going to pass out any minute.

It's no use trying to tell you what kind of emotions were racing through my brain because I just don't know, it was temporarily out of order.

One glimmer of a thought kept flickering in my mind, one single, constant, fleeting thought that recurred over and over until it took hold. I had to redeem myself! Yes! Somehow or other I had to make myself whole in his eyes. The only way out for me was to prove to him I was worthy of a second chance. That's it! If I could show him I deserved a break, I could still be saved.

I was grasping at straws, that's what I was doing, I knew that, but I had to give it my best shot! Silently, I began pleading for his forgiveness, I asked him to please, please forget all the fights we had had, Aurelio, show me some mercy please; Aurelio, I'm so, so very sorry I made you sick, Aurelio; I repent for all your suffering, Aurelio; I implore you, Aurelio; I beg you, I didn't mean to kill you.

I promised him I would recite a Rosary in his name every day for the rest of my life, I would attend Mass two, three, four times a week,

I swore I would use his short but noble life as the model for my life, I pledged I would lead a monastic existence in some goddamned cave somewhere. God! What I didn't promise!

I even promised I would stop jerking off, and that was a real toughie because I'd just learned how to do it and, man oh man! I loved it! But I promised that also!

And here's where things got **REALLY** sticky.

You see, when madness strikes, it's not a one shot deal, not with me at least. When frigging madness gets a hold of me, it starts as simple, ordinary madness, the kind every sane man gets now and then, but then it starts branching out. It begins playing a cat and mouse game, tantalizing like, it leaves for a moment then comes back for an encore, and then another one, and yet another one, it announces its retirement, then makes another glorious comeback, even gives a command performance or two. It will not leave for good until it is satisfied that permanent and irreversible damage has been done.

And this time was no exception.

After I had humbled myself, after I had beseeched him, supplicated, pleaded for his forgiveness, after I'd done everything but kiss his dead ass and all, for some goddamned silly reason I began to imagine him imperiously refusing to even look at me, to even acknowledge my presence, much less forgive me; can you fucking believe it?

And so, enter madness, round two, or three, I forget which. I began this totally insane silent conversation with him, making up my questions, all positive and conciliatory, and providing his answers, all negative and antagonistic, of course.

Now, despite all my previous humiliations, I still had some pride, and there was no way I was going to take his uppity ways without a fight. Hell, no! It had now become a test of strength, and I was going to at the very least get him to talk to me. I **had** to get him to come around to my way of thinking, no easy task because Aurelio's folks were from Calabria, the Italian Missouri.

And round four started. And I began this interminable see-saw dialogue consisting of me pleading, asking, begging, demanding forgiveness, and him rejecting my peace feelers over, and over, and over again.

Oh, you should have heard me! My arguments were so irresistible, so perfectly reasoned out, so impeccable in every detail, so totally and obviously convincing and irrefutable that I half expected him to sit up and applaud after every one of them.

But no, the bastard didn't see it that way! He had to be a prick even in death! Somehow, he'd wiggle out by finding all sorts of silly, totally invalid excuses, stupid *'non sequitur's'* like "Yeah! Maybe so, but what if it rains tomorrow? Then what?", or "But every time I passed you the ball you didn't score." That kind of shit.

Look, I'd never been at a loss for words but, believe me, I was fast running out of arguments. Worse yet, I was running out of patience.

At one time, after a particular inane repartee of his, I swear to Christ I was so goddamned mad I was just about ready to punch him in the nose and tell him to go roast in hell where he belonged.

But I decided to give it one more try, and I played my trump card.

I asked him: "How in hell do you expect to enter paradise if you still have hate, if you still have poison in your heart? You know damn well St. Peter won't even let you in through the front door, you'll be lucky if he'll let you go to Purgatory; you'll probably go straight to hell. Is that what you want?"

It was my ace in the hole—it had to work, or it was all over. And it did!

His attitude changed immediately, I could tell my argument had mollified him, I could tell his answers weren't so surly anymore, he was coming around, I could tell. He still didn't want to give in completely, the bastard, he still acted kind of hurt, kind of standoffish, but I knew I had made my point, I knew it was just a question of time now. I could tell that if I pressed him just a while longer he would have relented, and I was already envisioning me walking out of there in peace, my heart as pure and my soul as clean as the driven snow.

This give and take lasted just a few minutes longer and finally, victory at last!

Dredging out the best of my oratorical ability, I painted for him a glorious picture of what his entry in paradise would be like, with angels, archangels, cherubims, all the saints lining up to greet him, and him walking slowly until he was in God's presence. It was moving, beautiful, lyrical, I was almost in tears. And he capitulated.

I could see he was really touched, and he accepted my apologies. He even generously forgave me for having killed him at such a tender age. And to seal our renewed and everlasting friendship he grandly offered me his hand to shake.

And this is where things got **UNREALLY** sticky! You see, his fucking hand did not—hell, could not!—move, and I, in my stupor, actually reached out and grabbed it!

HOLY BLESSED IMMACULATE VIRGIN MOTHER OF THE DIVINE BABY JESUS!...

It was a piece of ice and it felt like... like what?... Like a dead man's hand feels, like waxy snake skin, and it brought me crashing down to earth with a sickening thud.

And what was earth? Earth was a lonely, flower filled, candle lit room with just one living thing in it—Me!—and one dead thing in it—Him!—and the hand of **Me** was holding the hand of **Him**.

All of a sudden I remembered he hated my guts and the feeling was mutual, and while we could have avoided each other when he was alive, there was no escape now. There we were, in this spooky room, our hands locked in a deadly embrace and he, being in the other world, had all the advantage and was pressing it.

Let me tell you, it was Panicsville all over again, downtown Panicsville this time!

Some sort of paralysis set in. Even now, after all these years, I can still recall that terrifying, that horrific feeling of being unable to open my mouth, to utter a sound, to stammer, to scream for help, to breathe, or even to throw up. I was doomed—it was pure, undiluted, primal terror, my mind incapable of formulating the most elementary thought, and my eyes just about ready to pop out of their sockets.

Talk about eyes, I couldn't have picked a better time to look at his fucking eye.

I swear to you, that slit had now become a half open eye—**HALF OPEN, GET THAT? NOT HALF CLOSED**—and don't anybody tell me that eye didn't open for one full second because it did, **IT DID, I SWEAR TO GOD IT DID!** It did open, I tell you, and it told me of unspeakable horrors, it revealed all sorts of unimaginable evils, it lacerated my soul as it screamed at me that I was a rotten son of a bitch, rotten, rotten to the core because it knew—**YES! IT KNEW!**—it knew all along that I had cheated him more than once when we had played with our bubble gum cards. And it was true, of course, I had cheated him, I used to cheat him a lot, and I got away with it because he wasn't just a prick, but a dumb one at that.

As a matter of fact, the last fight we had was because he had tried to cheat me, a bad move because I was a veteran at that sort of thing and I had caught him immediately. While I was eating crow with him a while before, the thought had crossed my mind that maybe he should have been the one apologizing to me because he had been at fault, on that particular occasion anyway. It was a clear-cut case, and he knew it. Hell, I had witnesses! He had even lost points with the guys because we had an ironclad—if somewhat skewed—code of honor; cheating wasn't allowed, but it was OK as long as you didn't get caught at it. He had been caught and, had he lived, he would have had a hell of a hard time being reaccepted by the gang.

Indeed, our gang had another clause in this screwed up code of honor of ours—your reputation grew in direct proportion to your **un**detected cheating. I was pretty popular because they knew I was good at cheating, I even bragged about it, but I never got caught.

Anyway, on that occasion, he was wrong and he knew it. Still, I felt that my cheating, even though undetected, had more than offset his clumsy attempt to cheat me, ten to one at least, and that's why I was the one apologizing. Plus, he was dead, and —come **ON**, now!—you had to give him some slack for that!

For some reasons, a few minutes earlier, while I was begging for his forgiveness, I'd felt he hadn't been aware of my cheating, even though in church they'd always taught us that once you're dead you get to know everything—you have 'inside' info, so to speak. But now, that eye...Oh, God, that eye, I can still see it...That eye was now staring at me accusingly, fiendishly, **KNOWINGLY,** and I could hear the malevolent sibilance of a voice, his voice, hissing at me, cackling at me, telling me that he knew, yes he knew, he had known all along, and now he was going to get his revenge, yes, I was going to pay for it, **NOW.**

In cases like that, time is suspended—a second, a minute, an hour, a day, or a month, it don't make no difference. As a matter of fact, a second might as well be a month, or a year, or a lifetime, so it's no point trying to figure out how long that scene lasted. Chronologically, I would say that less than one minute had passed from the moment we shook hands, but certainly the longest minute since creation.

What happened next is a bit fuzzy. I am sure that God, or whoever created us, equipped us with some sort of built-in mechanism that activates only when we get ourselves in deep, deep, very deep doo-doo.

In my case, that mechanism was an infinitesimally minute portion of my brain that had not become totally cataleptic like the rest of it, simply because it had never been used before. It had just laid there dormant, waiting for this emergency. I am positive it began functioning ever so slightly at that very moment because no living organism could have withstood the shock I was going through.

Those two or three brain cells—bless them!—slowly began cranking up and began mapping out a strategy for survival. They instructed me that—first thing first—I **HAD** to let go of that fucking hand that, **I KNOW**, was gripping mine.

Next, and equally important, they urged me—in fact, they screamed at me—to get my skinny ass out of that goddamned room and into a crowd, **PRONTO!!**

Those were the only two commands I understood—disengage and get the fuck out of there. And so, quietly and oh so slowly, to make sure

I wouldn't wake him up, I began to peel my hand away from his. That took the better part of a minute.

I then made a Herculean effort to break eye contact with him and that wasn't easy. I was in the same position of a baby rabbit in the presence of a snake—once the snake has him in his sights, the rabbit knows he is fucked. I mean, he could easily run away, but he is so terrified that he becomes totally paralyzed with fear, and in no time he becomes snake dinner.

I don't know how long that took, but somehow I did manage to break eye contact. Then I started turning around slowly, very slowly, very very slooooowly, like the second hand of a clock, and began to crawl out of that room. To this day, I swear to you I don't recall any actual motion on my part, you know, any actual putting one foot in front of the other, any—what's it called?—any walking, that's it!

Silently, sliding my feet ever so lightly, I found myself pushed out of that room. Yes, pushed! I could feel that eye staring at me, rotating clickety-clack in its socket, sending a malevolent laser beam glare that pierced me right between the shoulder blades.

I found myself out of that room, and then—**KABONG!**—I passed out falling to the ground like a sack of potatoes.

Next thing I knew, somebody was pouring liquor down my throat, and I was damn near choking to death. They had me laid me out on the floor and some lady had propped a pillow under my head to make me comfortable. I began making out all sorts of oooh's and aaah's, but I couldn't figure out what they were saying.

Eventually I came out of my daze, and then I began to cry. Ladies and gentlemen, let me tell you, on that day I covered the entire spectrum of human emotions. I cried tears of pain, joy, love, hate, relief, fear, remorse, anger, you name it. All of them! Whatever you can think of came out of my eyes in liquid form, ran down my cheeks, and soaked the front of my shirt, my pants, even my underwear.

My ears began to pick up bits and pieces of conversation here and there. One snatch of conversation caught my attention and damn near snuffed me out. This old witch was trying to explain my fainting spell to some other biddy. "Poor kid!..."—She was saying—"They were so close!"

Son of a bitch that I was even then, when I heard that line I damn near burst out laughing so hard I nearly strangled myself trying to hold it back. I couldn't hold it back entirely but I somehow managed to redirect the laugh, and it came out as a snort through my nose along with at least one pint of snot. As a result, I started choking even harder than before, and people kept slapping me in the back to make sure I wouldn't be keeping company to the guy in the other room, that's how bad it was.

Finally, I was OK. They started bringing out all kinds of pastries and stuff, and all the people there were falling all over each other trying to feed me.

Double son of a bitch that I was even then, I figured my luck had changed, and I kept on crying until I'd had my fill. You got to understand that in those days the only time you saw pastries was at weddings and funerals, and there hadn't been one of those in my family since I can remember. Hey!... A great chance like that comes by, and I wasn't going to let it slip by without a fight. And so I cried and I ate, I cried and I ate, and I enjoyed every single bit of it, and the hell with the dead kid.

If there's such thing as silent euphoria, I was experiencing it. I was with people now, real people, **LIVE** people, and I had already forgotten that goddamned eye and the trauma of a few minutes before.

My newfound euphoria was short lived, however. Yes, I had forgotten the eye, but I had also forgotten something else—a very simple thing really. I had forgotten that, inevitably, every goddamned day is followed by a goddamned night. And I had also forgotten that at night one goes to bed, and that I slept in a little room, **ALL ALONE!** That's what I forgot.

And so, ladies and gentlemen of the jury, in my summation I swear to you that for the next three, four months, maybe more, I did not sleep at all, not one little wink.

The minute the lights were turned off, the eye would appear, **THAT EYE!** Magically, as if suspended from the ceiling by an invisible thread, it would advance and retreat, it would sneer and blink at me, fiendishly, obscenely, cruelly.

And if the electric bill was so high in those days, it was me mom, it was me. I had to do it, mom, I had to do it or I wouldn't be here now to tell you about it.

And since then I still get the galloping heebie-jeebies when I see a corpse.

The Last Godfather

by Anthony Valerio

Anthony Valerio's piece, The Last Godfather,
is a story from his novel, Conversation with Johnny (1997; 2017).
This exploration of power and sensuality preceded the hit series
The Sopranos and the film Analyze This.
Here, though, the don is therapist.

Suddenly, about a dozen table lamps go on. The crystal chandelier above the dining room table lights up. It's as if the sun had been reluctant to leave Johnny and me, came down and installed itself in his home. Shading my eyes, I look around for the maid, the butler. There's no one here except Johnny and me. An automatic device was timed to activate the lamps and chandelier with the onset of darkness.

"Well, Johnny," I say with levity, "I'd better be on my way. Thanks a million, but before I go, I'd like to give you a copy of my last book. I inscribed it for you. Signed a personal note from me to you."

My trembling hand reaches into my briefcase and, while my head is bowed, I hear the crack of a firecracker, a bullet. I wince, close my eyes, waiting for it to go straight into my cranium. But I'm still alive when I look up, and see Johnny snap his fingers again. "Alfonso," he says low enough only for us to hear. Still, in walks Alfonso, a huge, hovering, mustached Alfonso, with the eyes and nose of a hawk, weathered skin white with lime, wearing a carpenter's apron strung with appropriate tools except for one, a .38 with silencer. In fingers the size and shape of hammerheads, Alfonso holds a microphone, speakers, roll of electrical wire.

"Johnny, how nice, you've planned some sort of pageant for my benefit."

"Also," Johnny says softly to Alfonso, "block off the ends of the street, use the police barricades in the cellar, and tell everybody on the block to throw open their windows. They're eating now, anyway. Anybody in cars, tell them to shut off the motors." Johnny turns to me. "I want to hear what you read at the college in Hoboken."

"Johnny," I choke, "in the book I'm presenting to you, there are twenty different stories. I've read them all over the country, South America, Palermo too, so when you read them in the privacy of your den, imagine I'm beside you."

His brows raise a fraction of an inch. Instantly, my entire outlook changes.

"You know, after I read in Hoboken, the kid professor came up to me and said, 'I learned something. Hot on hot's no good when I read as well as when I write. When you read,' he said, 'your voice is so soft, your rhythm so easy, natural.'"

Johnny's brows are still raised.

"It will be a great pleasure to read for you, Johnny. I really don't need all this light. See that marble statue behind your lovely snowball plant, that statue of Aphrodite and Apollo, the brilliant, muted lights around the base, those blues and yellows and greens, they're all the light I need. And please have Mr. Alfonso set up the statue and his mike at the head of the dining room table, I'll read from there. OK?"

Johnny sits back, content. Mr. Alfonso takes care of everything.

I breathe deeply, try to get up. False start. I try again. Suddenly, I'm overcome with a sense of work and duty, and love fills my heart.

They conjoin and I move, glide. Adjusting the mike, I say, "The second piece I read in Hoboken, Johnny, was called *The Last Godfather*," and then I read:

The Last Godfather

I am Pippo Napoli Sicilia and I am the last of the great Dons, the last Godfather. After me, after I join Dante in the empyrean, my family of thirty million or so will not need crime to get on, because in their dark souls and untrustful minds I have placed love and beauty and imagination and understanding. Their olive faces will be raised to the Crystalline Heaven. They will be at the point of assimilation into the American race, prepared to ponder the American Revolution and George Washington and Thomas Jefferson and Alexander Hamilton. They will look into one another's eyes and, instead of sensing alarm, will see brother and sister in Faith, Hope and Charity. For centuries in America, my Italians did not like how they felt about themselves and recognized their displeasure in one another. After pondering this state of affairs for decades, I decided to talk about creativity in general and then, in case I was not understood, to set myself as an example. People of all sorts, I said, have difficulty writing. You hear a lot, "I can't even write a letter!" and the common explanation is that the empty page or, in the modern age, the empty screen, invokes fear. But the problem is not the emptiness of the page or screen but their position, that is, opposite you, face to face, defiant, adversarial. And so from this moment onward, December 28, 2089, I say to imagine the empty page or screen not directly in front of you but *beside* you. Now in front of you and your companion is the whole of the universe, the sky and the moon and the sun and the heavens. Then, not waiting to see if I was understood, I set an example.

My last domicile is located on the lower west side of Manhattan in the building where my mother was born, on the corner of Houston and Sullivan Streets, across from St. Anthony's church. My room is small, a peaceful shrine nine flights up. When you cannot climb any higher, you have reached me. On my sill is a white scalloped bowl replenished each morning with fresh water for the sparrows. High winds blow my geraniums. One flower is wilted, in its demise looks down to the steps of the church. But one flower still faces the heavens, with its last breath bends on its strong thin stem, the flowers rich red, delicate and full. I am old, 94 years old and, if I can get up, I walk to the river. For the sake of unity, of appearing the same way inside and out, I wear the same clothes: Long johns, terry cloth robe, cotton socks and slippers. On the morning I set the example, Charlie Pino waited outside my door. Charlie owns the bread store on Bleecker Street, but in the morning, in order to pay his daily homage, he leaves his son in the store. Charlie reached up my robe for my right hand, but before it touched his lips and he could say, "Bless you this day, Don Pippo," I grabbed him around the waist and spun him around to a position beside me. Then I said, "Greet me, Charles, while looking at the church, and then let's walk side by side." I looked everywhere except down at our feet, in front and behind us, across the street, up at the sky. "Not a cloud in the sky today, Charles," I observed.

"Not a single cloud, Godfather," Charlie said.

We came to Father Demo Square on Carmine Street.

"Feed the pigeons today, Charles?"

"Yes, Godfather."

"Day old or fresh?"

"Fresh, Godfather."

"Good, Charles, good. You know, your son's pallor is that of your bread, and his expression of late is bland. It's not good for our sons to do as we do. My son, as you know, is an art historian."

"I'll tell my son to find something else."

"Good. Good."

A block or so from the square, about an hour later, we arrived at York's Ivory Jewelry run by Pretab Kamdar from Bombay, a short, dark, wall-eyed brother. As he approached with an outstretched arm, Charlie advanced and whirled Kamdar around until he was beside us. "Greet the Don from here," said Charlie, and we continued to the river. Yang the Japanese shoemaker and Bella the female butcher and Juan the Spanish fish vendor and Jake the Jewish pizza maker joined us in the same fashion. Down around West Street I reached into my deep pajama pocket for a wad of cash. "Pass this on to Kamdar," I said, and the money was passed along the line. "Kamdar!" I shouted, "no more killing of elephants for the ivory!"

"No, Godfather, no more."

We fanned out across the highway and looked at the river and the ocean beyond. I led the way to the vicinity of the parking lot about where the Hudson River washes into the Atlantic Ocean. For years I wondered exactly where the fresh water turns to salt. I expressed my wonderment to my family.

"I suppose the scientists have ways of finding out," said Kim, the Korean greengrocer.

Bella, the female butcher, said, "And why do you want to find out, Godfather?"

"I think about the fish," I said, "bass mainly who used to swim between the piers. Where in their desperation do the bass go? If they try a dash to the ocean, do they make the transition to the salt in a safe and healthy way?"

"If the bass die, Godfather," Juan, the Spanish fish vendor, said, "don't you think we'd see them on their bellies on the surface? I don't see any dead bass."

"Neither do I," said Samir, the gay Palestinian restaurateur.

"Neither do I," said Chang, the ice cream maker.

"Neither do I," said Gari, the albino Russian musician.

"Then the bass must be safe and healthy," I said. "Good." I turned and fixed my gaze on the parking lot attendant. "I'm drawn to that man," I said. "Let's regard him from here. He's not young, as you see, but he goes about his work with a youthful air, moving sprightly among his cars."

We were about nine cars away, and Charlie Pino said, "If you like him, Don Pippo, why don't we go right up to him?"

Every morning of every season, I explained, I contemplated asking that attendant whether he knew at what point the fresh water turns to salt. But in the end I decided not to burden him with a difficult question from, as far as he knew, an ordinary runner and then, in my old age, an ordinary walker. I did not wish to distract him from his diligent work of guiding cars to vacant spots and ticketing and making sure all the cars were parked straight as soldiers. Most of all, I did not wish to give him the opportunity of departing from the good cheer he showed me when I passed. I'd call out to him from afar, "And how are you this morning, my good man?"

He'd find me and tip his baseball cap and smile.

I saluted him going and coming, and did not pass on until he tipped his cap and smiled. One morning I succumbed to the temptation of learning his name.

"Jerry!" he called out.

"And where do you live, Jerry?"

"New Jersey," he returned.

Now I looked with infinite pleasure across the river to New Jersey. I was comfortable not desiring to know exactly where in New Jersey Jerry lived. Such a lovely man, certainly a happy family man, lived everywhere in New Jersey. Thus I resolved that there are at least two types of ignorance: intentional ignorance, from which I suffer, pray for me, Jerry! and pure ignorance. Jerry will ascend to Dante with the goodness he showed me preserved in his heart, purely ignorant of the knowledge that throughout all the days he worked his lot, I owned it, and the men and women he guided in and out may have appeared like teachers at that college across the highway or like businessmen of Wall Street, but they were my soldiers. And, at night, when Jerry was warm with his family in their mobile home in Jersey beside a peaceful wood, trucks marked *Wholesale Fish* came here and among the fish were the bodies of my enemies. They were unloaded into that dumpster there and then up, up, up and over into the river. The water below us appears stagnant and foul, but I know the tides. I know them from observing the piers that used to jut into the river busted up. Ungathered wood lingers here a while, then drifts out to the ocean.

TIZIANO THOMAS DOSSENA
— Editor of A Feast of Narrative —

Tiziano Thomas Dossena is the Editorial Director of *L'Idea Magazine* since 1990, and the founder and Editor-in-Chief of *OperaMyLove* and *OperaAmorMio* magazines.

He is the author of *"Caro Fantozzi"* (Scriptum Press, December 2008), *"Sunny Days and Sleepless Nights"* (Idea Press, 2016), *"The World As An Impression: The Landscapes of Emilio Giuseppe Dossena"* (Idea Press, 2020), and the co-author of *"Dona Flor, An Opera by Niccolò van Westerhout"* (Idea Publications, 2010).

His work as an editor and publisher at Idea Press, and his articles on Italian traditions, art, and music as well as his articles on Italian Americans, are aimed at divulging to the greater public the importance of Italians in the American society as much as to focus on the difficulties Italians had to face and overcome to be part of this great nation.

In 2012, he was awarded the "Globo Tricolore Award," considered the Italian Oscar of the publishing industry, for his outstanding work in the publishing industry and his journalistic work. In the same year, he was asked by the City of Yonkers to read poems at the 9/11 Memorial ceremony. Dossena is the recipient of the 2019 Sons of Italy Literary Award.

His works have appeared in more than 100 magazines and anthologies in Italy, France, Greece, Switzerland, India, Canada and the United States.

ABOUT OUR AUTHORS

PETER C. ALFIERI

Born in July, 1953, growing up in Brooklyn, and being raised by first generation Italian-American parents, Peter Alfieri and Madeline Sasso, Peter Alfieri enjoyed the family life and culture typical of other Italian-Americans of his generation.

After attending St. Francis College (BA, Sociology, 1975), and Fordham University (MA, Sociology, 1977), he accepted a position with the Department of Defense (DoD) in Human Resources in Northern New Jersey, where he worked from 1978-1992 in the areas of wage compensation and employee relations. In 1993, he accepted a management position with the Office of Personnel Management in Philadelphia, where he served until my retirement in June, 2019.

He lives in South Jersey, and has a daughter, Adelaide, who is also a member of the local chapter of the Sons of Italy where they are both active in the lodge and play on the bocce team, of which he is captain.

MARILYN
ANTENUCCI

Marilyn Antenucci is a second-generation Italian-American. In 1902, her grandfather, Salvatore, emigrated to the United States from Pietrobbondante in the Molise/Abruzzi Region of Italy. He settled in Pueblo, Colorado, where together with his wife, Angelina, they cultivated a truck garden farm and raised seven children. Marilyn spent happy childhood days running through her uncle's fields of Pueblo chili peppers. She has a B.A. in English and an M.A. in English/Creative Writing. After living all over the United States with a career in education and the Federal Government, she retired to the city of her roots. Each day she is grateful for the risks and sacrifices made by those she sadly never had the privilege of knowing.

LUCIA
ANTONUCCI

Lucia Antonucci always enjoyed writing and throughout her life she kept a journal containing her works of short stories and poetry. In 2013, when Lucia was age 83, her grandson decided to publish some of her works. This sparked Lucia to write more consistently. Fast forward to 2020, Lucia, now age 90, is an accomplished author of five books, and continues to earn five-star ratings on Amazon.com. Lucia gains inspiration from her life experiences, her strong faith and her Italian heritage. She has won the International Library of Poetry and Poetry. com's Editor's Choice Award for her poem entitled, "Park Angel," which was published in *The Best Poems and Poets.* Her vignettes and poetry have also appeared in various newspapers and church publications throughout New York City. In addition to writing, Lucia enjoys cooking, speaks Italian fluently and lives in Brooklyn, New York.

JOSEPH L. CACIBAUDA

Joseph L. Cacibauda is a retired elementary teacher living in Reno, Nevada with his wife Sue. He is the author of *After Laughing Comes Crying: Sicilian Immigrants on Louisiana Plantations,* Legas Press, New York, 2009; *Not For Self: A Sicilian Life and Death in Marion,* Legas Press, New York, 2017; and other books available at Amazon.com. He is a life member of the Arba Sicula Sicilian Society and has occasionally published in their journal and newsletter as well as written for Italian America Magazine of Sons and Daughters of Italy.

DEBBIE
DiGIACOBBE

Raised in an Italian American community in South Philadelphia, by parents of Italian descent, Debbie learned that family is at the heart of everything. Inspired by her parents, she learned the importance of hard work, persistence, and of her responsibility to help make the world a better place.

As a teacher, she has been committed to educating and inspiring her students. She has drawn on great books and literature to create programs that motivate students to read, write, think, and be curious. Currently, an adjunct professor at Temple University, she continues her goal to help young people reach their greatest potential.

She is an advocate for the homeless leading a ministry at her church, working with nonprofit organizations to help fight homelessness. She is a voracious reader and enjoys writing about issues that are important to her. Debbie is inspired by authors like Adriana Trigiani and Lisa Scottoline.

PATRICIA
RISPOLI EDICK

Patricia Rispoli Edick's grandparents immigrated to the United States in the early 1900s from Naples and Palermo, Italy where they were fishermen, rope makers and tailors. Her Father was an upholsterer and her Mom a seamstress.

She was born in Brooklyn, New York. Two months after her 17th birthday, and graduation from High School, she began work as a secretary in a Wall Street brokerage firm.

Patricia married in 1970 and is Mother to two sons, James and Michael.

She retired in 2014 as Office Manager of a Village Police Dept. and now has the time to write.

Patricia is President of the OSDIA Giovanni Caboto Lodge and is editor of The Caboto Lodge Newsletter, 'The Voyager.'

FRED L. GARDAPHÉ

Fred Gardaphé is a Distinguished Professor of English and Italian/American Studies at Queens College (CUNY) and the John D. Calandra Italian American Institute. He has published fiction in many journals and magazines. A collection of his stories has been published in Italian translation in: "Importato dall'Italia ed altri racconti dal vecchio quartiere" (*Translation by Silvana Mangione — Idea Publications, 2009*). His academic publications include "Italian Signs, American Streets: The Evolution of Italian American Narrative," "Dagoes Read: Tradition and the Italian/American Writer," "Moustache Pete is Dead!," "Leaving Little Italy, From Wiseguys to Wise Men: Masculinities and the Italian American Gangster," "The Art of Reading Italian Americana," and "Read 'Em and Reap." He is co-founder/co-editor of *VIA: Voices in Italian Americana*, editor of the *Italian American Culture Series of SUNY Press*, and frequent contributor to the *Fra Noi, L'italoamericano*, and *i-Italy magazine and television.*

CECILIA M. GIGLIOTTI

Cecilia M. Gigliotti is a writer, musician, and travel photographer, as well as the only Italian-speaking member of her family. Much of her work deals with pop culture, medical trauma, and things famous people have said when they thought no one was listening. Her essays, poems, short fiction, and photography have appeared in *The Atticus Review, The Route 7 Review, RiverCraft, Outrageous Fortune, Blue Muse, DoveTales, Uncomfortable Revolution,* and *Boudin,* among others. She also runs a culture blog called *Così faccio io* (cosifaccioio.com). A native New Englander, she is currently based in Berlin, Germany.

Find her on Twitter (@CeciliaGelato), Instagram (@c_m_giglio), and YouTube (Lia Lio).

JOE
GIORDANO

Joe Giordano was born in Brooklyn. His father and his grand-parents were immigrants from Naples. He and his wife, Jane, now live in Texas.

Joe's stories have appeared in more than one hundred magazines including *The Saturday Evening Post, and Shenandoah*. His novels, *Birds of Passage, An Italian Immigrant Coming of Age Story* (2015), and *Appointment with ISIL, an Anthony Provati Thriller* (2017) were published by Harvard Square Editions. Rogue Phoenix Press published *Drone Strike* in 2019 and will publish his short story collection, *Stories and Places I Remember*, in 2020.

Joe was among one hundred Italian American authors honored by Barnes & Noble to march in Manhattan's 2017 Columbus Day Parade. Read the first chapter of Joe's novels and sign up for his blog at http://joe-giordano.com/

SANDRA MARRA BARILE JACKSON

Sandra Marra Barile Jackson's maternal grandparents and paternal grandparents were from San Giovanni in Fiore, Cosenza, Italy. She is a retired school teacher married to Bill Jackson and has one son, Kenney. Her poem JESUS'S TEARS won Honorable mention in a Poetry Contest, while her short story THE LILAC PAINTING won in a writing contest, and THE WEEPING WILLOW won honorable mention in the 71st Annual Writer's Digest Writing competition. She loves to read, walk, ride a bike, write stories and bake cookies, and most of all she loves her dog Roxy.

MARY LOU
(AMATO) JOHNSTON

Mary Lou (Amato) Johnston was born and raised in the dairy country of southern Vermont. She was active in 4-H and church youth activities and attended local schools. She studied at the University of Vermont and Keene State College, New Hampshire where she received her Bachelor's Degree in Childhood Education. Relocating to sunny Arizona, she taught elementary classes for 25 years in Mesa Public Schools. She completed her Master's Degree at Arizona State University and was initiated into Alpha Delta Kappa honorary sorority for women educators. She has been a member of the Order of Sons and Daughters of Italy in Mesa for many years. Following retirement from teaching, Mary Lou spends her time making handmade paper for crafts, reading and sewing. An avid traveler, she has visited 104 countries to date. Twice widowed, she has a son who lives in Mesa and extended family in New England.

THOMAS LOCICERO

Thomas Locicero's short stories have won international, national, and regional awards. His poems have appeared on all seven continents in such literary magazines as The Satirist, Taj Mahal Review, The Pangolin Review, Roanoke Review, Boston Literary Magazine, Bindweed Magazine, Antarctica Journal, Poetry Pacific, The Ghazal Page, Birmingham Arts Journal, Boomer Lit, Hobart, and vox poetica, among others. He resides in Broken Arrow, Oklahoma.

C.J.
MARTELLO

C.J. Martello, is a Chicagoan residing in the Historic Pullman Community and he has been the author of the *Petals from Roseland* column for *Fra Noi* magazine. The column comments on current events and also takes a nostalgic look at growing up Italian-American. He is the author of the book: "Petals from Roseland: Fond Memories of Chicago's Roseland, Pullman, and Kensington Neighborhoods" a compilation of the best of ten years of his column.

As an actor CJ presents his one man show: "George Pullman: the man and his model town" for community organizations. He is a docent and historian of the Pullman National Monument and a member of organizations such as the "Spaghetti-Os," which keeps alive memories of Chicago's Roseland Community from years gone by, and OSIA Leone d'Oro Lodge #2700 that serves to keep alive our Italian-American heritage.

EDWARD ALBERT MARUGGI, PH. D.

Edward Albert Maruggi, Ph.D. is a second-generation Italian American and a Professor Emeritus from Rochester Institute of Technology, having chaired programs for hearing impaired students for twenty-one years. In 1980/81 he was a Rotary International Fellow who studied and conducted research in Italy. He is a diverse writer who writes a bi- monthly column for an Italian American newspaper, has authored seven college level textbooks and seven about Italians and Italian Americans. His memberships include the Italian American Studies Association, the Order of Sons and Daughters of Italy in America and Friends of Italian Genealogy.

In 2017, he was awarded the Literary Award by the New York Grand Lodge of OSDIA. He is married to the former Carolyn Baumgartner, a quiltmaker and quilt genealogist. Together with their two cats, they live at a lake-front community in Hilton, New York.

MARIA
MASSIMI

Maria Massimi holds a B.A. in French Literature from Mary-mount College, Certificat d'Etudes from Lausanne, Switzerland, an M.A. in Curriculum from Columbia University, and an M.A. in Administration from College of New Rochelle. Department Head of a public high school, she taught French, Italian, Spanish, with a knowledge of Latin. She served as advisor to clubs, trips, and honor societies; had co-ordinated a Sardinian middle school exchange program and headed the first American group to travel throughout that island, hosted by dignitaries and school officials there. The group was invited to the NATO base, Secret Service School, numerous sites, and to Caprera.

Upon retirement, she served as supervisor and mentor to new teachers, taught on a college level and in the Bronxville Schools. Founder of a private high school for girls, she served as its first principal. A first-generation born Italian American, she resides in Larchmont, N.Y. with her husband.

SUZANNA ROSA
MOLINO

Native Baltimorean, Suzanna Rosa Molino, is the author of *Italians in Baltimore, Baltimore's Little Italy: Heritage and History of The Neighborhood;* and *The Italian Immigrants' Daughter* (co-authored with her 86-year-old mamma, Gina Mossa Molino). Suzanna is the founder and volunteer director of the 501(c)(3) nonprofit organization, *Promotion Center for Little Italy, Baltimore.* What fuels her writing about Italian heritage is a rich pride and profound passion in being Italian as the granddaughter of four immigrants from Vasto, Abruzzo, and Luras, Sardinia, Italy.

SHARON NIKOSEY

Sharon Santamaria Nikosey is a second generation Italian-Irish American living north of Boston, MA. She and her husband Don actually did run the 100th Boston Marathon in 1996. She is a member of the OSIA Lodge 1732 in Wakefield, MA where she helps with photography and Public Relations. She works full-time at a healthcare company and part-time as a Track Official. She has two adult children, Eric and Marlena. This is her first short story.

MARGE
PELLEGRINO

Marge Pellegrino grew up in Tuckahoe, New York where she learned to make sauce cooking alongside her Nana on Sundays after church. She is an award-winning author and teaching artist who has facilitated workshops in school, library, and community settings. Her early chapter book *Too Nice* helps kids develop personal boundaries. Her picture book *My Grandma's the Mayor* celebrates community service. Her newest book *Neon Words: 10 Brilliant Ways to Light Up Your Writing* offers writing and craft activities families can enjoy together. *The Sculpture Speaks: A Refugee's Story of Survival* benefits the Owl & Panther Program for survivors of torture and their families. Then First Lady Barbara Bush bestowed Marge's Word Journeys afterschool program a *Coming Up Taller Award* at the White House in 2008. Marge and her family live in Tucson, AZ.

ANNADORA
PERILLO

Annadora Perillo is a novelist and poet. She was born in the home of her grandparents, a *palazzo* in the ancient fortress-city of Bari, Italy. On her first birthday, she sailed for New York, beginning her childhood in the Bronx where, thanks to her father's travel business, Italy was never too far out of reach. At 17, she went to study in the ivory towers of Marymount College and Richmond College in London, receiving a BA in English literature and the gold medal in creative writing from Marymount. She has won several awards for poetry; her manuscript, *Bella*, was a finalist for the Heekin Group Foundation's James Fellowship for the Novel. She works at *Perillo Tours* and in Library Youth Services. Her home is by the shores of the Hudson where she lives happily ever after: a reader, a writer, and a dreamer. She has two grown sons, a cat, and a broom.

ELIZABETH PRIMAMORE

Elizabeth Primamore is an author and playwright. Short stories are published in *Sweet Tree Review* and *The Opiate*. Her new book is titled *Shady Women: Three Short Plays* (Upper Hand Press, 2018). She is a recipient of the Bernard and Shirley Handel Playwriting Award and was a semifinalist for the Eugene O'Neill National Playwrights Conference. Her personal essays have been published in the anthologies *From A to LGBTQ* (650 Press, 2016) and *Pain and Memory* (2009). Primamore is a fellow at The Virginia Center for the Creative Arts and The Woodstock Byrdcliffe Guild. She holds a Ph.D. from the City University of New York.

TONY
REITANO

Tony Reitano was born in the Hudson Valley in Upstate NY to a Sicilian/Italian family (No, they're not the same thing). He attended State University of NY at Geneseo as a biology major where he auditioned for a play on a bet, kissed biology goodbye and entered the glorious, if not impoverished, world of show business. After many years in New York City he moved to Los Angeles where he did commercials, including over 50 spots as Vince the Crash Test Dummy in the award-winning Safety Belt Campaign. He is the author of the staged radio plays, "Young St. Nick," "Headless Tales, the stories of Washington Irving," and "Tales of the Emerald Isle."

He lives in Middleton, Wisconsin with his wife Leslie and his daughter Marguerite.

MICHAEL
RICCARDS

Michael Riccards is the author of 20 books, 15 verse plays, and a play on the well-known American poet, John Ciardi. Ha has been a college president of three institutions of higher education, a NEH Fellow at Princeton University, and a Fulbright Fellow in Japan. His latest volume of short stories is *The Ordinary Duties of the Day* and the upcoming *Growing Up Jersey*. He has three children and five grandchildren. Michael's family is from Benevento and Avellino.

ANIELLO (NEIL) RUSSO

Aniello (Neil) Russo is an 89-year-old retired elementary school teacher. He taught thirty-nine years in the town of Weymouth, Massachusettes, where he was born and spent his entire life. After graduation from Weymouth High School, he worked his way through Tufts University and graduated with a degree in sociology. While teaching, he attended Bridgewater State University and received a Masters of Education degree.

Both of his parents are Italian. His father is from Puglia and his mother from Avellino.

He had the good fortune to live in an Italian community, and did a Sunday paper route all through college, and the community customers supported him with enthusiasm and tips that they could afford.

For the past ten years, he has been writing an environmental article weekly for the local paper Weymouth News. In 2008, he self-published a mafia novel: "It's Just Business."

Aniello is extremely proud of his Italian heritage.

PAUL
SALSINI

The son of Italian immigrants, award-winning author Paul Salsini has written seven books—novels and collections of short stories—all set in Tuscany. Among them is the six-volume "A Tuscan Series," which follows a group of characters from World War II to the year 2000. He received the 2011 Sons of Italy's Leonardo da Vinci Award for Excellence in Literature.

MARK
SPANO

Mark Spano is working on a screenplay and developing two documentaries. He is traveling the U.S. and Canada with his feature documentary entitled *Sicily: Land of Love and Strife*. His recent novel *Midland Club* published by Thunderfoot Press has received two awards and significant critical acclaim. He recently adapted *Midland Club* for the screen at an artist's residency in Seaside, Florida. He is presently putting together a development team for the film of *Midland Club*. He is hoping to see his book *Kidding the Moon* published in the near future.

LEO
VADALÀ

Born in Genoa (Italy) in 1935, Leo Vadalà came to the United States as a student in 1951. In 1954 he enlisted in the U.S. Army to become an American citizen. Upon his discharge, he was employed by WSFS (Wilmington Savings Fund Society) where he worked in several executive positions. He retired in 1999 after 40 years of service. He lives in Elkton MD.

He has been married to Maria Flocco, a native of Torino di Sangro (Chieti) since 1964.

He has been active in the Italian community of Wilmington DE and has been a member of the Giuseppe Verdi Lodge, OSIA (Order Sons of Italy in America) since 1975 serving as Treasurer, Vice President and President. In 1995 he also founded the Lodge's monthly newsletter, "Va Pensiero," editing it and providing all articles for the first 7 years.

In 2019 Idea Press published his first novel, "Some Grief, Some Joy."

ANTHONY
VALERIO

Anthony Valerio is the author of ten books of fiction & nonfiction, including 'Conversation with Johnny;' 'Anita Garibaldi, a biography' and 'Toni Cade Bambara's One Sicilian Night.' His stories have appeared in the Paris Review and anthologized by Random House, William Morrow and the Viking Press. Mr. Valerio has taught at NYU, CUNY and Wesleyan University. He was a fiction judge at PEN's Prison writing Committee.

Made in the USA
Middletown, DE
29 September 2020